D0671391

Lucky Man, Lucky Woman

WINNER OF THE EDITORS' BOOK AWARD

Lucky Man,
Lucky Woman

A NOVEL BY JACK DRISCOLL

W. W. NORTON & COMPANY

New York • London

For my sisters, Gail, Maura, and Bean,
and for my brother, Toby

And in memory of my friend David Lemmen,
without whose inspiration this novel
could not have been written

And with special thanks
to Richard Jackson

Copyright © 1998 by Jack Driscoll
First published as a Norton paperback 2000
Published by arrangement with Pushcart

All rights reserved
Printed in the United States of America

The text of this book is set in 11 pt. Bembo
Manufacturing by the Courier Companies, Inc.
Book design by Jennifer Campbell

Chapter 2 appeared originally under the title "Hang Time," in *Witness,*
volume VI, no. 2, 1992

LC: 98-068048-0-8-X
ISBN 0-393-31945-8 pbk.

W. W. Norton & Company, Inc.
500 Fifth Avenue, New York, N.Y. 10110
www.wwnorton.com

W. W. Norton & Company Ltd.
10 Coptic Street, London WC1A 1PU

1 2 3 4 5 6 7 8 9 0

If three and four were seven only
Where would that leave one and two?
If love can be, and still be lonely,
Where does that leave me and you?
Time there was, and time there will be,
Where does that leave you and me?

—Townes Van Zandt

Chapter 1

Perry Lafond wakes early, though he's the one who stayed up late, reading the underlined sections in Marcia's *Portable Nietzsche*, an old college text he found while rummaging the bookshelf for something to help his insomnia. He reaches down now and picks up the book from the floor, and rereads that same passage he thought about while finally drifting off to sleep: "When marrying, one should ask oneself this question: Do you believe that you will be able to converse well with this woman into your old age? Everything else in marriage is transitory. . . ."

Lately, Perry and Marcia have been arguing much too often, followed by hours of the silent treatment, each avoiding the other in the apartment, and each refusing to be the first to speak, as though whoever does has lost some slight but essential edge. He's determined to ease up, to stop swooping down on her. He hopes the change of scenery will help.

They are both covered to the waist by a pinstriped blue-and-white

L. L. Bean flannel sheet. Marcia is naked underneath—Perry is certain of this without even looking. If he were to lift the edge, because Marcia has turned on her side during the night, her legs tucked up, and is facing away from him toward the open window, he would see the needle tracks on her backside—there's barely enough light, but there is enough. He's the one who put them there, injecting her for twelve consecutive mornings with Pergonal, derived, Marcia's obstetrician, a fertility expert, explained to them, "from the urine of postmenopausal Italian nuns." Almost no medical talk surprises Perry anymore—lazy sperm or borrowed grade-A eggs or zygotes in the fallopian tube. But he wondered, losing eye contact with this doctor, and then staring at the detailed blue-and-red diagram of a woman's reproductive organs behind Plexiglas on the wall, who it was who asked those nuns, celibate their entire lives, to pee for this purpose in a jar. He couldn't, and cannot now, imagine them consenting.

And yet he has consented to injecting Marcia, who hates shots, at $150 a whack, paid for by Betty Benoit, Marcia's mother, who has the money and believes, as she often says, that "God's delays are not necessarily denials."

"Amen," Marcia's twin sister, Pauline, said to that. "Amen."

Perry has never gotten used to Betty's handouts. "Maybe I do sound like a broken record," he's insisted over the years to Marcia, "but I hate sponging like this. It's never felt right to me."

The handouts started before they were even married, Perry agreeing to let Marcia help pay his grad school expenses at Trinity. She referred to it as an investment in their future. Until meeting Marcia, Perry had never considered applying to schools out east, but that's where she was headed, back home to be with her family. And there was the teaching job already waiting for her in Mystic.

On weekends, he'd take the train from Hartford, and Marcia would be there waiting at the station to pick him up. During the two years of their engagement, he felt a bit of a pauper in the Benoits' house, the odd man out. They all liked Perry, an awfully sweet young man, but oh, that submissive midwestern shyness. It's not that they'd ride him about it or anything—they weren't like that, not ever—but he could always sense that he came from some other place that they didn't care much about.

Pauline, who was there least, always made the biggest effort, asking Perry about his family, about cherry farming, and about Lake Michigan, which she'd crossed one time by ferryboat on her way to Minneapolis.

Pauline has two children, a nine-year-old named Virtine, and her younger brother, J.J. Virtine, like her mother and her aunt Marcia, is a leap-year baby. She likes to count up the years of her life even when she has no calendar birthday, but Marcia does not, meaning, she says to Virtine, that next February 29 they'll both turn ten. Virtine gets a kick out of that and says maybe she'll stop counting, too, but not until she's eighteen. Or possibly twenty-one, she says, but for sure before she gets as old and short-tempered as her parents, who have grown past loving each other.

Betty Benoit is visiting Pauline and the grandchildren in Boston because Pauline's husband, Neil Schwerk, has recently walked out to be with another woman. That's all Perry knows—he hasn't been clued in on the juicy details. But he has, from the very first time he met Neil, his only brother-in-law, thought of him as a single-minded, niggling little prick whose primary reason for existing is to bust other people's balls—or, at family functions, to list publicly his considerable assets. "Aw," he remembers Neil, all singsongy, saying. "Aw," and smirking and playing his imaginary "you're a goddamn sap" violin for anyone in the family who tried to turn a conversation away from investments toward anything the least bit heartfelt.

Perry and Marcia are not alone in her mother's house. Security at Groton Long Point is tight. The Chippendale and rose medallion and

Tiffany are heavily insured. No triple locks or dead bolts or fancy alarm systems—those are unnecessary precautions. The real reason he and Marcia are here is to enjoy the beach, and to dog-sit for Basket, part Chihuahua and part who knows what. Chihuahua and channel rat, Perry believes when he's thinking clearly. Or, because of her protruding lizard eyes and thinning hair, Chihuahua and miniature space reptile. He stifles the impulse to say, "Sorry about the mutt" to anybody seeing her for the first time. He knows that Basket knows this. It's the way with homely dogs who get spoiled—they're usually too damn smart and spiteful. She still nips at Pauline's children, at all kids, even when they're attempting to make friends, saying, "Good girl, good Basket." And she detests grown men. Perry's family always owned retrievers— outdoor dogs, shiny black and square-headed, who loved to please.

Although the bedroom door is open, Basket has not come in. Perry, who has just kissed his wife's tanned, smooth shoulder twice, and is now sitting at the foot of the bed, his bathrobe and slippers on, can see all the way down the hall to the kitchen, where Basket keeps eyeballing him, her awful nails clicking on the linoleum in front of her bowl. She's been running in place from the moment she heard Perry begin to stir. He gets up and tiptoes out of the bedroom and closes the door quietly behind him, letting Marcia sleep.

"Basket Case," he whispers, greeting her. He says, "Here's the deal today," but he doesn't finish with the threat. He just stands glaring down as she continues her obnoxious tap dance by her bowl. It's not for food. Her leash is kept above her head in the cupboard drawer— she is demanding to be walked, about fifteen yards, around to the other, always cooler, always shady side of the house. Perry has learned, as recently as yesterday, that what Marcia's mother told him, incredible as it sounded, is true—that if he pushes Basket with his foot onto the porch, no matter how gently, she will go to the bathroom right there— "And this a dog, Marcia chimed in, "who has never had an accident

✳ 4

on the porch or in the house, not in twelve years." Or worse, the dog will hold it until she's let back inside, then make a beeline for the Oriental rug in the living room and pee and poop on it, underneath a glass end table. "This creature," Perry told Marcia, who helped clean up the mess, "this martian canine, has no shame."

The coffeemaker has been programmed for 6:00 A.M., and it is dripping in a thin stream into the pot right now, Beanery blend. His pack of Camels stands on end on the countertop, and a book of matches that says "Mr. T's" has been slid, upside down, behind the cellophane. Perry does not light up, nor pour himself a cup of coffee. He bends over and snaps the leash clip to the ring of Basket's collar and is led outside and down the stairs and around to her spot. But this morning, she does not sniff and circle and linger in her deliberate, pain-in-the-ass style. Instead, she stops and begins to shiver. The fog has rolled in so thick during the night that Perry can hardly see Basket in front of him, her hair not unlike the colorless, fine texture of fog. But he can feel in his hand the tiny trembling in the leash, which he drops, and he says, "What?" He says, "Hey, what's the matter?" and he stoops and picks her up, something else Betty Benoit, the first time Perry ever reached out to Basket, said couldn't be done by any man. Strangely, Basket relaxes in his arms. She cannot weigh five pounds. And stranger still is how, across the waist-high, flat-topped hedge, the neighbor's house begins suddenly to reappear, first the green shutters and, right below them, though he cannot yet make out a flower box, the bent heads of oversized white begonias. And what he sees next, magnified behind the wavy glass of the only window visible, is an Airedale he's never laid eyes on before, its teeth bared as if, any second, it will grab and violently shake something to death, simply to get the day started. Which explains, all of a sudden, why Basket refuses to walk out here alone.

"Huh?" he asks her. "Is that it?" He lowers his face and she licks him on the mouth and cheeks and forehead, along his hairline. It is the tiniest tongue he has ever felt.

"Watch this," he tells her, and he raises his middle finger, his arm extended full length, and flips the Airedale the first-thing-in-the-morning bird. "Up yours, bucko," he says, silently mouthing the words as the fog breaks up in swirls and lifts above the faded cedar shakes to the roofline and out of sight. Two gulls are perched on the chimney, staring down, their wings partway open, as if they're expecting Perry to toss some bread crusts into the sky. Basket does not growl at the gulls—she growls at the window, where someone is pulling a shade in front of the Airedale's face.

"Okay," Perry says, "see?" and he kisses Basket between her pointy ears, on the top of her head, and not offhandedly. He means it, and does not pretend otherwise—not even when Marcia, her lips pressed to the screen of their bedroom window, says, "You're going to make a wonderful daddy. You know why?" she asks. "Because you know how to protect and forgive."

He believes she's mostly right about forgiveness—it's the protection part that's a stretch. But he nods anyway. And Basket, hearing Marcia's voice, wags her tail madly as Perry, both hands around Basket's potbelly, lowers her, like a new puppy brought home from the pound, for the first time onto the grass.

They keep the Pergonal in the refrigerator, the disposable syringes in an empty Penn tennis ball can on the bureau. It's that time, and Perry shakes the small vial slowly back and forth as he walks toward his wife. She is wearing his shirt, unbuttoned except for one button, and nothing else, her elbows pressed against the doorjamb, her head tilted slightly, so that her hair falls just beyond her left shoulder. She reminds Perry of that Bugle Boy ad he likes on TV, the one in which the woman says to her husband, who's sitting on the edge of the bed, "The only thing I'd change about you are your clothes." In this pose, Marcia does not appear like a woman about to be given a shot. She hates them, refusing each winter to get one to prevent the flu, or to travel abroad, remembering as a schoolgirl, she says, how she'd start to cry as soon as the nurse, holding a bottle of rubbing alcohol and a single cotton ball, approached her on squeaky soles. And how she fainted every time she was inoculated—polio, tetanus, diphtheria, whooping cough—and how queasy and depressed she always felt waking up sweaty on that narrow infirmary cot.

"Ready?" Perry asks, and Marcia nods and hands him the syringe, then falls across her mother's mattress, arms outstretched in front of her, the way she does often, diving from the raft anchored offshore at Main Beach. For years, she used to be the full-time summer lifeguard, whistling and signaling the kids back who ducked underwater and surfaced on the outside of those bright yellow lifelines.

She glances back and says, "Excuse me? Yoo-hoo, are you still there?" and she smiles at him sitting beside her, but it's a nervous smile, and she turns quickly away, her face splashing again into the rippled indentation of the pillow. She cannot help tensing up, the muscle of her rear end hard and twitching.

"Relax," he says, "and it won't hurt so much. Remember?" And he begins to massage her bottom lightly, then the backs of her legs, and she says, "Go on, do it—save the foreplay for later."

He's nervous, too, as always, and he says back to her, "Right, okay." He's balancing the syringe between his thumb and index finger, like a dart. "Okay," he says again, concentrating on a spot between two small purple bruises, and takes close aim and pricks her with the point and pushes, carefully and slowly, that clear, cold liquid beneath her skin.

For breakfast, Marcia fixes herself a toasted blueberry bagel with margarine and marinated artichoke hearts. From Pauline, Perry has heard

7 ✳

stories about the weird cravings of pregnant women—rhubarb with chocolate syrup and iced tea, which is no crazier than Marcia's combo. Even Basket, for once in her life, is not at the table begging for scraps. She's out on the front porch in the sun, curled up asleep on a wicker chair.

Marcia stabs the last artichoke wedge from the jar with her fork and holds it out to Perry, but he says, "No thanks, it's all yours."

"Sure?" she asks, and he nods yes, he is. He's enjoying finally his first cup of black coffee and first cigarette of the morning, and reading last night's *New London Day*. There's an article about a doctor in Texas, indicted for performing abortions without any anesthesia.

"Here," Marcia says, "use this for an ashtray," and she slides the lid from the artichoke jar across the page to him.

He flicks his ashes, which hiss slightly as they hit the thin film of oil on the inside. Perry notices the ad there: "The Art of Cooking with Cara Mia—50 Cents Postpaid." He looks up at Marcia, who is not a good cook, and who weighs the same as she did in college in Ann Arbor, where they met in 1976, he a junior, she a senior. One hundred and eighteen pounds. Playing four corners, or H-O-R-S-E, or one-on-one with him in the gym, she can hold her own, as she boasts she can against any man. Until two summers ago, she played with Perry in the men's softball league in Mystic, hitting leadoff for Seaport Canvas, a contender that year. Tennis, biking, water polo— she does them all. And this, lately: this leaning back in her chair, like now, the fingers of both hands spread open and pressing down on her stomach. Even pushing it out, she has no bulge—it's flat and tight, the kind of stomach most women her age would kill for.

"Did I ever tell you how much weight Mom gained when she was pregnant with me and Pauline?"

"Seventy pounds," Perry says without looking up, and Marcia says back, "Imagine me like that. Just imagine it."

✳ 8

Perry can't, not really, not anymore. He's losing the nerve to believe. Time, he argues, is running out for that. No, absolutely not, Marcia counters whenever Perry talks that line. She claims it's possible these days to trick the biological clock, and she's been bringing home, and saving in a folder, magazine articles about childbearing women in their fifties. Not an image that excites Perry and, by extension, the vision of himself as a grandfather father, some little tyke fatiguing, in fifteen hyperactive minutes, this gray-haired guy with an inhaler and a smoker's cough. "Then quit smoking," Marcia responded. "Damn you," she told him back then, raising her voice. "Goddamn you, Perry, I want a baby."

So he has agreed reluctantly to these fertility drugs, and Marcia has agreed, at least for the time being, not to discuss the next step—the miracle doctor ransacking her body to remove eggs from her ovaries, Perry's jacked-off sperm spread over them in a petri dish. It's not the way he wants to start or even talk about a family—this desperate, terrible lingo he's been forced to speak.

But this morning, it's another language—light, happy for a change. There's that soft breeze through the windows, and the smell of seaweed washed ashore that he likes. Marcia's legs are crossed under the table, one foot on top of the other on Perry's lap, her toenails painted red. She is retelling that story about Pauline and how, when she was pregnant with Virtine and experiencing motion sickness for the entire final month, and feeling like a hippo, she'd tell Neil, without warning, to stop the car, and she'd get out and lean back inside and say, "Now run me over."

Perry still gets goose bumps from the voltage in Marcia's giggle, girlish and, as it always has, turning him on.

"How 'bout we—" Perry says, and before he can finish his sentence, Marcia leans toward him and says, "C'mere you," and they kiss.

"The postman always rings twice," Perry says, but they do not make furious love on her mother's kitchen table like Jack Nicholson and Jessica Lange, though it's Perry's all-time favorite lust scene. Instead, they go back to the bedroom, where the bed is flooded with sunlight. And they slowly lower themselves in, as they do two, sometimes three times a day, now that the timing is crucial.

Chapter 2

Perry is shooting hoops again in the small gymnasium of S. B. Butler Elementary School, where Marcia teaches second grade. It's almost midnight on July 3, and he's left her alone in her mother's queen-size bed, watching *Mystic Pizza* on the VCR for what Perry exaggerates to be the hundredth time. Perry's a film buff; he and Marcia own over three hundred videos, and this is the only one she's brought over to the beach house.

Marcia actually appears in the film, about halfway through, for a grand total of maybe four seconds, a local background stand-in. When anyone asks, she smiles and says she plays a "Mystic person," meaning simply that she was born and raised and, except for five years away at the University of Michigan in Ann Arbor, has lived in the area all her life.

Perry, riding his high horse, argued with Marcia, even before the semis and film crews and the Guild actors and actresses arrived, that, unlike most New England coastal towns, Mystic's diners, thank God, had still not *all* gone quiche and cappuccino. He was dead against it being transformed into a Hollywood set—Main Street roped off for the swarms of tourists, the local traffic snagged and rerouted along I-95. Stand up against the glitz, he'd said, against the gross oversell of showbiz.

The truth is, he's a Julia Roberts fan, which makes it impossible for him to trash the flick totally. And, like Marcia, *he* sometimes entertains the fantasy of stardom, which is why he's wearing Marcia's Walkman and slam-dunking to Van Morrison's "Brown-Eyed Girl" and pretending he's Michael Jordan. The bright orange rims are only eight feet high, thus the illusion of good hang time, and it is good, he tells himself, for a guy who is thirty-eight and smokes Camel straights and is overweight through the gut by a few flabby pounds. But not over the hill—he's got a high sperm count, 30 billion a year, what Perry, after getting the initial test results from the health clinic, referred to as his "wicked jizz." But that was more than two years ago, and Marcia is still not pregnant, and Perry does not joke about it, not to anyone, not anymore.

" 'Hey, where did we go,' " he sings, " 'days when the rains came?' " and dribbles the basketball between his legs, behind his back, head fakes, and then drives suddenly right and pulls up, this time popping from just behind the foul line. It's a buzzer beater, all net, and he yells, "Yes," raising and shaking one fist in triumph to this final winning shot of the night.

In his imagination, he's been unstoppable, showboating to the cheers of a full house, scoring almost at will, and, his dark chest hairs glistening, he has rebounded every missed shot, going back up hard each time to the basket for what he calls his "two-handed gorilla stuffs." He has even hung on to the rim, chinning himself, his legs kicking out into a midair splits the instant after his hands let go. But when he turns off the tape and slides the earphones away from his ears, letting

✳ 12

them hang around his neck, the gym is perfectly quiet—except for his own breathing.

His throat, as always after a workout, is dry, but there is a single long-neck on ice in the small cooler inside the saddlebag of his motorcycle, which is parked outside where the teachers park their cars and minivans during the school year—it's a Harley-Davidson that Marcia hates. It's just that it's so dangerous, she says, it worries her half to death. It's been one of the long-standing snafus in their marriage.

Perry is not walking toward the bike, though, not yet, but, rather, toward the gymnasium stage, where the light switches are, on the partition of wall behind the partly drawn curtain. He does not like going up there, but he goes and, stopping on the top stair, begins to sweat badly, a kind of after sweat—runnels of it down his neck and ribs—that has nothing to do with exercise. Nor with this late-night heat. It's as though he's been invited to speak to an assembly of little kids but has forgotten what it is he wants to say—something simple maybe, something about how much he hopes their parents love them? Something about good touches and bad touches? Or how a second grader named Marvin Ants was kidnapped last month from the playground in Ledyard during recess, not far from here, and has not yet been found? And until then, wasn't that a funny, sad name—Marvin Ants—and how they should never, ever trust a stranger. What he whispers is, "Holy Jesus Christ." And then louder, "C'mon, move, move your ass," but he doesn't. He can't. "Freako" is how Perry's best friend, Wayne, describes these irrational fears—bona fide freako. And the cure? "Will it the fuck away," Wayne always tells him. "Perry, listen to me, will it away."

This time, it works, because when Perry turns slowly around, he is facing nobody, only the empty fold-out bleachers. And the gymnasium is emptier still a few seconds later when the overheads blink off and what's left to see by is the slant of moonlight through the single wire-mesh window high up on the tiles. The light splays and glitters on the newly waxed and buffed hardwood floor. Like a ballroom floor, Perry thinks, and just that quickly, in the emulsifying semidarkness, he imagines a lineup of tiny boys and, backs pressed flat against the opposite wall, girls in white dresses. He can't make out the faces, but he knows they'll move from the shadows soon because Marcia, at center court, is smiling and waving in slow motion, waving them toward one another for the first awkward dance of their lives.

Outside, there are no ghosts, only the stars and the full moon and a half circle of giant maples silhouetted against the sky. Straddling the Harley, Perry adjusts the strap of his goggles so they fit tightly around his eyes. There is no traffic, the way he likes it, and you can see, because he wears no shirt, that, unlike Wayne, he is without tattoos on his arms. Perry is a parole and probation officer, licensed to carry a gun, but he does not have one with him now. Nor a helmet, which means, when he turns onto Island View Avenue, he is breaking the law. The beer has disappeared in two gulps, and, because it's intended when he cranks half throttle and pops the clutch, the wide front tire lifts a few inches from the pavement. By the time he hits third gear, he's roaring past the abandoned Mystic Ice Company. And the basketball? Somehow it stays balanced on the metal-flake blue gas tank between his knees, even at seventy-five or eighty miles an hour down the long, empty straightaways.

This is the kind of night when Wayne might say, "Let's ride." And Perry has, for almost half an hour, through what he calls the small "shitstorms" of insects along U.S. Route 1, all the way to Westerly, Rhode Island, where, gearing down, he comes finally to a stop on the road's gravelly shoulder. It is here he lights a cigarette and cleans his goggles, rubbing, in small circles with his thumb on the lenses, the red kerchief he has just untied from around his neck. To his right, in the low-tide salt marsh, a single white skiff floats motionless below the end of a long dock. Perry knows the skiff is tied there—oars still in the oarlocks—but he cannot see the rope. There is no house in sight, and no electric lights—only the slow drift of the moon and the ancient nautical chart of the stars.

Tomorrow evening, he and Marcia and Wayne will motor out of the harbor on Wayne's houseboat, almost a mile down the Mystic River to the mouth, where Wayne will cut the engine and they'll drift with the currents out into the Sound. They celebrate every Fourth of July this way, just the three of them, drinking rum on the deck of the boat and grilling hot dogs or burgers over the coals. Wayne seems to know, within minutes, when the first brilliant red canopy of fireworks will explode above Fishers Island, and sometimes, before it does, depending on his mood, he'll start to name in Vietnamese the constellations he can still remember in that tongue. Then he'll go silent, leaning back in his chair and staring up. He has been back from that war for over twenty years, since 1971. Perry figures the fireworks remind Wayne of tracer fire, but he's not sure—the two of them don't engage in conversations like that anymore, truth sessions that Wayne says only go toward weakening or embarrassing a man. He distrusts most people, especially shrinks, saying he's learned somewhere, somehow, to fall more in love with the edge than with the therapist. His first one, right after coming home from Nam, was a single woman, lanky-limbed and maybe forty and, as Wayne told it, very, very pretty. She insisted at the first session that he open right up to her, just go ahead and spill his guts. Then she spoke to him about war as if it were sex—being drafted, she'd said, was like involuntary intercourse. His recurring nightmares about land mines were only wet dreams gone bad on the DMZ. "Mind Fuck," Wayne had called her, and he made clear in a letter to the Veterans Administration in D.C. that that kind of New Age rehab bullshit was wasted on him.

Perry, ever since he was nine years old, has suffered both panic

15 ✳

attacks and nightmares, though he'll go months sometimes without one. And then, like last week, he'll have two or three, and scream himself awake in a cold sweat. Or Marcia will be there to reach over and shake his shoulder, calling, "Perry, Perry, I'm here, I'm right here. . . . it's all right." She doesn't ask anymore if it's about his sister, Janine, because it always is, always. It begins every time with Perry climbing up onto the tractor and riding away with his dad, Janine waving good-bye to him in slow motion until they're completely out of sight. Their older brother, Hank, is there, too, but he's not waving—he's angry that Perry has taken his spot.

Then, from all the way down in the lower orchard, after his dad turns the tractor off, Perry, who does not follow him through the avenues of trees, can hear Janine. Her voice is very faint, but he can hear her clearly: "Help me, Perry." Always to him—never calling to their dad or mom, never to Hank, who is there specifically to watch her. During the time it takes Perry to run back up, the yard has turned into a lake. Hank is asleep on an inflatable raft, just offshore, but Perry cannot wake him. Hank is a good swimmer and Perry is not; he won't be for years yet. So he exhausts himself getting out to where Janine's been kicking and splashing, but she's not there. She's sinking right below him, her hand extended—he can never reach it, no matter how long he holds his breath and breaststrokes away from the surface—her eyes wide open and staring at him.

Hyperventilating, he'll sit on the edge of the bed, and Marcia, returning from the bathroom, will dry him off with a towel until he stops shivering, and she'll hug him and rub his neck and back until he falls deep into sleep again, his breathing back to normal.

Wayne seldom comes ashore anymore. "Landsickness," he calls it, and, like Perry, he hates the summer tourists invading in full force, taking careful aim at the harbor at sunset with their new lightweight video cameras. He'll venture out only at night, on recon, he says, for cigarettes and booze, now and then to pick up a woman in the bars, and fresh limes at the Farmer's Market. Or sometimes to ride behind Perry on the Harley, most often when Wayne is stoned or half in the bag on hot, humid nights like this one. Then will come that grin of his, and he'll say, "Yeah." He'll say, "Perry, my man, it's time to cool off." Followed by Perry's instructions for Wayne to hang on, and Wayne does, wrapping both arms tightly around his friend's chest, the two of them shirtless. At some point—let's say while leaning into the curves on Pequot Trail—their laughing and joking will stop, and Wayne, as though he needs to hide, will press his forehead, his long hair wind-combed straight back, right between Perry's shoulder blades and begin to hum. Perry can feel the tunes on his skin—always something jumpy from the late sixties—Moby Grape or Mott the Hoople or the Electric Prunes. It's the only music Wayne will play on the houseboat—scratchy, worn-out 45's at maximum decibels.

If Wayne were with him now—and Perry wishes he were—they'd stop for a nightcap at the Portuguese Holy Ghost Society in Stonington. Wayne's last name is daSilva; he's a lobsterman by trade, a one-man operation, a lobsterman extraordinaire. Without him, though Perry would love another cold beer, he will not go into that bar. Perry's French and, yes, he does fish, but not for his livelihood. Some evenings after work, or on weekends, he'll cast artificial baits for stripers or blues from the rocks just down from his mother-in-law's at Groton Long Point. Wayne claims there are tagged bluefish worth ten thousand dollars apiece swimming out there. Perry would sure as hell keep one of those, but whatever else he catches, he releases so he does not have to clean or fillet them. What he likes is the slow-reel, absentminded retrieve as he stares out at the sea. Then that sudden, violent strike, just when he's sure there's nothing feeding in the shallows. And wherever he is lost in thought gives way to that one clear second it takes him to set the hook hard, and again a second time, burying the sharp barbs

17 ✳

deep into the fish's jaw and fighting it until either the line breaks or the fish, exhausted, rolls sideways on the surface, allowing itself to be hauled in.

Perry takes a final, long drag and, holding the smoke in his lungs, tosses his cigarette butt on the ground and grinds it out under one of his shoes—high-top Nike Airs. And fifteen minutes later, he is dribbling the basketball again, this time left-handed while riding slowly in first gear across the Mystic drawbridge. Through the ribbons of iron grating, he sees the deepwater green phosphorescence like schools of tiny minnows below him. And not only can he hear but he can also feel the ball's hollow reverberations bouncing back off the flat black surface of the water. It is not the first time he has done this, and once again he forms a picture in his mind of a game of B-ball on motorcycles, and how the hoops are thousands of miles apart, one on each coast, and he all alone on a breakaway, the dimly lighted store windows on Main Street a blur now that he has picked up speed past Jackeroos and B. B. Dairy and Raven's Child and is roaring out of town, closing in, he believes, for that one big shot he'll take at the edge of the ocean.

Chapter 3

Perry's reading Marcia's *Portable Nietzsche* again, a section called "Preparatory Men," though the particular passage he likes has not been underlined: "For, believe me, the secret of the greatest fruitfulness and the greatest enjoyment of existence is: to live dangerously!" Perry dog-ears that page just as the phone rings out on the porch, where he and Marcia have been drinking their morning coffee. Perry's dressed in a pair of purple-and-white Umbro shorts, a present from Marcia, who likes the baggy look—she likes Perry's legs.

"Hello," he says. It's Wayne on the other end, chanting, as he does at least once every Fourth of July to celebrate his own independence, the Country Joe and the Fish cheer.

"Gimme an F," he says. "Gimme a U, gimme a C," and then a pause, and then, "Everybody, c'mon, gimme a K. What's it spell?"

Nothing is duller for Perry than old politics, so he gives Wayne the har-dee-har-har treatment, and trying to change the sixties drift, he says, "So where it were?" meaning the current action. The second half of their standing phone joke, the response, should be, "In my pants.'" Private men's talk. But this morning, Wayne's wired—he's all Country Joe.

"Fuck," he shouts, and Perry holds the receiver away from his ear. He has been staring at Marcia, who's sitting on the top stair, sideways from where he is, her eyes closed behind her tortoiseshell sunglasses, head tilted back. It's the sun she's after, and it could be any decade and it wouldn't matter, and this moment wouldn't change. He can't pinpoint it exactly—maybe it's her hair, still wet and shiny from the shower and combed straight back, or what Perry refers to sometimes as her "Mariel Hemingway lips." Whatever it is, he's never seen her more radiant. The ocean behind her is deep blue. He hopes she won't move.

"It's in the *Random House Unabridged Dictionary*," Wayne says, "alongside all those other well-behaved, all-American words. Fathers use it in good taste these days in front of their sons. Go ahead, look it up. It's a goddamn good word," Wayne says. "Fucking-A right!"

"You need help," Perry says, "big-time."

"Big-time, small-time. By the way," he says, "what the fuck time *is* it?"

He's the only person Perry has ever met who does not own a watch or a clock or, at least for decoration like the people at GLP, a sundial.

"It's the holiday happy hour," Perry says, "so sit tight and I'll come rescue you from yourself, and we can retreat back here out of harm's way and wage our private war on a pitcher of Bloody Marys—a little Worcestershire, a touch of Tabasco. Whaddaya say?"

Now Marcia does move, shaking her head no, though she's sure there's little danger of Wayne agreeing to come out to the Point. He's made clear too many times in the past that there's more soul in one inner-city soup kitchen than in all the posh homes in Connecticut.

Marcia's not up to listening to him harangue about the rich folks again—it's tiresome discourse, and Perry knows she does not wish to occupy her mind that way. A book entitled *Infertility* is bent open across her thigh.

She loves Wayne dearly, but handles him best in small doses. They've had their share of flare-ups, Wayne explaining to Marcia how her life has been too sheltered, and she firing right back at him about how Vietnam has been over for almost twenty years and that he should rejoin the world, and Perry silent and trapped in the cross fire. To listen to them argue is to realize they are both, in their separate ways, out of touch.

"Naw," Wayne says. "Invite me next time there's a hurricane. I'll bring my binocs and a case of cold ones and we'll kick back and watch her come on."

"Or him," Perry corrects, reminding Wayne that the last big damage was done by Hurricane Bob.

"That's so goddamn ass-backward," Wayne says. "So Mickey Mouse. The sea is a woman, for Christ's sake, always has been."

The first two people of the morning walk by on the boardwalk. The woman carries a stuffed wicker beach bag, the guy a newspaper tucked under his arm. Both are wearing flip-flops and shades and they are holding hands. Perry can see the color—Day-Glo orange—of her bikini through the gauzy fabric of her beach top as she passes. Her legs are long and very tanned. He mentions this detail to Wayne. He says, "Hey, check it out."

"She got a husband?" Wayne asks.

"Somebody—husband, boyfriend. He's got a ponytail, just like you." Which is true, the guy does, though without the thick strands of gray.

"Yeah," Wayne says, "but with no religion in it. Yuppies without Christ. Just a lot of expensive mousse—just another rich, cocksure

Dobie Gillis. Nerdsville, man. Now gimme an F," he starts again, and Perry hangs up.

For the few seconds it takes for Wayne to redial, Perry thinks about the one thing his friend has right—there's a ton of money down here, trendy money some of it. BMWs and Saabs and Mercedes, a Rolls-Royce or two, most with New York or Massachusetts license plates. And all with GLP parking stickers on the rear bumpers. It's private and exclusive and safe, "a refuge," Betty calls it, from the poverty and crime and loneliness Perry sees every day in his work. He can pick out probationers and parolees anywhere—at amusement parks or at Foxwoods, the new Mashatucket gambling casino, where he's been only once, or in the supermarket. That obvious criminal element is not alive here. But as Wayne would argue, wealth is simply a different kind of crime, and worse, and bigger, and always premeditated. It's in the genes, he'd say. Fine, Marcia is always quick to point out, but it's the rich who spring for the lobsters he sells to the Harbor View or the Fisherman or Ye Old Tavern.

"Ask him what he needs us to bring for tonight," Marcia says when the phone rings again, and she points out at a schooner, its red-and-yellow-striped spinnaker suddenly filling with wind. Perry wonders from where. Onshore, there's only that same light breeze, barely enough to lift the hair from Basket's back as she sleeps.

"Well?" Marcia asks after Perry places the receiver in its cradle and walks over and stands right behind her, his hands in his pockets.

"My pistol," Perry says.

"And what else?" Marcia says back, that edge to her voice that means, Let's get serious for a minute so we can make some plans.

"A box of ammo," Perry says. "And some cherry bombs."

Wayne has not asked for sparklers, but Perry tosses two boxes of those into his knapsack, too, along with the inchers and ladyfingers and, against his better judgment, the cherry bombs. He buys his fireworks from a guy stationed at the submarine base at Groton, who says they're the real McCoy, smuggled all the way from China. He guarantees no duds.

Perry keeps rummaging through the hall closet of their apartment on Elm Street, what Marcia, who is waiting for him in the car, referred to last week as their "Nightmare on Elm Street." Cockroaches and silverfish coming up, the exterminator explained, through the drain in the kitchen sink. On his knees like this, Perry cannot smell the insecticide—he smells gunpowder, which he likes.

Marcia's ready to start house hunting, and she says as soon as she gets pregnant, they're breaking their lease. She'd like to buy into the new subdivision overlooking Palmer's Cove, right at the end of the cul-de-sac where the joggers, stopping to check their watches, run in place. Perry's not sold on the location—he claims all joggers remind him of Mystic's famous marathoner, Jim Fixx, who died of a heart attack in full stride. Perry cannot remember the year, but he can remember it happening, and he has thought about jogging as body abuse ever since.

Rent is not cheap anywhere in Mystic, especially for such a quiet and spacious apartment: ten-foot plaster ceilings and refinished hardwood floors in the hallway, a chandelier in the dining room. And a five-minute walk to downtown. Perry, after all this time, still likes driving up to such an enormous house, with its multipeaked roof and elaborate cornice work above all the windows. But during the fourteen years they've lived here, the apartment's wainscoting has faded from honey color to a darker, and now it seems, bleaker brown. Nonetheless, there's a large bedroom and a bathroom with a claw-footed tub and, in the living room, an alcove where you might expect to see a caged bird, a cockatoo or a parakeet. There's a piece of pink ribbon tied and hanging from the end of the string, which Perry yanks to turn off the closet light. The windows have remained closed because of the fumigation, and Perry figures it must be at least a hundred stinking degrees. The stand-up oscillating fan does nothing but circulate the hot, dead air.

So he exits quickly, the knapsack of explosives hanging over one shoulder, but no gun. Even so, he has an image of himself as a revolutionary, clomping down the steep back stairs outside, though he seldom entertains that kind of destructive ambition. Unlike Wayne, who is eight years older, Perry, to make a point about *not* being a sixties rebel, would gladly admit to feeling at least a little bit patriotic on this day. As would Marcia, relaxing and looking very middle-class in her Mercury Sable. Cruising the lots last year, she made it perfectly clear, after what the Japanese said about Detroit's autoworkers, that she'd consider buying only American. "Fine by me," Perry had said when they finally got in to test-drive the Merc. "I'm all for it, but how do I get this goddamn tilt steering wheel off my balls?"

Wayne is wearing cutoffs and ostrich-skin cowboy boots with red heels, no shirt, and a baseball cap turned backward that says KGB. The tarantula tattoo on his left bicep is green and blue. He's squeezing, with both hands, what's left of the can of Gulf charcoal lighter—a thin, spitting spray of fluid. Before he lights the fire, he rattles a box of snakes—what he calls his "lawful" fireworks—and scatters the black pellets, all of them, on top of the briquettes. Although there will be no loud bang, Marcia covers her ears and stands back as Wayne lights a stick match by flicking the blue sulphur head with his thumbnail.

"Ladies and gentlemen," he says, and tosses the match a few inches, igniting, in a single poof, the entire inside of the grill. Then, cupping his hands around his mouth, he hisses, and it's as if he's awakened the snakes in the flame, all of them erupting at once into a writhing tangle of thick black ash.

✳   24

Marcia, a lit major in college, says, "Eek, God, it looks like Medusa."

"Mah who?" Wayne asks.

Marcia, starting to explain, says, "Never mind."

"Greek mythology," Perry says, and Wayne, who is reaching into the cooler of water and ice for another beer, nods.

Marcia says she has to have a picture of this, and she reaches for her camera on the flattop of the piling. When she does, there is a small girl staring down at this magic from the sailboat in the slip next door. It's called the *Venture Capital*, from Newport News, Virginia, and it's flying Old Glory from the starboard stay. Perry has been reading the names: *Screws Up*, *The Doris Dawn*, *TopKat*. And the yawl that's been waiting for the drawbridge to go up, *The Dancin' Machine*. Wayne refers to them all as *The Money Pit*. He says lobstermen are different—always using a woman's name, that of the woman who somewhere, some out-of-the-mind time, forever and ever broke your heart. His lobster boat, moored over at the Fort Rachael Marina, is called *The Greta Garbo*.

Perry notices, on board the *Venture Capital*, a moped and a pogo stick and what he knows to be a pink Mongoose with knobby white tires, identical to the bicycle he and Marcia bought last year for Virtine on her birthday.

"Hi there," Marcia says, and the little girl, make-believe tapping an invisible computer keyboard with one finger—*her* magic—pauses and says, "That's my name I just spelled."

"Do it again," Marcia, the schoolteacher, says. She loves playing at these kids' games. Perry is certain, if this exchange were to go on for an hour, Marcia would show not the slightest sign of boredom. Nor would she be bored.

"Okay," the little girl says, and this time Marcia counts the taps—eight of them.

"Carmella," Marcia says.

"Nope, wrong."

"How about Mary Beth?"

"One name," she says. She's correcting this adult, who should know better. "Not two. Mary Beth is two names, a first and a middle." Her hair, tied back in a braid, is bleached almost white by the sun, the rounded front of her shoulders a color between deep red and bronze. It almost glows.

"Gertrude," Marcia says, the name she's picked for her first child if it's a girl, after Gertrude Stein.

"Yuck," the little girl says, and Marcia turns toward Perry and smiles and shrugs. He smiles back, then follows Wayne inside. "Give me a hint," he hears Marcia say, and then he stops listening.

The interior is all one room, minus the bath, and narrow. As Perry heard Wayne describe it one time in the bar, "You could piss across it with two good strong pisses." Which is probably true, but inaccurate, meaning that the image of someone actually doing that is all wrong for this place. Perry has spent more than a few nights here after arguments with Marcia, once during an electrical storm in December, when he and Wayne lifted and carried the couch up close to the sliding glass door and watched, side by side, the blue arcs of lightning dance and crackle across the water, all the way upriver and under the bridge. They socked down, in less than an hour, a fifth of rum. And no talk, nodding instead to toast their lives after each loud thunderclap.

It's dark at this moment, not just because they've come suddenly out of the late-afternoon sun but also because Wayne has already unhooked the power cable from the dock. They're about set to shove off.

"Here, take this," Wayne says. Perry, reaching out, can't see what *this* is, but he can feel it's Wayne's slingshot.

"And this, too," Wayne says. "It'll get chilly out there mighty quick." It's a sweater for Marcia, who is wearing shorts and a halter top.

✳ 26

"Francine," Marcia says as Perry steps back onto the porch, the fragile skins of those snakes having lifted and blown away over the river with the smoke. The little girl, hands on her hips, shakes her head slowly back and forth. "No," she says, pretending exasperation as Marcia shrugs again as if to say, What's the matter with us lamebrain adults that we can't guess a common eight-letter name? Marcia doesn't give up.

"Shirelle," she says. "Victoria, Caroline, Samantha, Marjorie." Not even close.

"Gretchen," Perry interrupts, and he can tell from the girl's silence that he's right. "Ah, one for the good guys," he says, and touches his fingertip to his tongue, like it's a pen, and makes a check mark in the air.

"Whoopee," the little girl says. "It doesn't take a genius." She's staring down at him as if he's just ruined all the fun.

"Ship ahoy," Wayne yells, Perry's cue to unfasten the tie-lines from the metal cleats on the pilings.

"Where you going?" Gretchen asks, and Perry tells her to the New York side to watch the fireworks.

"That's not till dark," she says.

"Well, that's true," he says, "but we're going to eat and relax out there. We'll see you later."

"Later when?" she demands, and Marcia fields this question, diffusing it by asking to take Gretchen's picture.

"In case we miss you when we get back," she explains, "I'll have a photo to remind me that we had this nice talk. Okay?"

She's not thrilled, but she agrees, and when Marcia frames her inside the yellow lines of the viewfinder and says, "Ready?" Gretchen strikes a facial pose that reminds Perry of faces he has seen in certain snapshots that come across his desk. Something in the eyes—it's not fear exactly. More like resigned, abandoned gazes.

But when the shutter clicks, it's as if Perry has blinked away this image, obliterated it, as he's forced himself to do more and more lately, especially since he and Marcia have been trying to have a baby. Marcia has never flip-flopped on the subject of having kids: for her it's turned into a mission. But more often than not, Perry's secretly relieved whenever another month passes and Marcia's still not pregnant. Today is the crucial time in her cycle, so once again Perry's on edge, moody and distracted, but functional and smiling when he needs to. He turns briefly and smiles at Marcia now as the houseboat begins to float backward, Wayne manuevering it with a twenty-five-horsepower Johnson outboard into the slow, heavy current. And because Gretchen knows they are all still watching, she shows off, life preserver and all, with a shaky, off-balance cartwheel.

"Cute kid," Wayne says, shifting from reverse to neutral to forward, then opening the throttle halfway, the propeller churning against the resistance of so much weight.

Marcia, who is still waving and yelling, "Hooray, hooray," agrees with Wayne—the child *is* cute. And much too young to be left unattended like this—Perry knows all too well about that. But he moves away, up to the front so he can help Wayne navigate toward the flotilla of yawls and catches and souped-up powerboats they will do their best to avoid before entering the open water, wanting this night to themselves.

Not burgers. Skewered lobster tails, split lengthwise and buttered and seasoned with pepper and paprika, and grilled eggplant basted with olive oil—Wayne showing some razzmatazz for once on the grill. And Marcia answering to Wayne's nickname for her whenever he's stoned and feeling good—Angel, he says. Or Angel darlin'. She's got her arms crossed under the sweater, the empty sleeves hanging straight down by her sides.

✳   28

What's left of the charcoal is an orange glow, and Perry, on a sea that has flattened out during the past few hours, keeps hearing what he believes are the end notes from a saxophone, though no other boat is close by and they are floating maybe half a mile off Clubhouse Point.

"Must be the Sirens," Marcia jokes. "Or the papaya and rum," Wayne chimes in, but Perry says, "No, listen," and they all do, to the slow rhythmic lapping of water underneath the hull.

Which is another kind of music, so Wayne, having finished his joint, gets out of his chair and asks Marcia, still leaning against the railing, to dance.

Perry, at Marcia's request, has given up marijuana; Wayne, honoring this decision, has offered him none. Marcia never started, unless, as she says, you call toking one time on a hooka in her college dorm smoking dope.

"Ma'am?" Wayne asks in his exaggerated cowboy drawl, squinting and bleary-eyed in what's left of the twilight. "May I?"

Spare me, Perry thinks, but Marcia says, "You may," and she curtsies, and Wayne drapes her empty sleeves over his shoulders, one on each side, so that it appears to Perry as if she's hugging his friend around the neck. But when her hands appear, they hold Wayne's waist, and he her elbows through the tattered wool. He lifts one pointy toe of one boot, then taps his heel as though counting beats before he and Marcia square-dance around and across the green planking of the deck.

Perry half expects to hear a fiddle, and a caller—"Swing your partner and do-si-do." He's attended such hokey goings-on back home in Michigan, and he detects in himself the slightest pang of nostalgia for the couples, his parents included, who lived for those Saturday nights, and how they'd be blown away by the crazy notion of a floating dance hall.

There's no allemande left or California twirl—Wayne is almost immobilized, his wiry body leaning on Marcia now, and Perry does not resist the urge to cut in, tapping not only Wayne's shoulder but Marcia's, too, and they drift apart just enough to include him, a tight huddle of three.

Marcia is giddy from the one drink she's had, and she's laughing at Wayne, who's mumbling something about an ad in the newspaper for Vietnamese potbellied pigs, over in Deep River. Overhead in the distance, the first airbursts spray apart into a slow-falling parachute of red. Perry wishes he were closer. As a kid, because his dad was friends with the fire marshal, Perry got to stand behind the guy who set the rockets off—he could hear the shells hiss out of the tubes, then that zigzagging fizzle the fireworks always made as they dissolved high above him in the air.

"Wow," Marcia says, "hurry," and she lines up three foldaway chairs, the middle one for herself, and with her fingertips, she taps the vinyl padding on the seats of the other two. "Hurry," she says. "Hurry up, you guys!"

Perry, as Wayne likes to say, parks his sorry excuse for an ass immediately down, but Wayne does not—he's headed off by himself.

"Wayne," Marcia yells over her shoulder to him. "Wayne, you're missing it."

"Over there, look," Perry says, and he points, not across to Fishers Island, but even farther away, down the coast toward New London. What resembles a giant time-lapse spider mum blossoms outward into a shower of lavender, followed by smaller, more rapid bursts of green and blue and gold superimposed. Then darkness again. Marcia claps her hands quietly between her legs, then leans over and kisses Perry on the temple. Except for the distant, intermittent pops, the display from each shore is silent.

Which, a half hour later, makes the high-pitched hoots and screeches from the party yacht approaching, not forty yards away, seem loud and irksome—an intrusion. They are motoring painfully slowly, as though

✳ 30

on patrol. Wayne has not returned, par for the course, and Marcia has stopped calling for him after Perry suggested they leave him be, just leave him alone.

"Aren't they awfully close?" Marcia asks, and Perry says, "We're okay; we're fine." The houseboat is unlighted and floats heavy in the water, like a miniature barge. Perry knows that all he has to do is hit the switch that Wayne has rigged to a DieHard battery and the lamps in the windows will all come on. He makes a mental note of where the switch is and, in a pinch, he believes he can find it in the dark. And anyway, there is little danger of being rammed. So when he yells, "Holy shit," it's because someone has just launched two Roman candles directly at them from the stern of the yacht. Perry and Marcia actually duck—it's that near a miss—his chair toppling backward and slamming closed against the deck.

"Hey, over there!" Marcia screams from her knees, and then more fiercely at the top of her lungs, "Hey, hey, hey," until a wavering beam of a searchlight finds her flailing her arms like a panicked swimmer, blinding her. She waves the light away, off to the side.

Someone, and Perry can see he's wearing a captain's hat and cupping his hands around his mouth, yells, "Sorry, mate," but the background laughter makes the proportion of such an apology an insult. The yacht is overcrowded and tilting, now that people, and there must be twenty of them, have gathered on the one side, the women, Perry realizes, in evening gowns, the men in white dinner jackets. He's almost certain it's going to capsize, or that the shit-faced passengers will begin to topple overboard, champagne glasses and all.

"If you're Haitians or Cubans, we'll reload," the same guy hollers over, the joke applauded with cheers and the shrill squawks of party blowers. Perry cannot make out what is said next, something about survivors and boat people, and Wayne says down to Perry, "Deep-six the pricks." He seems even taller and thinner up there and, with the tip of his cigarette, he touches the fuse of a cherry bomb alive, then slingshots it up and out into the sky.

Nobody's expecting this kind of bang. It's louder than any gun Perry has ever fired; louder than he remembers the stubby half sticks of dynamite his dad detonated to blow up stumps in their cherry orchard, Perry and his older brother, Hank, cheering each time the heavy, dark clods of sod flew apart into the leaves of the standing trees. But this noise, reverberating back at them point-blank off the water, has really frightened Marcia—she's crying, and harder with each new blast, her hands covering her ears, her forehead pressed against Perry's chest. He's holding her tightly, rocking her in the wake the yacht has left, motoring lopsided and hurriedly away.

"Make him stop," Marcia says. "Please make him stop." But Wayne, like a raging Dennis Hopper, keeps shouting crazy stuff about Tet and the Year of the Monkey from up on the roof. He has not lost his sea legs—even half-blitzed, he stands erect, not shouldering a bazooka or an M16, but holding a goddamn slingshot. The houseboat has shifted angles, and Perry can see, above and beyond Wayne, the sky ignited now nonstop in its leadup to the grand finale in this annual celebration of war and victory.

Wayne finally collapses spread-eagle on the roof, but Perry does not go to him right away. He stays with Marcia, who is still shaken but asking already if Wayne is all right, if they are all all right, everybody. She has never witnessed one of Wayne's freak-outs before, the aftereffects hard-core, like a seizure, and Perry knows Wayne will sleep up there and that he'll remember nothing about the night from this point on. He convinces Marcia it's true, but he does not expect what she says back. She says, "It's the time—I can feel it low in my stomach. I can feel it right here," she says, and she lifts her sweater and places Perry's palm over the spot, his fingers spread apart under the elastic of her panties. "I don't want to wait until we get home," she says.

Perry is the one who will pull-start the motor and navigate back, following the buoy markers into the channel between Mouse and Ram islands and up the river past the Jesuit monastery that cannot be seen from the water. Even people who have lived for years in Mystic do not know it's there.

"Right here on the floor," Marcia says, "under the stars," and Perry thinks, Not the Year of the Monkey, but the Month of Getting It On. Even meant as a joke—though it's not all joke—it would sound too crude, so he says nothing. He watches Marcia step out of her shorts and panties and pull the sweater off over her head. Then the halter top drops by her feet.

"Wait a sec," she says. "I want to see you better." And she pulls a single sparkler from the box and reaches up and wedges the thin stem into a hanging flowerpot. "Light it," she says, and Perry does. Then he closes his eyes against the shower of sparks and imagines not cherry bombs but cherry blossoms, and that blunt underground rupture of dynamite, and the way he and Hank and his father would drive back home, all three of them in the cab of the pickup. And he imagines the lilt of that saxophone again, the only instrument he ever played, and not well, and how simple and sad and romantic he believed each note sounded back then. At moments like this, he's scared out of his wits that he won't ever father a child to link to that past, to that early part of his growing up. And it's with this in mind that he turns back to Marcia and she can see it, through the dancing shadows, clearly in his eyes.

"We have to keep trying" is all she says.

He's being unfair when he asks her, "What for?"

"Curly hair."

"Meaning?"

"Meaning like yours. That's what I want," Marcia says, "just one baby with dark, curly hair." Then she lifts one breast as if to show

33 ✳

Perry how she'll feed that baby, and he bends to kiss her. She stops him and takes his head between her hands and forces him to look directly at her. "Curly hair," she says again, and aroused by the possibility of this, they both lie down.

Chapter 4

Perry does not refer to these people he sees, as some agents do, as clients; he calls them what they are, parolees or probationers. At least in public. But sometimes, in his own mind, for a clearer distillation of type and crime, he uses these names: down-and-outers or deadbeats or losers. Lowlifes, self-righteous slackers. Crooks. Bottom feeders. Scat mongers. Wackos. Gutterballers. Slow-witted dreamers, usually B and Es, toothless at nineteen and splitting firewood with a cousin part-time for a living. A balanced diet of cheap beer and beef jerky. Nothing storybook—the wallflower in remedial English who drops out in tenth grade with a gripe against the world and, deciding finally to settle the score, steals, over in Old Lyme, a Sony camcorder and a stereo TV he can't carry any farther and drops and leaves it in the tall beach grass behind this expensive summer place, his smudgy fingerprints plastered all over the picture screen. Boneheads, peckerbrains, cretin stooges, usually nabbed within hours of the break-in, the stolen goods displayed big as life in their tiny prefabbers or trailer homes. Wives or girlfriends, watching these arrests, stand back, their arms folded, and say nothing. Perry reads about such details in the police reports, because he's never there at the scene playing cops and robbers. When he meets these people, it's usually in the county jail, behind bars. He listens then to their side of the story, and yes, over the course of weeks or months or years, he might even grow to like them and, on their behalf, offer friendly testimony to the court for early discharge from probation. He has not done this, though, for Roland Knudson, who is in trouble again for violating curfew, and whom Perry will drive out this morning to see.

And there are the hateful sorts—louts and sickos; in Nietzschean terms, "evil for nothings." Garbage, scumbags, the ones who hurt and shame the kids, the child sex offenders.

Perry never takes his Harley on home visits—it sends the wrong signal. Because he did not stop at the apartment last night to pick up his Subaru, he is using Marcia's car, the volume juiced up on the tape deck for his favorite John Prine tune. Perry sings along: "'Life is a blessin'/it's a delicatessen.'" True enough, he guesses, and reverses the tape and replays that one, and before he realizes it, he's tailgating a woman who has slowed on the Gold Star Memorial Bridge, for what reason, Perry doesn't know. For once, there's no traffic merging left or right into the funnel of those heavy rubber dunce-cap construction cones. She glares at him in her rearview mirror, and he backs off, reading the bumper sticker on her Saab Turbo: IF YOU'RE AGAINST ABORTION, DON'T HAVE ONE. He hits his blinker and pulls out to pass and raises his coffee mug, nodding to her in absolute agreement with such a levelheaded admonition.

She refuses to look over, or even acknowledge him. She's attractive and annoyed and just girlish enough still to be under thirty-five. A career woman—he'd give odds on it—no fluff, no frills. He can tell all that simply by the way she cranes her neck, as if to demonstrate how, at 7:45 A.M., it's already been a long and irritating day, and now this goon. "You're way off base on this one," Marcia would say if she were with him. She'd say, "You don't have a clue when it comes to women."

Still, even during such a brief highway encounter, Perry cannot resist working up an imaginary character profile in his head: cashmere and pearls, a strict no-bargain shopper—Liz Claiborne all the way. Definitely a second husband, older, who has never squeezed the trigger of a caulk gun, and who hauls out, at cocktail parties, the trophy in his study to relive, insufferably detailed for his guests, his freaky midmorning hole in one at the country club. One preschooler— evidenced by the car seat in back—and more than likely a live-in nanny. And, because this woman leans slightly away from the window, her arm on the armrest, Perry concludes: frigid, aloof, treacherous in an affair, possibly the *Fatal Attraction* type. He stays in the passing lane and does not glance back, wishing she had smiled or waved, anything to prove him wrong.

Perry is not wrong about Roland Knudson, who is out of jail after serving six months in Montville for passing bad checks. Last week, he failed to report for a urine screen. His flimsy excuse? His truck wouldn't start and he couldn't locate a ride, this conversation a day later over the telephone. Perry did not say, "Horseshit," nor did he say to Roland, "You'd sure as fuck have found a goddamn ride if you were holding a winning lotto ticket." It's not in his personality, nor is it in his job to play the heavy—he's been trained to diffuse confrontation, to appear nonthreatening. What he said was, "Don't botch it, Roland. C'mon, don't start that sneaking around."

Perry has his own office in the New London County courthouse and, in the adjacent room, a part-time secretary. He likes being isolated in the old section of the building, which dates back to 1784. It's Colonial—clapboarded and picturesque—and does not feel so penal. Like most agents, Perry has his college diploma and certificate of appointment framed and hanging on the wall. He was advised, when he first accepted the job, not to decorate with any personal-interest items—no photographs of wife or family or Harley-Davidsons. And no movie posters: Marlon Brando or James Dean or King Kong. Keep it bland, he was told. Keep it official. Since then, Perry has hung, suspended by wires from the ceiling, the polished shell of a sea turtle, a gift from Wayne, who found the turtle floating dead in the Sound. Perry calls it his "icebreaker," and it has worked well.

On Monday mornings, before heading out on his home visits, Perry always checks in. On his desk already this morning, a police report. Subject? Roland Knudson. Perry reads it standing in front of the window that overlooks the intersection of Huntington and State. When he's finished, he slides open the heavy bottom drawer of his file cabinet and, for the next twenty minutes, prepares a charge form.

Roland lives out past the New London–Waterford airport, originally, and not long ago, farmland. All private planes, single-and twin-engine jobbies that take off and land directly over Roland's house, an aluminum-sided ranch with no garage and a brownish lawn and a picture window with the curtains usually drawn—against the noise, Perry suspects. But they are not drawn now. Across the road, a field of thistle and napweed and goldenrod, and in the field a red Firebird with yellow-and-orange flames painted along both sides. The hood and trunk are popped up as though the car has been sandwiched in a demolition derby and then left to rust. Roland claims it was in decent shape before he left to serve time; then one night some asshole or assholes took after it with pellet guns—the windshield and windows and headlights, even the glass on the dashboard, he said, the mirrors, inside and out. "Maybe you can locate the son of a bitch that did all that," Roland said the very first time Perry stopped out. "Maybe you could make that a goddamn matter of public interest."

Roland's wife, Angela, answers the door. She's wearing tight jeans with ankle zippers and a light blue Mystic Seaport T-shirt, a V neck that is not tight, and cross-trainers like Marcia's. She says right off that she does not know her husband's whereabouts, and she invites Perry inside. She calls him Mr. Lafond and offers not a cup of coffee, which he could use, but a can of Faygo orange. Perry's policy is to converse at arm's length, out on the porch, where he can simply verify residency and ask Roland how things are going—the readjustment, his job over at Junior's Frame and Front End Alignment. Then perhaps shoot the breeze a few minutes about the Pawtucket Red Sox, whether so-and-so's sinker or fastball is live enough for a shot at him being called up midseason to pitch with the parent club—a touch-base conversation. Which this one would certainly not be if Roland were here this morning. The visit is no longer what is referred to in the business as "relaxed" supervision. Roland is on the hook.

"Sure," Perry says to Roland's wife, whom he has met only briefly once before, but whom he remembers well. "Yeah, a cold drink sounds great."

Though Perry has not yet filed it, he has with him the petition for a bench warrant and parole-violation hearing. It's dated today and signed and there is no question in his mind now that he will file it this afternoon. Roland's full name is typed in the box under "Defendant." Under "Judge," the Honorable Frank A. Collins, who sentenced Roland the first time, and who is death on repeat offenders. Perry's name is listed, too, and the violations. "Term Three: Failure to report on June 26, 1992," the regularly scheduled report day for that month. "Term Seven: Failure to pay—defendant has not made his last two payments of $38.00 per month to the Court." And now this one, "Term Eight: Failure to observe curfew—defendant was seen leaving Lamperili's Seven Brothers bar at 12:05 A.M. on July 4, 1992, by New London police officers, one hour and five minutes past his 11:00 P.M. to 7:00 A.M. curfew."

Perry has been in the house before, one day when it was raining. He ought to recognize its interior, but, to the contrary, it seems all different—the couch he's sitting on, the color of the walls and the macrame hanging there, the new playpen, where the baby, Corey, is asleep on his back. A mobile of pink and green fish flutter and turn slowly in the air currents above his face. He's wearing a diaper and a white pullover jersey with snaps at the shoulders. His tiny fist is up to the second knuckle in his mouth.

Angela carries a tray from the kitchen—on it the can of Faygo orange and a clear plastic glass with ice cubes. She places the tray on the coffee table in front of Perry, then sits opposite him in a La-Z-Boy, reclining it to the second notch, her hands folded in her lap.

"Thank you for coming," she says, as though she has asked Perry to drop around, and, as soon as she closes her eyes and exhales a single deep breath, he knows she is going to cry. As she does, Perry says nothing, wishing that he had not come in. He pours the Faygo into the glass, and he can feel the cold carbonation on his upper lip before he actually takes a sip. When he does, it is much too sweet, a kid's drink. He wonders if that's what's in the baby bottle in the corner of the playpen.

"I'm sorry," Angela says after a couple of minutes. "I just have no idea what to do anymore. Mr. Lafond," she says, "I'm pregnant." She says it as though Perry were the father. "My son's not even ten months old and I'm pregnant again. The one night I wasn't careful," she explains. "And Roland knowing it but refusing to let me get up to go into the bathroom."

Perry attempts a sympathetic smile, but he's not at all sure it's the right response. He asks her if she's told Roland. She nods. "Want to know what he said? He said, 'Is it mine?' No kidding, he did, and of course I said yes, because it is his. Not exactly conceived in passion, but his just the same. 'Maybe so,' he said, and stormed out, and I know where to. Lamperili's Seven Brothers, to dance with the navy wives. Their husbands," she says, "go off for three months at a time on maneuvers."

Perry knows what ship she's talking about, the minesweeper USS *Fulton.*

"He came home real late," she says, "with that stamp still on the back of his hand. You know those stamps I mean? The ones they give you at the door after you pay?"

"Yes," Perry says, and he remembers how they glowed purple in the dark under ultraviolet lights in the college bars in Ann Arbor.

"Brilliant, isn't it?" she says. She throws open both hands and says, "Look, we redid the entire living room because I was tired of living tacky, always so tacky, and we can't hardly pay for any of it. Roland said any color was fine for the walls, as long as it was yellow. So I settled on eggnog. Do you like it?"

"Yes," Perry says, "I do—I like it a lot. It's soft."

"He's going to jail again, isn't he, Mr. Lafond? Isn't he?" Perry wishes she'd call him by his first name, though he's not sure why, and he's not going to ask her to.

"We're in crisis mode," Perry says, "and Roland has to come talk to me. He has to come in on his own or call me from wherever he is; then maybe there's a chance I can help him. It's all he's got left."

The recliner thuds, coming back into its upright position, Angela's legs uncrossing. She leans forward and stares Perry directly in the eyes

41 ✳

and says, "Sometimes I used to have this wishful notion that someone—I don't know who, a miracle man—would just appear and offer Roland a better-paying job, something secure and respectable, a job he'd like for once—a foreman or something. He keeps saying he'll score one sooner or later, but he won't, not anymore, not with a police record." She looks over at Corey, whom Perry would like to pick up or play peekaboo with and make smile. He loves the fat bowlegs of babies this age.

"Roland's been a good father," she says, "and deep down he's a decent man, too. But he refuses to play by anybody else's rules—he's always been that way, kind of carefree and crazy, which I guess was fine until it started making us both so unhappy. Don't people have to settle down sometime? Don't they have to stop throwing caution to the wind?" When Perry doesn't answer, Angela, embarrassed, smiles and asks, "Can I get you another soda?"

"I've got to get going," Perry says, and Angela gets up and, self-consciously, shyly, straightens her hair. It's cut short, Jamie Lee Curtis–style, and accentuates her high cheekbones, her long and, he thinks, graceful neck, a dancer's neck. She is narrow-shouldered, slender but not skinny, and Perry is finding it difficult to think of her as Roland's wife.

"Pregnant and losing weight," she says, and giggles and shakes the excess of her belt back and forth, the silver trim on the tip clicking against her thumbnail. "The all-grief diet," she says. "Nerves and worry and distress."

Perry, on impulse, does something he has not done to a woman since his one and only affair—he reaches out and brushes Angela's hair back from her forehead, and immediately it feels all wrong in a way that both frightens and excites him, low in the solar plexus. Angela closes her eyes at the touch, arms limp at her sides, making this as awkward a moment as Perry has ever felt on a home visit, awkward and in slow motion, like a dream. He wants to wake from it and be gone, and all he can think to say is, "Listen, you take care, you hear?"

For a few long seconds, he believes she's going to remain standing like that, her eyes still shut, waiting for whatever he says or does next, waiting, he thinks, for him really to come on to her. He clears his throat louder than he intends and says, "Good-bye," and starts to leave. He is almost to the door before Angela says, "Can Roland call you at home?" Perry realizes he has no choice now—he's opened himself up for this, and already he regrets it.

"Here," he says, walking back to where she is. "Give him this," and Perry jots down his mother-in-law's phone number on his card and hands it to Angela. Until now, he has always kept his work at a safe distance from his family and out of his private life.

"Roland does trust you," she says, "and almost nobody else."

"After six," Perry says back, "and for this one night only. After that, he's out of time and out of chances."

Perry does not date or make any notes about this visit in his road book. At least for now, he leaves the space blank, as though he has not been here today, and drives away past the junk Firebird and weedy fields, trying to decipher the strange place he's drifted toward in his mind. He wonders if this is what Nietzsche meant by "dancing on the feet of chance." You're no Fred Astaire, Perry tells himself, so pull it together, just pull it the hell together—a philosophy simple enough that even he can understand.

Except that he keeps having flashes about Angela, the rest of the day is routine, everything on the up-and-up, as it should be, needs to be. He finds Milton Sparks, not in his room at the Good Samaritan Housing Project, but outside, to the left of the door, where, because this is a converted motel, you might expect to see a canvas linen cart. Perry does not believe the sheets get changed much around here, at least not in number eight, the end unit. The doors are still all painted different colors; Milton's is mustard. It's open enough for Perry to see the green Naugahyde arm of a couch, and he can hear screaming applause from some TV game show.

"How's tricks, Mr. Deputy?" Milton says through that permanent smirk on his face, as though he has to endure these next few minutes talking to a fool. He wears no shirt and stays seated and bent forward on a bucket of driveway sealer, thumbing a Victoria's Secret catalog, his elbows resting just above his knees. He still hasn't bothered to pull the weeds growing up through the cracks in the pavement. "Came in the mail," Milton volunteers, "honest Injun," and he turns the catalog sideways and reads on the back cover, "Allison Arvo. Nice name but wrong address," he says, "or maybe I ain't had the pleasure yet of bumping into her." Coming from him, this sounds like a threat. He's out of prison after serving four years for assaulting his girlfriend with the butt end of a pool cue, then squirting lighter fluid on her legs and setting them on fire, her wrists bound with duct tape. Perry has his Basic Information Report with him, but he does not need it to recall these details, nor the conditions of the plea bargain—dismissal of attempted murder for admitting to the lesser charge. He remembers the number of jail credit days—156—and how, during sentencing, he hoped this slime would be locked away for good.

Milton's boots and pant legs are splattered black to the knees with sealer. In the back of his Ford pickup, cracked squeegees and crusted rollers. He says to Perry, who's looking back there, "We be fine on that score—I ain't outta work . . . just between jobs, which you gotta figure for, what with the economy and all. It ain't nothin' permanent."

Milton Sparks is a parole failure, and guaranteed, Perry predicts, to be back in the slammer within six months. Perry wishes it were sooner, except he knows, of course, that there must be another victim first. He hates standing here at the edge of this parking lot, the sun hot on his back, while Milton Sparks, sitting and grinning and squinting up at Perry from under the overhang, says to him, "You really oughta do me some good before you depart, and go knock on my wop neighbor's door and ask him real pleasantlike to stop blasting that wop Bon Jovi music every goddamn night. I got rights. Jumpin' Jesus," he says. "For the love of Christ, let me remember my stay here as part of the glory days—you know, it being the time I learned to behave and all. I'm making real inroads—cross my heart and hope to die." And Milton Sparks does cross his heart, and says, "You oughta cut me a little slack for good behavior—positive reinforcement, so to speak."

Perry won't, not ever; he'll help bury this self-serving reprobate if he gets half a chance.

"Cigarette?" Milton asks, leaning back and sliding a flattened pack of Marlboros from his pants pocket.

"I quit," Perry says. He hates responding at all to Milton, even with a lie.

"Yeah?" Milton says. "Me, too," and he lights up and inhales deeply and, holding the smoke in his lungs, says again, "Me, too."

As always, when Perry turns to leave, he can hear Milton Sparks, just under his breath, singing a line from Bob Marley's "I Shot the Sheriff."

Perry stops for a late lunch at Thames Landing—a blue-cheese-and-bacon burger and a tall glass of lemonade. What he craves is a cold Miller draft, but he never drinks—not even a single beer—on the job. He knows it's 2:45 exactly because, through the window, he's watching the Orient Point ferry back out of its slip, heading to Block Island. He and Marcia make that same trip, but always later in the summer, after the jungle of tourist traffic tapers off. He wishes they were on that ferryboat with their bicycles now, crowded or not, simply so they'd be going someplace away from the heat of the day, the heat of the past several weeks.

Although he does not finish his burger or chips, he says, on his way out of the restaurant, "Fine," addressing the receptionist, who has asked him how everything was. And incidentally, he imagines saying, did I mention that these fingertips brushed the hair back from Angela Knudson's forehead this morning, in front of her sleeping kid? This is not a confession—he understands that—but it is part of the growing hysteria he's feeling again. "It'll pass," he whispers once he's outside, and for a little while he's right.

He's parked out front on State Street, directly across from the Garde, the newly renovated art center, where he's promised to take Marcia to see *Tartuffe* in August. But he's not thinking spoof right now. Nope, he can't think of a single funny thing, least of all Walt Bolobas, his last appointment, about twenty minutes away on the Boston Post Road, just this side of Niantic.

Walt, as always, is already walking toward Perry the instant the car enters the driveway. Perry has never been inside Walt's house—the porch in bad weather is as close as he's gotten—and he has certainly never been offered a Faygo orange by Oleida Bolobas, who Walt insists keeps getting more and more frightened of people. "She's afraid," Walt says, "of what they might do to *me*. Oleida," I tell her. "Oleida, please."

"They who?" Perry asks, and Walt says back, "They who break your spirit and your heart and leave you like this—like me, empty."

Walt is a transfer-in, meaning his crime was committed elsewhere; then he moved here to the country, where no one knows him, where he and his wife of forty years have tried to begin their lives over again. "Doesn't work," Walt has said repeatedly to Perry. "How could it?"

His crime, tax evasion, and for it he has spent nine months in the can and has since made full restitution to the court and to the IRS, the biggest of all thieves, Perry is convinced. He's going to recommend for Walt's early discharge, something he has done only once before.

Walt Bolobas has more than paid his debt. Perry can see it, a remarkable clarity deep in the man's dark eyes.

Walt is old enough to be Perry's father—he's sixty-two and does, in fact, have a son in his late thirties, whom Perry has often heard about but never met, a solar-home architect who lives in West Hartford, not more than half an hour's drive.

"He won't speak to me, not yet," Walt says, forever updating Perry on that front. "One lousy mistake in this life, and for that I go unforgiven."

But not by Perry, and it is never his intention to hurt or intimidate or humiliate anyone in front of family or friends or neighbors, which is why he's happy to conduct this business out back under the horse chestnut trees, rare around here anymore. Like the elms, they're quickly disappearing. But these are old and healthy. Perry makes the point often of wishing aloud that he, too, was blessed with this kind of green thumb, and Walt explains each time that it's Crisco he's spread on the tape circling the trunks in a wide band—protection against the gypsy moths. The leaves in the distance are shiny green.

Last October, under the weight of his boot heel, Walt split a spiny greenish brown shell, then, peeling it back with his thumbs, exposed the chestnut, moist and glistening and a color Perry has only ever truly seen on a horse. That was the same afternoon Perry noticed Oleida watching the two of them from the kitchen window. He's certain now that if he were to turn around, he would see her peeking through the bend she always makes with one finger in the venetian blinds. Perry's confused by what further torment she's expecting to endure—Walt on his knees perhaps, his face pressed to the newly mown and watered lawn, wrists twisted and handcuffed behind his back?—such an incongruous image to conceive of in this place where Perry one day counted twenty ruby-throated hummingbirds as they hovered among the bell-shaped fuchsia and trumpet vines. Not that Perry knew those names, at least not until Walt identified each flower as they walked the grounds. A crash course, Perry thought, in the succulent, sweet seductions of nectar.

There must be at least a dozen birdhouses on the premises or, as Walt refers to them, "bird hotels"—six or eight small openings in each. He builds them in his fully equipped woodworking shop in the shed. He says the hotels attract a steady clientele of swallows and martins. And, flying even higher up, is an American flag on an aluminum pole.

It smells like some exotic greenhouse here, especially in early summer—honeysuckle and wisteria and, directly ahead, Walt's living fence, a hedgerow with thousands of voluptuous pink roses. Perry, as he gets closer, cannot stop staring at them in the soft breeze as they appear to tremble between shadows and tunnels of light.

"No more wait and see," Walt says. "It's way past that. Self-preservation's the order of the day now that we're without angels and saviors."

Perry nods, but it's not his usual good-listener nod. It's more to affirm in his own mind that yes, we *are* on our own—every last one of us lost and haunted by our checkered pasts—and to save ourselves we must take immediate charge of our lives. Make the difficult choices and shame those demons of distraction and desire.

"Simple, really," Walt says, and Perry wonders, What is? What's simple anymore, and why can't he blot out this sudden vision of Angela running toward him from under those high, vaulting branches of the horse chestnut trees beyond the roses? The fragrance reminds him of perfumed soap, and why should this cause such an acute sense of guilt?

"Because that's always the first step," Walt says, "always, always, always," but Perry has lost complete track of their conversation, concentrating instead on the redness of Angela's lips, those sad eyes, and also on how deeply he has suffered once before the consequences of a seductive woman's approach.

"Another year, maybe two," Walt says, "I'm never sure." He says,

✳ 48

"Oleida cries and cries into the void, and I'm no comfort." He says something about staying busy, something about compost and a posthole digger and, as always, gives the ritual pat on the back as Perry passes first through the neatly trimmed opening in the living fence.

Then it happens—he remembers the time of the lies to Marcia. And he remembers the biggest lie of all to himself, that the affair would teach him to love Marcia more. Such a cruel lesson when what you really learn—and Perry has—is that there's this dark place in yourself that can never be trusted, that doesn't give a good goddamn about truths or lies or much of anything. He's afraid, if he moves, that he'll enter that place, pawing the walls for a light switch, but there won't be any light—there never is, not there—and nobody who will be able to hear or help him.

But he can hear someone calling his name now. "Perry? Hey, Perry, are you all right?"

It's Walt's voice, Walt who keeps squeezing his shoulder and asking the same question of Perry, who's bent over and covering his eyes. "Perry, what's wrong? Talk to me, Perry."

"Jesus," Perry says. "Wow, it must be the heat. I guess I just felt dizzy for a sec. I'm okay though. I'm fine."

"You don't look all that fine, or at least you didn't a minute ago," Walt says. "Let's go sit down." Perry focuses on the wooden bench Walt built last summer and is now pointing to by the paddock. Sometimes the two of them will sit there in shade for well over an hour. It's always been good for Perry's soul. Until now it has, but now he just wants to get away.

"You look like you've seen a ghost," Walt says.

"No," Perry says, "it's nothing like that." Not anymore it isn't, because the only movement Perry sees is Rocky, Walt's Shetland pony, a gift for his two grandkids, whom he hasn't seen in nearly two years, not since the day of his arrest.

Rocky is certainly not the color of horse chestnuts. Perry can see

Rocky's white mane and tail. He can see that the small barn is newly painted—red with white trim—and that the cupola is, naturally, on the roof, sun glinting off the shiny bronze weathervane skiff pointing east toward the ocean.

Both men remain mute as Perry observes these surroundings, attempting to get his bearings again, his composure, a grip, for Christ sake, a direction.

It's obvious from the look in Walt's eyes that he believes Perry needs some looking after. "Go home to your wife," Walt says. "We'll talk soon as you're feeling better."

It's the first advice he's ever gotten from Walt, and he listens.

Chapter 5

"Mom's staying with Pauline for a few more days," Marcia says. "What a fiasco. I told Pauline on the phone, 'Dump Neil—end it and get custody of the children and move down here closer to us.'"

"He'll be back," Perry says, not meaning to defend Neil, but merely to predict the obvious, and sounding a little too self-righteous, as though a statute of limitations has excused his big cheat.

"I'd have the locks changed," Marcia says, attacking. "He's an idiot, and I'd no more let him in . . ." She doesn't finish her sentence, just continues to water the geraniums in the hanging flowerpots on the porch, pinching the dead leaves off and dropping them over the railing, behind the shrubs.

"Who's the woman?" Perry asks.

"What, are we playing twenty questions? The woman's the woman," Marcia scoffs. "I don't know—Helen of Troy. What difference does it make, for God sake?"

"Just asking," Perry says, raising his arms above his head as if in surrender.

"No, no you're not—you're grilling me, Perry, and for all the wrong reasons."

"Grilling you? Fine, end of interrogation," he says, and gets up abruptly to leave, but she blocks his path into the house, her palm open on his chest.

"I'm sorry. I didn't mean to snap at you like that. Take two," she says, as though she's just screwed up the filming of a scene. "Let's try it again. Sit down, okay? I'm sorry."

Perry does, and Marcia says, "Evidently, all Neil's revealed about her is that she's—get this—'earthy.' A sculptor or potter, from somewhere out on the Cape. Truro, I think. Maybe she can throw a clay penis on the wheel in his honor."

"A penis and two globby ape balls," Perry says, following Marcia's lead and imagining suddenly how unattractive Neil must be without his clothes. The man's got more hair on his shoulders and back than Perry has ever seen on a person.

"Why can't grown-ups grow up?" she says, placing the watering can on the floor in the corner, next to Perry's snorkel and mask and flippers. It's Angela's question, though cattier, and now Perry does not respond.

He'd like to get into his swim trunks and wet-suit vest and take the Jet Ski for a ride into and around the calm surface of Mumford Cove before they eat—fresh bluefish from Abbots on the grill, and what Perry calls his "famous potatoes," a kind of cottage fry basted with butter, pureed garlic, and fresh ground pepper and served with sour cream. But he cannot leave the phone; he needs to be here if Roland calls.

An hour later, it rings, but it's a wrong number, a young girl's voice asking for Donna. The second time, it's Betty, who reminds Perry to be sure and remember to put the trash out—pickup is once a week, on Wednesdays. "Betty, I have the memory of an elephant."

Then she tells him that an ounce of example is worth a ton of advice, but he's missed the context and says, "Here, let me put Marcia on," and he walks toward her into the kitchen, where she's tossing the salad greens in a wooden bowl.

Back outside, Perry bends on one knee and turns the knob on the propane tank clockwise, hears the gas hiss in the copper tubing, then presses hard three times with his thumb on the red igniter button before the grill finally lights. He adjusts the flame to medium, then lowers the cover and watches the fire a while through the rectangle of filmy glass on the front. The sky has already turned salmon color low in the west, and Perry realizes he is exhausted by the crisscrossing of emotions all day, how he both satisfied a powerful urge as well as frightened himself by touching Angela Knudson. At this very instant, he is fighting ineffectively against the bullying and irrational and, he knows, destructive desire to drive out there again tomorrow. Or worse, to drive over there tonight.

"Don't react," Marcia says as she backs out the screen door, the bluefish wrapped loosely in foil on a platter, the phone cradled between her neck and shoulder. "Hang on a sec. Here," she says to Perry, "take this," and he steps forward and reaches up and takes from her their dinner to cook. Once it's on the grill, Perry lifts the edge of the fillet and punctures several tiny holes in the foil with his fork to drain the oil and let in the smoke flavor. Fish on the grill is his specialty, and he's glad to be busy preparing it.

Marcia, sitting on the stairs, signals to him that she'd like a glass of wine by cupping her hand and tipping it to her mouth. Half a glass, she indicates now. Perry knows from the conversation that it's her sister on the line, and on his way inside, he yells hi to Pauline.

"Hi back," Marcia says. "Pauline says she misses you."

Because he and Marcia are not in the bedroom, Basket is, on the middle of the bed, imitating a miniature Sphinx. She growls at him when he enters to get a new pack of cigarettes from the bureau top.

"How short-lived the loyalty," Perry says, and on his way out, he turns and says to her, "Stunning pose."

He brings the wine out to Marcia—chilled Claude Moret—in a long-stemmed glass. When he hands it to her over her shoulder, she tilts her head back and to the side and smiles up at him and nods, then takes a sip.

"He's critical about everybody," Marcia reminds Pauline. "You, me, the children, Mom—everyone. He's the master at dishing it out."

"Plus, he's a loudmouth bore," Perry chimes in. "An infidel."

Marcia repeats it; she says, "Perry says Neil's a loudmouth infidel." Close enough, Perry thinks, squeezing the juice from half a lemon onto the bluefish.

They eat dinner at the card table on the porch, more silence between them than usual. Perry does not often display, outside the routines of ordinary, small affections, how much he truly loves this woman who sits across from him and who, at this moment, is wiping her mouth with a linen napkin and leaning back in her chair, saying she's completely stuffed. But he has never once lost the nerve to confirm to himself, even during arguments—and there have been some doozies over the years—that she matters and has always mattered more to him than anybody alive and that nothing can change that.

"You betcha," he says to her question about whether he's happy that they get to stay alone here for another few days. Perry's in no hurry to get back to the apartment—since the fumigation, it depresses him. After work tomorrow, he'll stop there and open the windows and vacuum whatever chemical residue he can suck up from the carpeting. And replace the batteries in the smoke detector. The exterminator explained that the clouds of poison would set it off. And he'll uncover the furniture and bring those sheets over here to wash. He and Marcia don't own a washer/dryer. Marcia likes doing the laundry at her mom's—it guarantees at least one visit each week. And as crazy as it seems, Perry agrees with Marcia, who believes there's a better chance for her to conceive in this house where they can hear the ocean at night as they sleep and wake and dream. It also frightens him.

"You're awfully quiet tonight," Marcia says, and he's not lying when he says he needs a full-fledged vacation, and not simply a long weekend, from the job. "I'm picking up two new cases on Friday, one for child abuse. Maybe it's really time," he says, "to pack our bags and head out for the Galápagos Islands."

"Do you wish sometimes you'd stayed with the teaching?" she asks, and Perry shakes his head. "Nope," he says, "mostly I don't," his standard reply. But it's true that working as a parole and probation officer was not a career choice, but, rather, the result of scoring so high on a civil-service exam and being offered immediately the job in New London.

Perry had been commuting every teaching day to Bridgeport, where he was associate professor in the criminology department at Sacred Heart University, and where he became involved with a woman who taught literature there, her specialty George Eliot, whom Perry has never read, though Marcia has, and loves. The affair was short-lived, and the aftermath of guilt and depression—at its worst, crying jags on the drive home—forced Perry finally to confess to Marcia, who just shook her head, not only in disbelief but also to signal that she did not want to hear any more—no names or places, no more weak apologies. "Is it finished?" she asked, and when Perry said, "Yes, it is; it has been," and promised that it would never happen again, she stood eyeing him for a long time. Then she said neither of them, for any reason, was ever to mention this, not ever again. And what wasn't said as she walked into the bedroom and closed the door was crystal clear to them both: a second affair would immediately end their marriage for good.

For six years, he'd offered classes such as Crime and Delinquency,

Social Stratification, and the Sociology of Deviant Behavior, the kind of credentials that appealed to the Department of Corrections.

In junior high and high school, though he did not then understand the impulse to fail or destroy deliberately, Perry was fascinated by those brooding kids who, standing backward to the bathroom stalls in the boys room, kicked, as they boasted later, the shit out of the doors with the heels of their engineer boots. When they arrested them a few days later, the cops said they probably used that same method to topple headstones in Saint Jerome's cemetery, Perry's grandfather's headstone included. "Who'd do such a shameful thing to the dead?" Perry's mom asked at dinner, his dad silent and shaking his head. Although he didn't say, Perry knew they were kids like Rory Mulvaney and Howie Greenspan, kids growing further and further every day into the full ugliness of their adult faces. Now Perry's mom, because of her stroke, labors to ask a different question—she wants to know why he, why in the world anybody, would want such a dangerous job. Maybe it would be dangerous in Detroit he tells her, but not here in Mystic, a logic only he understands. Marcia claims the job has spawned in him an unhealthy skepticism, a singularity too distrustful of everybody he doesn't know well. Maybe so, he concedes, maybe so. The reason he stays, he says, is that the little boy in him is still amazed to go up against that world of hoods. Or he shrugs his shoulders and, like his father does so often, says nothing.

He does that now when Marcia asks him if he feels like walking to the Casino for an ice-cream cone. Despite its name, the only stakes wagered there are gentlemen's bets on what time the last *Wall Street Journal* will disappear from the shelf, or the Sunday *Times*. But there's a soda fountain, where the pistachio rarely runs out, and some evenings Perry and Marcia do stop in for cones—sugar for him, plain for her— and sit on the deck that overlooks the lagoon of cabin cruisers and sailboats. Neil claims, with the collapsing East Coast real estate market, that a guy could snap up one of these houses on the lagoon for a million and a half bucks. Perry listens with benign amusement whenever he hears such crazy figures tossed around. Betty's house, on the ocean side of the Point, is worth even more. Almost worth hanging around for, Neil said one time to Perry. Marriage, he said, can be a beautiful thing, a genuine cockteaser.

"I guess not," Perry says about the ice cream. "Not tonight." Which should be a small thing, but his refusal brings disappointment to Marcia's face. They're looking at each other across the table. Behind Marcia, in the neighbor's yard, a boy about J.J.'s age begins to fine-spray a hose and laugh at the Airedale, who keeps jumping and snapping at the water, twisting so violently in the air that Perry believes the dumb dog is going to perform a paralyzing backflip onto the lawn. He's about to yell over for the kid to knock it off, but a man, the kid's father, Perry guesses, is already on his way out to rebuke the little shit. He drops the hose, but when he does, it loops on the ground in a contortion of rapid spasms, the nozzle wide open now and aimed directly at the man's crotch, soaking him as he attempts to sidestep and back away on the toes of his shiny black loafers. He's wearing creased white slacks and a red polo shirt, as though he's dressed to go out to dinner—attire for the relaxed summer atmosphere of the Wharf.

The charade might even be funny if the man or the boy or the woman, who is turning off the knob on the spigot, were smiling, or if the wiry-haired Airedale were licking the man's hands instead of cowering, its head turned away, haunches quivering. And what happens next happens quickly. The man slaps the boy across the face, then shakes him hard, at which point Perry gets up and steps to the edge of the porch, letting the guy see he's there watching. The worst part is that the boy does not cry and the woman does not go to him. She hurries back inside; this is strictly between father and son.

"Don't," Marcia pleads, touching Perry's arm, "don't interfere." But Perry does. He says over to the guy, "Enjoying the evening?"

"Such as it is," he says back. He's holding the boy too tightly by his bare arm, squeezing it. "Bruno," he commands, "get inside," and the door swings open just as the dog, on the run, reaches the top stair of their porch. "Torments that animal all day long," the guy says, "drives it nuts. You get inside, too," he says to the kid, who's peeking up at Perry, this strange, intervening adult. He obeys and, with his arms folded, he walks into the house.

"You're a fuckup parent," Perry wants to say. He wants to tell him there is no good reason ever to lambaste a child like that, not ever. He's waiting for the guy to speak.

"Hi ya," he says, noticing Marcia, who is also standing now, her hand on Perry's elbow. She nods but says nothing, and the guy, attempting to maneuver the conversation toward a safer, neutral place, says, "We're here renting, from New Delhi. Pennsylvania," he says. The joke's a flop. Perry's staring at him as if to say, Who gives a good goddamn where you're from—you're still a worthless asshole. "Wow," the guy says, "listen, this is a hell of a lousy way to be introduced. I'm sorry you had to see that."

"You should be sorry you did it," Perry says, his anger expanding in his chest and legs.

"Let's go inside," Marcia says, "please." She says, "I don't want this."

"Right you are, missy, right you are," the guy adds, looking down at himself like someone surprised to find he's just peed his pants. "Folks," he says, "have a good one," and Perry, who's been holding and fiddling with the wine cork, fires it at the back of this bozo's squarish head, and the shot doesn't miss by much—a couple of inches. "Fuck you," Perry yells over, but the guy doesn't turn around or say a thing. Both hands stuffed deep into his pockets, he keeps walking leisurely away, the smart move when you're on vacation and laid-back and trying to enjoy the long, easy summer days.

★ ★ ★

Perry sits alone on a bench at the far end of East Dock, which extends out from the shore for almost fifty yards. He cups his cigarette in his hand, the waves swelling and pounding underneath against the pilings. It has taken him twenty minutes to walk here. The lightning he sees in the distance above Stonington is heat lightning, not a storm.

But it's a storm he's thinking about. It's a downpour, and Perry, for the very first time, has allowed Janine to follow him up the ladder into the barn loft, where neither of them is supposed to be. They're lying side by side on their backs in the hay, the rain falling harder now and sounding like snare drums against the corrugated metal roof.

Janine reaches out and touches Perry's arm, and then she says, "Perry, it's too loud," but she's all right with her brother so close. She is until the rain turns to hail, and then Perry has to sit up and cover her ears against the clamor. It's so relentless and loud, he can hardly hear Janine, between sobs, calling his name: "Perry, Perry." But it isn't until the storm finally passes that she's able to finish her sentence. She says, "Perry, I don't want you to come up here anymore."

But he can't help going there, because in a sense he has never left. It was the last time they were together alone, and what happened half an hour ago next door makes Perry want to hold on to her and protect her forever.

The cigarette burns his finger, and Perry's suddenly back at East Dock, the moon shining brightly on the water. He no longer expects or cares if Roland calls. He doesn't much care at this moment what any adult needs him for, Marcia included.

"That's reassuring," Perry had said sarcastically to her when she argued that maybe what they'd witnessed was simply a case of someone losing his temper—he hadn't exactly beaten up his son, had he?

My God, yes, of course he did, and how utterly incredible what passes for acceptable, and how easy the renaming of motivation and events—poor judgment or indiscretion, or how so-and-so is going to have to live with himself now, the ultimate justice. Or this—Let's get the incident behind us and go on, the response from a mother whose baby died last year in New London from thirty-five broken bones. Thirty-five. Femur, kneecap. A ruptured spleen, et cetera, et cetera. The abysmal mentality of saving face, making do and protecting her marriage. The guiltier one? Her husband, a classical musician, a violinist, slightly bucktoothed, who committed this crime over several months, whenever the baby interrupted, by crying, the Bach or Debussy during the practice mornings at home. Bach, Perry thinks, Debussy. He cannot listen to either anymore. The musician's wife—it's true, because this is the world—is a successful environmental lawyer. Perry has seen the autopsy photos; he has read every vile word of the forensic exam. The ordinary person, as it should be, has absolutely no comprehension of the clarity of such things, nor do they really want to know, and Perry does not, will not, even if asked, describe for them the grisly details.

Marcia reproached him: "You overdid it when you threw that cork. Only a ninny would do that—what gives you the right? My God. And what's next? Are you going to scramble over there and beat him up? That's what you're doing to us, Perry, you're beating us up, and I can't take it anymore." At which point, Perry left the house, not storming out, but plenty angry. He did hesitate, shouting back at her after the screen door slapped, "You're wrong, dead wrong on this one."

Now he's watching the slow-moving incandescent glow of a scuba diver's light under the water, someone most likely spearing flounder, eight or ten feet down, as Perry used to do alone some nights before he sold his tank and regulator. He has seen long, fat black eels down there, and stripers and blackfish. Shutting off his light, he has felt rescued by the enormous dark silence of the ocean. And he has let himself sink in slow motion into the deeper water, where, on his back on the kelpy bottom, he has stared up at the wavering moon. Or closed his eyes, and he could not now swear that he didn't, for a few minutes, sleep there. And dream. The year? It's 1964. Mid-July, maybe a month after the hailstorm, and what his dad kept calling a bumper crop. He'd hired outside help—not migrants, but, rather, the sons of growers who'd already sold off their land to developers, but not so long ago that the harvest wasn't still in their blood. Perry can't recall their names—a second shaker and two haulers, and everyone working fast because of the weight of the fruit on the branches.

Perry's dad never played favorites with his three kids, though maybe Hank saw it that way when Perry got to ride on the tractor all the way down to the lower orchard, their mom upstairs in a cool bath, her way of dealing with the afternoon heat. Hank had just turned twelve, and his job, for only half an hour, was to watch Janine, and *not* to fall asleep in the hammock. But he did, not fifty yards from where the thousands and thousands of pounds of tart cherries were soaking in the water tanks already forklifted onto the co-op flatbed. At first, nobody thought to look there, concentrating instead on the barn and the outbuildings and under the front porch of the house, the obvious hiding places. Followed by searching the scarier ones—along the roadside—and one of the hired guys lifting up and sliding the well cover off to the side and shining a searchlight down there, his voice a trembling echo as he spoke her name. Then the sheriff's department deputies arrived, and a few minutes later the sheriff himself, everyone asking Hank the same question: "Where did you see her last?" Hank, stunned and holding out a Lincoln Log, said, "Underneath me. She was building a tower in the dirt right underneath the hammock."

"Hank—son, listen to me, d'you—" Perry's dad started to say, but he stopped whatever the question was going to be and turned suddenly away and pointed at the flatbed, and Perry, standing right beside his brother, knew. Knew not how she climbed up there but that she had. And the image he always returns to—and this time almost thirty years have passed—is not the image of his dad running full speed and screaming Janine's name, but the way his two muscular arms plunged into and divided that mass of red cherries and water, first in one tank, then in another and another, Perry's mom shaking her head no, dear God, no, this cannot be.

But what was, and is still, and always will be are the silence and the guilt and the grief that surrounds this family.

Now, watching the diver's light, Perry wishes he hadn't sold his gear—he'd like to go under awhile tonight. He had never once gotten caught in the undertow, though he had been warned at the dive shop that it was there, as strong as any on the coast, at dead high tide. "Dead is right," Marcia had said on their way out to the car, but she accompanied him each night and waited on the dock while he stayed down, his private lifeguard, he joked. But it worried her equally as much each time, each second, she said, until he'd surface and take off his fins and walk toward her out of the water.

He cannot tell right away that it's Marcia riding the mountain bike down the path and onto and down the center of the dock. He can hear the spokes spinning and the brakes wheeze as she slows to a stop, the front wheel almost bumping his knee. Her breathing seems strenuous, as though she's pedaled hard to get here.

"The police called," she says, and stares out at the water as if there's been a drowning, as if the diver who is heading toward them is searching for the body. "Why are they calling here, at Mom's? What's wrong that they need to talk to you so late?"

Perry holds his cigarette by the end and drops it through the space between the boards, and he stays in that position, head lowered, and Marcia says, "Perry, please?"

He doesn't want to talk or even move. Only to light up again and slowly smoke his next Camel, staring down for no reason other than to do it. There is just cause for this—the day has run out of options and he hasn't the energy left to solve or settle or respond to much of anything.

"The impression the police gave is that someone's in trouble and needs you," Marcia says. "It must be somebody we know, somebody who knows we're staying here. Is it Wayne? Perry, please don't do this to me."

She's going to persist, so Perry stands and straddles the front tire and grabs hold of the handlebars so that he's facing her. Her left foot rests on the high pedal, her heel angled downward, and Perry sees in the moonlight the tight muscle in her thigh. She's changed into a leotard top and cutoffs, and wears no shoes.

The diver's light, directly below them, moves farther under and toward the other, shallower side of the dock, where the barnacled cement stairs are. "I hated when you used to do that," Marcia says.

"That's why I stopped."

"Because you love and don't want to scare me," she says, and puts her arms around Perry's neck. "But you're scaring me tonight. You're all hollow-eyed and distant and angry, and you refuse to talk to me. The police have never called you at home before, never once in all these years, and you don't even seem concerned. There's something wrong, isn't there? And it's not just that idiot lunatic next door."

"That's a lot of it," Perry says.

"Only because you connect it to so many other things."

"Exactly right," Perry says, "because it *is* connected. It's like an early scene in a Bergman film, setting you up for the big nightmare violence."

"I hate Bergman."

"That's my point—you think the whole world is *Mystic Pizza.*"

"And you think the whole world is *The Seventh Seal.*"

"Which you walked out on," Perry reminds her, "and sat in the car."

"And locked all the doors," she says, "and waited for you in that parking lot for over an hour, half-frozen because I didn't have the ignition key. When I asked how you could sit through a movie like that, you told me it was brilliant."

"Funny," Perry says, "how we can remember so clearly a conversation that took place almost twenty years ago."

"We talked a lot more back then," Marcia says. "Even when we disagreed, I always knew where you were, where you were coming from. But you've gone careening off somewhere and I can't find where that is anymore."

"You found me here," Perry says.

"No," she says, and taps his forehead. "I need to figure out where you've gone in there." She looks beyond him and says, "Heat lightning," and stares at the sky.

The first time Perry visited her at GLP, she took him that afternoon here to East Dock—picnic, sunbathing, some important quiet talk—a break from the family madness. And showing off, he got a running start and performed for her his madman cannonball, shouting "Geronimo" on his way down.

"Graceful," she'd said. "Inspiring." And wearing a white one-piece bathing suit, a Speedo, she climbed onto the end piling and stared down at him. From where he was treading water, she seemed as high up as a platform diver. He was certain, if she dared at all, it would be feetfirst into the brackish water. But she bent her knees and pushed out into the most perfect swan dive he had ever seen—back arched, her nipples pressing against the stretch of the nylon. She entered with hardly a splash, surfacing behind him maybe thirty seconds later, and laughing. "Don't scare me like that," he'd said, but he had never felt more alive in his life, licking the salt from her lips and teeth. He needs that kind of resuscitation now.

"Kiss me," he says, and she leans forward. He does not hold her breasts as much as he cups his hands around them, lifting and massaging with his thumbs.

"I can feel the wine," Marcia says, and she unbuttons and unzips her shorts and, with her toe, lowers the kickstand. Since the injections, she has never once refused Perry, never once said, "Later," or "Wait," or "Not here," though he's suffered bouts of impotence more and more, blaming it on the sex overdose. But he has no trouble this time, Marcia sitting on the edge of the bench now, and Perry on his knees, and the diver sloshing toward shore already, maybe dragging a stringer of fish. All that gear to haul back to his car—all part of the risk and the enormous effort that Perry knows it takes sometimes to make of the night what you will.

Bond is set at ten thousand dollars, for which Roland must come up with 10 percent. Perry's not sure he can, but, not taking any chances, he requests and is granted over the phone a seventy-two-hour detainer to keep Roland behind bars. He's there this time for drunkenness and resisting arrest—not biggies with the jails so crowded, but certainly enough to get him another thirty days if Danny Higley, the arresting officer, whom Roland took a swing at, decides to push it. Perry's guessing he won't, if for no other reason than to avoid the paperwork. But Perry's convinced that Roland is itching to jump, and this time, if he's freed on bail, he'll light out to points south or southwest, Galveston maybe, where he's still clean and where a friend, as Roland tells it, has a good-paying job waiting for him on a shrimp trawler, working way out in the Gulf.

"Dreamland," Perry has told Roland. "Phantom employment. Fool's gold."

"Is that right?" he said back. "Well, you must've been raised something different from me. You must've never really needed to run bad enough."

Not from the law, Perry thinks. From boredom now and again,

for which the penalty usually means a hangover, though he admits those keep getting harder and harder to bounce back from, so he's been drinking less. Wayne has accused him recently of deserting the ranks of the deranged and the restless. Goddamn stick-in-the-mud, he called Perry, a goddamn pansy. First purging the good reefer, and now this. Next, a dipshit, dry-humping khaki and crewneck man. Just another sorry white-assed and willing victim of the great American middle-class crapout. But regardless what changes, one thing stands— should Perry ever need an alibi, Wayne will always cover for him, swearing up and down and across his Purple Heart and his live, pounding heart that Perry was at the houseboat, fucking-A right he was, for a couple of harmless brews and a chance to chew the fat.

After getting off the phone, Perry has explained to Marcia how he's climbed out on a limb to protect a probationer named Roland Knudson, whom he'll see tomorrow, but who might not, after all, be worth the trouble. Only a passing mention of Angela and baby Corey. And yes, after the lovemaking, followed by the "more like old times" talk, Marcia has fallen sound asleep. Perry, leaning against the headboard, has stopped stroking her hair. Because he *can't* sleep, he's been waiting for *The Tonight Show*, but as soon as Jay Leno begins his monologue, Perry aims the remote at the screen and listens to Jay's opening joke speed-funnel into a disappearing white dot of electric static.

What he cannot make disappear is the image of Angela standing before him in her living room, and it's those high cheekbones he imagines again as he quietly closes the bedroom door and dresses in the kitchen. A few minutes later, he's pushing the Harley out of the garage and down the street, past Venetian, all the way to Beach Avenue, where he stops on the bridge above the narrow inlet of the tidal marsh. He's breathing openmouthed, leaning forward on the gas tank, and trying to catch his breath. He does not immediately turn on the key and push the electric start for two reasons: first, cruising Angela's house at midnight is too fucking dumb to be believed, and secondly, Perry has just caught a glimpse of something moving up from the spongy, low-tide bottom ground and through the sharp blades of the marsh grass. He makes no mistake that it's a fox, the bushy tail straight out as it passes head down under the streetlight and telephone wires and angles directly at Perry.

He tries to place the weirdness of this scene in his mind—a man half-exhausted from sneaking out on his wife and pushing a Harley hog at midnight onto a bridge in the center of a resort community surrounded by ocean and the flat, rhythmic slapping of waves. Tennis courts he cannot see but knows exist behind the high chain-link fencing. The Casino white and empty and dark inside. Something right out of Kafka or Robbe-Grillet. A place without mountains for the beasts to come prowling down from, howling their nightmare choruses of grief. Not as odd as a seal or a zebra, Marcia's favorite animal, but a fox here is odd enough to be disbelieved, especially the way it stops, not twenty feet away, and stares at Perry. There's something in its mouth, and Perry knows what when he hears the sudden and unmistakable sharp, whining shrill of a rabbit that he can now see kicking to free itself from whatever, even harsher cruelty it is being carried toward.

If Perry had his pistol with him, he would not open fire the way he has seen his dad open fire across fields at dusk. He would do exactly what he is doing now, nervously wetting his lips. Nothing else. If this were a dream, perhaps he would chase and shoot at the fox from his Harley, down Atlantic and across Bridge Street, then reload and pursue on foot into the estuary, knee-deep in mud and screaming himself like an asylum escapee to let the rabbit go. The truth is, Perry has never seen a fox so close, and it is truly a beautiful pose, more so because of the rabbit's high-pitched-frequency terror. Perry's brother, Hank, used to raise them in a hutch behind the barn, then kill them with a silver cleaver—a single blow between the ears—and hang them on hooks and skin them and sell the meat to a limited but steady clientele. Perry is not squeamish about such things.

And because this is not a dream, the cop who has spotted Perry is real and the cruiser approaching with its lights off is real, too, and Perry, pointing to where the fox really did stop and stare at him, appears suspicious. Since he has no GLP sticker on the Harley and no wallet with him, he is told to sit tight, hands on the handlebars, and answer a few questions. No problem. Perry says he understands.

The cop is holding a flashlight out in front of his forehead, the beam shining down not into Perry's eyes, but dead center on his chest. There's been no radio for backup because this cop has seen Perry on the Point before—it's a routine check, a soon-to-be chat, Perry guesses.

"Betty Benoit," he explains, "is my mother-in-law—over on Shore Avenue. My wife and I are staying in the house while she's in Boston, probably for a few more days."

The cop nods like he's got the picture. Let's everyone relax a sec. We'll just have a look-see at what's in the saddlebags. It's his job, nothing personal you understand. He finds exactly what he expects to find—no booze or dope or weapons—only a socket set and an extra taillight bulb and, wrapped up in a chamois cloth, a can of McGuire's Mirror Glaze.

"You married one of the twins," the cop says, making it sound like an accusation, like he's about to link this discovery to something else, something illegal.

"The older one. Marcia," Perry says, clarifying for the record.

The cop turns off the flashlight, folds his arms, and says, "They had a lot of fanfare when I knew 'em in high school. Swam one-two on the varsity squad, or two-one, or one-one—I never could tell them apart back then. Great behinds," he says, and, no offense, but they were identical in that department, too, no way you could choose between them.

As if this baboon butt ever had a choice, a prayer, or a clue, but Perry does not respond. He watches the cop peer back at the cruiser, but it's only static on the police radio. Perry can see, in the perimeter light from the streetlamp, that there's no shotgun barrel poking up above the dashboard, no iron grate separating the front seat from the back—no need, not patrolling here. "Those two together," the cop continues, "hell, they made mincemeat out of the competition, and I don't care where in the state they were bussed in from. I figured sure I'd see 'em both someday in the Olympics. Christ, the way the water swelled around them in the lanes when they butterflied side by side. Like porpoises. Naturals," he says. "And real nice girls." He shifts his weight. "Kids?" he asks.

"Pauline, she's got two—a boy and a girl," Perry says, and it's as if he's implied that the two sisters are as identical in childbearing as they were twenty years ago, breaking the surface water in the high school pool with their exquisite behinds.

The cop's instincts are surprisingly good. "But not you," he says.

"Not yet," Perry tells him, and immediately he tries to sense what the cop is thinking—like, We're all approximately the same age here, bub, so who's kidding who? And by the way, where are you headed so late, and who's shackled with the big inadequacy to procreate, you or her?

But Perry's dead wrong about this guy—he's not here to pry or harass. "That's no federal offense in my book," he reasons. Then, amending that, he laughs and adds, "Course, down here in kiddie paradise, you'd think it is. Kids are status. You ever seen so many kids? Me, I'm a 'one time to the altar' kinda guy, and I'm not what you'd call anxious to open the floodgates on all that raising a family stuff. Time's time, the way I look at it, if you catch my drift."

Perry lies and says he does. "A confirmed bachelor," he offers as a kind of odd congratulations, then changes the subject and asks this cop, whose job it is to patrol and observe, if he's ever seen a red fox on the Point.

"The foxes!" he says, a spontaneous but feeble imitation of Steve Martin and Dan Aykroyd. "Red foxes, blond foxes, gorgeous brunette foxes." And, he says, and this is strictly off the record, there are foxes in certain windows lighted brighter than a New Orleans peep show, and nothing cheap, he emphasizes, about these ladies.

And here's Perry, sitting on a motorcycle in the dark, and doesn't this smack just a tad of your typical late-night Mr. Peeping Tom?

"Don't even think it," Perry says, and the cop laughs and shakes his head and advises Perry right. No driver's license or registration or helmet, no real route to resume.

"Go home," he says. And just as Perry heels the kickstand up, the cop adds, "Hey, no kidding, you should've seen your wife swim— there wasn't a guy alive didn't wish he could come out of the stands and hand her a towel when she climbed dripping wet out of that pool. Or Pauline. Either one. That's good stock."

"I'll tell them that," Perry says, and he starts the Harley, which chugs as he makes a U-turn but smooths right out throaty and clean after he picks up a little speed, only to kill the engine and coast the final forty or fifty yards in neutral through the open door of Betty Benoit's garage—where he stays a few minutes until he hears Marcia's feet padding from room to room, then her voice calling his name, which was never famous, nor ever will be, as far as he knows. But he answers, and then he goes in.

Chapter 6

What Roland is not short on is belligerence and judgments and surges of great uncertainty about almost everything important in his life, as well as schemes to change it, which inevitably mean leaving for someplace else. Texas most recently; before that, Fort Lauderdale, to work maintenance for a new condominium development. And early last spring, the frost gone from the ground, the opportunity of a lifetime, he said, to go equal partners on a used backhoe with a guy in Wisconsin—digging out irrigation ditches for the beet growers. He's twenty-nine years old. When the dispatcher buzzes Perry through into the consultation room, Roland, who's already seated behind the table, looks up. He's red-eyed and badly in need of a shower and a shave. He looks like he's been sick—hair sticking out on one side and in back, and there's a welt on his left cheekbone.

"Let me guess," Roland says. "You brought the blindfold and a length of rope to tie me to the firing post."

Perry takes the hard line—he's abrupt and all business and says,

"Let's cut the crap." Message delivered loud and clear. Roland closes his eyes, leans back in his chair, and lowers his chin to his chest, remaining unresponsive for the next several minutes while Perry talks at him nonstop. A regular storm trooper, and then he backs off. "You agree to attend AA and a continuing-education class, and maybe you walk this time—there's an outside chance."

"Two things I ain't," Roland says, his arms folded so that the knuckles of each fist push up against his biceps, "an alky and a student. Me," he says, forcing a laugh, "in a goddamn encounter group or a classroom. I don't take to that kind of stuff in a big way, and I don't much care if it's real school or evening yoga or whatever the hell you got in mind. C'mon, man, that's like reheated sauerkraut—it don't go down so good."

"Then swallow harder," Perry says.

"What you mean is, I should eat more shit." He's staring at Perry now, shifting his weight and leaning forward and resting one forearm on the table edge, a gesture to show he's not backing down one lousy inch. He purses his lips, and by doing this he's saying with his eyes, Let's bag the whole discussion, because here's the bottom line, plain as fucking day—the joint or a program I can't handle, so what's the point? What's left to rehash?

"The point," Perry says, as though Roland has actually verbalized the question, "is that you'll go stir-crazy doing push-ups in here, waiting for your court appearance, and I'll make sure the good judge sets a high bail at least until you decide you want to talk to me."

"And life everlasting, amen," Roland says.

Perry keeps fast-tapping the tip of his ballpoint against a yellow legal pad. "Write this down," Roland says. "Write down that I'm a bad boy and that badness is in my blood because I got the shit kicked out of me by my old man when I was seven or eight or nine or whatever the hell year it is you realize that age don't mean diddly—

what matters is that it's your own father hates your ugly guts and you ain't got the foggiest notion what for. For nothing, as it turns out, that's what, except you're you and maybe like some parasite you're gonna multiply and contaminate the whole civilized world. So, Mr. Lafond, let's talk, but in your heart of hearts you know the medicine you prescribe ain't got enough punch to cure me of that past. Even the shrink told me that. You gotta nip it in the bud to stop the disease, but nobody did. For your information, I take notes, too, mental notes," and he taps his temple with his forefinger, "and I got words for what you are, all of you blue bloods, if you're ever interested and decide someday maybe you need a review."

Perry's been over and over Roland's character profile: short-tempered and shrewd, outspoken, outraged about what his life's become. It's all clinical and simple enough and blatantly true. And most likely irreversible. Let's go through the motions again, Roland is saying, but let's also be up front about it and admit you people don't know squat about where I been, and he's not talking about his case history—runaway and ward of the state at fourteen, foster homes where there's always room for a troubled boy: take 'em in, turn 'em out. He's talking about someplace inside himself he can't quite name or describe except by taking a swing at the arresting officer, who decides to shake him down. Or by pointing at a pellet-riddled flaming-red Firebird in an old cow pasture across from his house, pointing and nodding, as if to say, There, right there, do you see it? Not what's left of the car—not that exactly—but the open passenger door into the weeds. Imagine there's a boy, he's saying, who's been hiding in that junk, any junk and anywhere, and that the boy is one Roland Knudson, and it's 1969 or 1970 and his own father has just chased him all the way down the embankment and has caught him finally, whipping long welts across his bare back and shoulders with the broken-off radio antenna. Fathom that place, Roland's anger demands, and forget the

73 ✳

station wagon where a father, sliding in—last evening or last year or anytime—says to his son, "Scoot over," and they drive away alone, just the two of them after dinner, for double chocolate dips at the Tastee-Freez, followed by a quick trip to Family Home Video to rent *Home Alone* or *Hook* or *Who Framed Roger Rabbit*, whatever the kid wants.

Perry clips the pen back into his shirt pocket and tosses his pack of Camels onto the table between him and Roland. "Let's begin again," he suggests. "For openers, can I offer you a cigarette?"

Roland breathes in deeply. "Yeah," he says. "Yeah, thanks," and Perry hands him the book of matches, the striker on the back. Roland, lighting the match, cups it in his palms as though protecting the flame from the wind. It's a method and it's a look. But Roland has spent the night in the drunk tank and he's got a bad case of the shakes. "Jesus," he says, holding out one hand to show Perry. "Jesus Christ."

Roland then gives his version of last night's events, which is not so different from the police report, except that the cop refers to Roland as the suspect and Roland refers to the cop as both the mental midget and the schmuck. "You want we should eliminate the guesswork?" Roland says. "Fine, here's the night in a nutshell. One: my wife drops me the big bomb that she's knocked up and I blow sky-high. With me so far? Two: I vacate the premises—see, I've learned the legal lingo—and I get into my pickup and head for Lamperili's Seven Brothers, believing there's enough free military nooky there to transport me smiling into the hereafter. Number three: I get absolutely blasted instead on shots and beers, a freebie for every three I drink. And finally, your eager-beaver law-enforcement officer with the flattop and the earring pisses me off when he decides to frisk me, and you've already pieced together what transpires after that. Who'd believe it, a goddamn cop with an earring." Roland inhales and tips his head back and blows three perfect smoke rings at the ceiling, each ring tighter and passing through the one in front.

"You plead no contest," Perry says, "and you call the judge 'Your Honor,' and *not* 'Your Majesty,' and you offer an apology to him and to Patrolman Higley and we go from there." Perry remains up-tempo. He says, "We get you out of here and back home and back to work. And no additional jail time if we're lucky."

"If we're lucky," Roland corrects Perry, "Angela doesn't have the baby. In front of God and the mortgage company, we're forever half a payment away from losing the house. Since the day we bought it we've been riding a roller coaster between flat broke and almost broke, those bounty hunters from the collection agency constantly breathing down my neck. It don't excuse that I wrote those bogus checks—I ain't saying that. I'm just trying to make real clear that this is the wrong time to consider raising a second kid. D'you fathom what I'm saying? There's still welfare abortions in this goddamn state, right? Gimme a real chance to get on with this life of mine—think about that for me, Mr. Lafond, and see if you can get my wife to contemplate what I'm telling you. I don't care right this minute about the chickenshit charges or about getting out of the slammer. I got bigger problems to confront, problems that *really* hurt and that I'm sorry as hell about. This stuff, it ain't important, not finally. Talk to her for me."

Roland seems on the verge of tears, but they don't come—if anything, his eyes begin to brighten through the redness, to sparkle. Perry does not have to turn around to know it's Angela leaning against the thick glass panels in the outer room. And he would not be far wrong if he guessed she was leaning with her left shoulder and waving baby Corey's tiny hand back and forth, and baby Corey suddenly smiling and reaching out with both arms, now that he's recognized his daddy.

Then these alternating images: Roland being escorted back into the cell block, and Angela, the impounded pickup released to her, steering with both hands onto the dirt road to her house. Roland dressed in prison blues and lying on his back on the jail cot, hands behind his head, eyes open or closed on the mountain vistas he imagines in places like New Mexico or Arizona, places he's never been. And Angela changing out of her dress and staring from the bedroom window at the rusty chaise lounge on the small ground-level back deck. Or trying to compose herself in the bathroom mirror, a cold washcloth pressed against the pulse under her chin. Perry does not allow himself to take the scene any further and instead plunges headlong into the nondescript tedium of the paperwork on his desk.

When he does see Angela again, it's here in the safety of the office, late in the afternoon, the air conditioning so cool that she asks to borrow his sport jacket, which is draped across the back of his swivel chair. "Yes, of course," he says, and gets up, but he does not walk behind her, holding the jacket open. Her sundress is sleeveless, and he's nervous that his fingertips might brush against the bare skin of her arms or shoulders. "Here you go," he says, reaching across the desktop.

"Thank you," she says, and swings it around her like a cape and sits back down, pinching the lapels closed at her throat. "You'd think in summer nothing could be too cold. Funny," she says, "in winter it's the exact opposite. I wonder if there's any place the climate's perfect. I read once—I can't remember what in, some magazine—that women adapt better to the heat than men. But not me—my joints swell up when it gets too hot. Look, I can't even slide my ring off. I feel best at around seventy-two degrees. Except in the shower," she says, "especially outdoor showers at night. Then I like it at whatever temperature it is you get steam, and your pores open up and you feel really good and clean."

There's an outdoor shower at the beach house, and the image in Perry's mind now is a white towel hanging on the hook and, because of the space between the ground and the bottom edge of the clapboard stall, a woman's narrow, perfectly arched feet on the slat-wood pallet, then a hand reaching down for the dropped bar of Ivory soap. And the sound of the nozzle spray, and yes, there's steam rising.

"How'd you find Roland to be when you left?" Perry asks. "Did he seem okay?"

"Both okay and not okay," she says. "Temperamental as always—furious one minute and then remorseful, though he kept his voice pretty calm 'cause he was cradling Corey in his arms the whole time we stayed. Corey's taking a nap at my friend Brenda's house—I dropped him off before I drove over here. He's been a handful ever since we left the jail, crying so hard once I thought sure to God he'd choke. And sweating bullets—you wouldn't think a baby could sweat like that, but they do if they're upset enough. Plus, he's developed a diaper rash on both legs. I guess in this family it's a good day to be miserable," she says. "I mean . . ." She doesn't finish; she bursts into tears, covering both eyes with her free hand, then with both hands, the sport jacket sliding off her shoulders. Perry does not look away. He snaps a couple of Kleenex from the box and walks slowly around to her.

"Here," he says. He says, "Angela, listen to me," and he crouches in front of her, his hands on her wrists; he can feel the heat of her body, and he does not shy away when she presses her forehead against his. "Angela," he says again, but she shakes her head no. She wants only to stay the way they are, huddled together. He hopes nobody knocks on his door, and nobody does, and as he lets go of her wrists, Angela grips his hands and squeezes. "Help us," she whispers, sniffling. "Please help us—help me," she says, her lips wet when she sits back halfway and blows her nose. Perry's almost certain it's red licorice he smells on her breath—it's sweet like that. He clears his throat and swallows, but still his voice sounds raspy when he speaks. He says, "This is only a setback, Angela—the bottom has not completely fallen out. It was a dumb stunt—it's typical Roland, you know that—but I haven't thrown in the towel on him, not by a long shot. It's best I keep him locked up until tomorrow morning—he still needs to cool down more. I'll be talking with the magistrate before I leave, to see if he'll rescind bail. Everything will be back to normal in a day or two. I'm sure it will."

"I'm numb from what's normal in my life," she says. "*This* normal. Trouble and debt and food stamps Roland's embarrassed to use, or to let me use, and trades instead at half their value for cigarettes and beer—that's all normal, too. Normal means all mixed-up in our household, Mr. Lafond. What you're saying I know I need to hear, but nothing makes any sense anymore. Especially another baby." Perry does not have to wonder long if she means to add abortion to that list of normals. "Don't misunderstand—I'm going to have the baby," she says, "even if it ruins my marriage, which it might. I love Roland, but I'm already dreading the next time he screws up, and the next, and the next. That's no way to live, and I won't forever. When I leave your office, I'll be driving a pickup truck that sputters and stalls. I'm not even sure I can get home in it."

"I'll follow you," Perry offers, standing again, then half sitting, half leaning against the edge of his desk. "I'll meet you back here in forty-five minutes," he says, Angela staring up at him as if to ask if she can wait right here, if she can wait quietly for him until he is ready.

Her friend Brenda lives in a duplex over on Masonic. Perry is parked behind the pickup, baby Corey's car seat next to him. The pickup has oversized tires—not monster-truck tires, but big and wide—and pink windshield wiper blades and a cargo net where the tailgate used to be. A woman driving this rig, Perry thinks, should have big teenybopper hair and be fast-cracking big gum and *not* wearing a lightweight summer dress and carrying a baby down the walkway toward him.

Angela opens the passenger door and straps baby Corey in. Perry does not mean to, but with Angela bending over like this, he cannot help seeing down her cleavage.

"There," she says, "all set to ride with your uncle Perry," which is what J.J. and Virtine call him. "Oops," she says when baby Corey reaches one hand out to her. "Can't forget this," and she takes from her pocket a pacifier and slides the nipple into his mouth. Then she repeats what she's told Perry about reaching over and tickling the baby's knees or ribs if he starts to cry. "Sometimes that works," she explains. "If not and you need me, just honk and I'll pull over, but I have a hunch he's going to be a good boy. Right," she says, and kisses Corey on top of his head.

Perry has never driven a car alone with a baby so young; he has never had a baby seat in this car before, in any car. J.J. and Virtine were old enough for seat belts the first time they went anywhere with him—to the dive shop in Groton, if he remembers right. He felt like an uncle. But this feels different—this feels a lot like something else, and he knows what when he stops at the first traffic light, baby Corey wide-eyed and watching him. "Hi there," Perry says. "There's your mama ahead of us. Look, up there," and he points at Angela, who's waving into her rearview mirror, as much, Perry believes, at him as at her son. To anyone observing, they could easily be a two-vehicle family in tandem, heading home. Angela has scattered a handful of doodads on the front seat—a set of measuring spoons on a ring, a rattle, a plastic Oscar the Grouch. Ejecting John Prine, Perry plays the Hap Palmer tape Angela has borrowed from Brenda. It put Corey to sleep, she said, and it does again, before Hap even finishes singing "Walter the Waltzing Worm," who wiggles and squiggles and squirms.

Which is a little like what Corey does when Perry lifts him from the car seat, but he immediately settles into Perry's arms, never once opening his eyes. "You're so good with him," Angela says, asking

Perry if he'll carry him into the house. "This way," she says, and he follows her to the side door and watches her unlock and shoulder it open when it sticks. Perry steps inside and she closes it behind him. "Through the kitchen," she says, "first room on your right. Or thereabouts," she jokes, touching Perry's elbow, guiding his first few steps.

The peacefulness in the weight of this sleeping baby makes Perry want to hold him longer, and he pictures himself as the father, browsing the shops on Main Street in Mystic, or walking the boardwalk at the beach, Marcia beside him, pushing the empty stroller. But he knows, lowering Corey onto his back into the crib, that a quick exit is a must. Just leg it on out of here, he tells himself. This time do the smart thing.

But it's Angela with the leggy stride, heading back to the house with the car seat and toys, and she says to Perry, "Won't you stay? I'm going to pop a couple of egg rolls into the microwave—I haven't eaten all day. Are you hungry?"

He's already standing in the driveway, his car keys in his hand. "For just a few minutes," she says, and she does not take her eyes off him, not even when she drops the rattle onto the hard-packed gravel and sand. Perry crouches and picks it up and, upright again, shakes it, "La Cucaracha"–style, a few times back and forth beside his ear, the beads soft-sounding against the plastic, more like rice inside. The little song-and-dance routine is short-lived when Angela doesn't smile, and Perry, sticking the rattle into her dress pocket, says, "I can't really. I've got to go."

"I know," she says, averting her eyes and staring over at the faded gray plywood outbuilding, a red snow fence stretched and staked in front of a pile of old boards and cinder blocks and a tractor chassis. "There's no hiding what this life is," she says, "and it's unfair of me— I know it is—to ask you in. Not now, but someday when the timing is better, I'll have to give you a blow-by-blow on how I met Roland and what I believed back then, what we both believed. I'm not sure why Roland—Brenda calls him my 'hoodlum husband'—insisted we buy this house in the middle of nowhere. Y'know," she says, pausing, "how sometimes you're saying one thing but trying hard to say another? That's what I'm doing, just not very well."

"You're doing fine," Perry says. "Here, let me take that," he offers when Angela shifts the car seat so that its weight balances on her hip.

"No, you go," she says. "That other thing I'm trying to say—it'll only complicate what's already complicated enough. Not that we need a chaperon, Mr. Lafond—we're grown-ups, after all, and I think faithful to what's right—but I can't pretend I'm not attracted to you, because I am. There," she says, "all done and harmless enough except for a touch of the heebie-jeebies in my stomach." In Perry's stomach, too. Then she says, "Ugh," and exaggerates a gulp and blushes, and Perry, the sun hot on the back of his neck, senses that if she rises on her tiptoes and kisses him, he will not resist. He provides her that chance— he busies himself toeing the ground between them, studying the slightly frayed left cuff of his Sun-Tans. Then his eyes move to the hem of her dress, then gradually upward past her breasts and collarbone, until he is staring her in the eyes, which, in this brightness, he notices are deep blue, a full shade deeper than Marcia's, and sadder by far.

She touches his lips with one finger, as if, in deference to his initial instinct to be gone from her, she means to shush him. And now Angela repositions herself, taking a step back. She says she'd better check on Corey and, shading her eyes, increases the distance between them by glancing up and commenting on how downright hot it still is out. "Hotter than Hades," she says, but she does not offer Perry a Faygo orange, which he would actually like for the road. She has made it easy for him to leave. Still, it takes every ounce of resolve he can muster and every intelligent brain cell sparking before he goes. He knows, of course, that Roland will come home to his wife and son tomorrow, just as Perry, nodding to this woman as he passes, goes home to Marcia now.

Chapter 7

Perry calls it "eternal composure," a magic that Marcia displays no matter what she's doing: serving a tennis ball, or clicking open a barrette with her teeth, or the flutter dance of her eyelids in dream sleep. Or like now, the way she reaches into one of the grocery bags on the kitchen table and lifts out a box of S.O.S.

Her body parts all seem so uniform, right down to the tendons in her wrists, the perfect extension of her fingers when she writes a letter or postcard. Unlike most women Perry has known, she looks as good undressed as she does dressed, equally seductive at twilight or high noon, winter or summer. There's still not the slightest sag to her eyes or lips.

Perry believes that, unlike his mom, Marcia will never know stroke or paralysis, a walker or wheelchair. She'll continue to age beautifully, the envy of both men and women half as old. But there's no question that she'd trade way down in the looks department for the experience of childbirth.

Having taken the day off from work, Perry has just returned from an hour walking the beach. He's still in his swimming trunks, his shoulders greasy with sun block, and he's forcing himself to sound upbeat in the conversation that always upsets him most: "One way or another—we'll consider plan B if we have to, but let's give the injections another month."

Marcia's come back downstairs after trying one of those home pregnancy tests, the results negative.

"I was so sure I felt something," she says, turning around to him, and Perry sees now that her face is lopsided, straining against the flood of tears. She bought the pregnancy kit after finding and playing the Hap Palmer tape Perry forgot in the deck. She thinks it's his—she thinks he's been practicing up to be a father, after all. There is no lie he can concoct to convince her otherwise, and he will *not* tell her the truth. When he has a chance, he's going to check under the seats of the Sable. But for now, he improvises.

"It's a tad infantile for my tastes," he jokes, "but it's a heck of a cute tape. I don't know—I guess I was just curious what's on the market these days for kids. I'm not hedging my bets or anything like that, and I sure didn't mean to get you all upset again." That last part's true, but he feels like a lout, saying what he's saying. "I should have hidden it in the glove compartment or something."

"Hidden it! No," Marcia says. "Perry, no, it's a lovely funny-funny tape. I love it and I love you for buying it. We've been under so much pressure, too much, and little things like this, they really help."

She wipes her eyes with the back of her wrist and, remembering half a verse, she says, " 'In three-quarter time / he slithers and slimes.' " And then she's half laughing, half crying, and staring at the floor, she inhales, short, quick breaths, followed by a long exhale, like what she demonstrated for Perry after attending Lamaze classes with Pauline when Neil refused to go, an hour drive each way for four consecutive Fridays.

"God," she says, "I'm a complete wreck—so irascible and moody and . . . I felt fine a few hours ago, and now look at me. Next time, I'll pee in some Drāno and save the fourteen dollars. Pauline says if the Drāno turns green, you're going to be a mom."

Less scientific, Perry thinks, but certainly more colorful than what a woman reveals under the harsh aisle lights in pharmacies.

"We'll keep trying," Perry reassures her, hiding that part of himself that *is* relieved that she's not pregnant. "Gotta keep up appearances, right?"

He didn't mean right this second, but Marcia stops unpacking the groceries and says, "Fasten the hook latch on the screen door and close the curtains."

Perry doesn't protest, and when he turns around, Marcia's shorts and undies are already on the linoleum and she's sitting on the kitchen counter in only her T-shirt, her heels braced on the edges of the half-open top drawers. He has never seen Marcia's feet in stirrups at the gynecologist's, but it's that image that comes to mind as he walks toward her.

Marcia's shoulder blades are pressed against the cupboard door where the vanilla extract and sunflower oil and jars of honey are kept, but she doesn't reach for any of these when Perry, his hands on her knees, can't get an erection. He can feel the heat on the insides of Marcia's thighs, the smooth skin of her calves, her hair damp against his face.

"It's no good," he says. "I can't—I don't know what's wrong. . . ."

"Nothing's wrong," Marcia says, "nothing," and she spits in her palm and reaches down between Perry's legs and whispers in his ear, "Perry, please. Yes," she says, "yes," but it's not until he imagines Angela's voice that he rises on his tiptoes, and it's her house he's entered, her kitchen, her. She's holding him tightly, breathing hard and rocking back and forth. And Perry, in sync finally and thrusting

* 84

faster and faster into the motion, savors this fantasy until the very instant he calls out, opening his eyes and concentrating hard to be sure that it's Marcia's name—and it is—that they both hear.

Perry's still out in the garage, vacuuming the Merc's interior with Bob Benoit's Black & Decker. No toys or pacifier, no additional incriminating evidence—everything seems shipshape, back on an even keel. Except for Perry's conscience.

It was right here that he declared to Bob Benoit how much he loved Marcia. That was over a decade and a half ago, back in 1974, three years before Perry and Marcia got married. Bob had already lost all his hair to chemo, as well as his spirit, Marcia had told Perry, trying to prepare him to meet and not be too uncomfortable around her father.

"Bob Benoit," he said, pushing himself forward on the couch, where he was listening to "All Things Considered," and holding out his hand to Perry.

"No I haven't," Perry said when asked if he'd had the grand tour, but by the way Bob eyed him, Perry wasn't sure if he meant the grand tour of the house or the grand tour of his daughter.

"Follow me then," he said, and led Perry directly out into the garage, where they talked. "My wife, Betty, is a good housekeeper," he said, "and I'm a stickler when it comes to home repair. So you'll find everything in order: clean towels at the foot of the guest bed, and no loose grout between the shower tiles. Drains that all work, a full fridge. Sound good so far?"

"Sounds good to me," Perry said. "Sounds great."

"Yes, it does, but what I have to say next, young fella . . . well, this is what I have to say—you and I won't get a chance to set any oyster traps on a bed only I know about, a secret spot. I've got the boat up for sale—down to Palmer's Marina. But then again, you wouldn't know anything about that, correct?"

"No, sir, I wouldn't. I mean, yes, you're correct, I don't know about the boat or the oyster bed. I wish I did. Listen, I'm really sorry. Marcia mentioned—" But Bob did not let him finish. He said, "Mentioned that I'm about to caddie for the Almighty Himself, maybe have a heart-to-heart about what life's like down here for the earthlings, while He aces every par three, four, and five to the infinite decimal on heaven's impossible back nine. I don't even own any clubs," he added. "Except for Sammy Snead and Arnold Palmer, I despise the sport. I drive this golf cart," and he pointed to it, "to the Casino and back because I can't walk that far anymore. I keep the battery charged. I wave to people who say I'd look pretty damn snazzy if I'd stick a few golf tees in my hatband." He paused then. "It can all end like this," he said. "I'm the one to tell you. You wake up one day and get the bad news and poof, in your face. Remember that."

Perry has. He liked Bob Benoit, who meticulously arranged his affairs before he died so that, as he put it, he'd keep the Mayflower moving van idling for the rest of eternity at the end of the street. There's a framed color photograph of Betty and Bob on the mantel above the fireplace. Bob's got a full head of dark hair, dark and heavy like Marcia's and, before she had it highlighted, like Pauline's. Betty has her arm around Bob's shoulders, and Bob's arms are folded across his chest. They're standing in front of the Sands Hotel in Las Vegas, Betty smiling, but Bob wearing a scowl, showing he's just lost a wad of cash at the blackjack table. Truth is, he was smiling—you can see it clear as day all over his face, the way he smiled at Perry in the garage and said, "Sit with me," and Perry did, the older man gripping the steering wheel of the golf cart and talking about whatever came to mind—just things in general, Perry told Marcia that night when she asked. It was his first lie to her. Hindsight has convinced him a thousand times over that he was right to do that. Listening and watching Bob Benoit as he talked was as private a time as Perry had ever spent with anyone, or has since. He remembers how Bob patted him on the thigh as a grandfather might, and how, when he pointed at the twin stroller still in the garage, his bottom lip quivered half a dozen times, like a little boy determined *not* to cry. And he didn't, not even when Perry explained how he worshiped Marcia and that he'd always love and take care of her.

Three months later, as Perry knelt at the casket during the wake, he could hardly believe how Bob had deteriorated bare-bones. "But hell," he'd said to Perry before the two of them entered the house together that evening from the garage for dinner, "I got no serious gripes. I married the woman I loved and had two gorgeous daughters I taught to swim. Whatever else you might hear about my life is either inaccurate or overrated. Remarkable," he said, pulling back on Perry's sleeve, the door not yet open. "You find out you're going to knock off early—you got six months max—and what you remember best is the race in which your twin daughters touched the pool's blue edge at exactly the same instant in the state finals, a photo finish for first in the butterfly, and how, when they hugged, sinking underwater, your wife could not stop squeezing your hand. This one," he said, raising it, and Perry reached back and squeezed it, too, Bob Benoit nodding as if to say, That's good. With so little time together, we both got said what we had to.

Perry switches off the vacuum and jockeys the floor mat into place underneath the brake and gas pedal. Then he applies Armor All to the dash, the leather steering wheel cover, both visors. Marcia's off the phone after spending almost an hour talking with Betty and Pauline. The whole clan will arrive tomorrow. Since the call, Marcia's been spiffing the place up. The big news—Pauline has seen a lawyer. Surprise, surprise. Thus begins what Perry calls the hack-and-slice time, the nasty days. Aspirin and Pepto-Bismol. Betty, he's positive, will be more spiritual, hopeful, churchy even, though she is not a regular parishioner anywhere. She'll say something like what she said to Perry shortly after Bob died, that no one ever became an expert navigator on calm seas. But the ocean is flat this evening—pink skies, sailor's delight—and Perry walks back inside and through the house and out again onto the front porch. The dinner plates have been cleared from the card table, and there's a clean white towel draped over the chair back. There's no sign at all of the renters next door—back to New Delhi, no doubt—so there's no reason to keep glaring over there, to stoop, as Marcia said earlier, to that idiot's level.

There's another kind of idiocy that Perry has not been able to resist, though he's plenty smart enough to understand this much: it can only lead to trouble. It frightens him that he can't shape things more clearly in his mind. "Dumb-fucker syndrome," Wayne calls it, meaning no perspective when you're up to your eyeballs in denial and deceit. Wayne should know, Perry says to himself. Wayne should sure the hell know all about that.

At first, Perry does not see Marcia swimming away from shore, but as soon as he does, he picks up the binoculars from the windowsill and twists off the lens caps and focuses, his elbows steadied on the railing. He watches her roll effortlessly onto her back and do a flutter kick, arms at her sides, racing nobody and no stopwatch, beautifully buoyant in the salt water. Her swimsuit in the last of the sunlight is navy blue.

Down the beach, gulls keep screeching and fighting over something washed up into the foam and seaweed at the tide line, a rubbery stingray or a skate or a spider crab—Perry cannot make it out. Otherwise the beach is deserted.

Perry watches the blur the ocean makes through the binoculars as he swings them back to where Marcia should be. But she's not there, not when he stands, not even when he starts, slowly at first, down the stairs and across the lawn to the boardwalk. She could not possibly have swum out of sight. He lays the binoculars on the seawall and cups his hands around his mouth. "Marcia . . ." he yells, and this time he's not pretending she's another woman. It's his wife he's calling back, but it's not until after he leaps down and is running full speed across the sand that she surfaces.

His shirt and shoes and jeans are still on, but he doesn't stop when she waves to him, maybe fifty yards away. He high-steps it through the shallows, then plunges facefirst into the ocean, his strokes weak, his feet heavy like stones.

He insists to himself he hasn't panicked, but this much is clear: only her touching him can slow his crazy breathing. He's standing now, collarbone-deep, the pulse at his temples racing. He will not risk another step, forward or backward or to the side. Instead, he closes his eyes and tips back his head and waits right there to be rescued.

Chapter 8

"Thirty-year bonds! I told the broker, 'What are you, nuts?' I'm eighty-four years old—I don't even buy green bananas."

Perry, having stopped by the apartment for a change of clothes, has been listening impatiently to Gorman Yack, the landlord, an older and just slightly more angular version of Wilford Brimley. Charlie Sullivan nicknamed him "Yackety-Yack," and he always sings that song whenever the old fritz leaves. The truth is, he's seldom around, and never snooping. But if you alert him to a problem, he's Johnny-on-the-spot. Today he received the exterminator's bill, so he's stopped by to check that the apartment is indeed free, as he says, of hell's critters.

Perry can recall the exact day that Yackety refused to climb the stairs anymore. It was weird how for years he always seemed the same—agile, even spry—and then one Sunday, the oomph had disappeared; it happened that fast. Now he knocks on nobody's door. Instead, he folds an aluminum lawn chair and waits in the shadowy light outside the detached four-car garage for whomever it is he's here to see. That's how many apartments there are in this ex-mansion—four of them.

But only two are rented. Yackety keeps the entire first floor vacant in case the zoning changes. If it does, he intends to open a funeral home. Marcia said absolutely not, that she wouldn't consider renting here, no matter how much they both liked the apartment, not until Perry checked with the zoning commission to make sure she'd never see a hearse parked in the driveway, or smell hothouse flowers, or believe for one second that Yackety could store caskets in those empty rooms.

"But wakes are such quiet affairs," Perry joked. "We wouldn't even notice." Marcia, no pun intended, she said, was dead serious—she refused to live in a house with cadavers.

"It's the economy. What we need's a change," Yackety says. "It's death these days in business unless, like me, it's business in death; then times are always the same, always good. Death," he says, "takes a backseat to no one." The reason he's got money to invest is because he's a principal shareholder in the largest chain of funeral homes in the country, a chain of six hundred. "Some folks kill bugs," he explains, "like we got here. Or beef or trees, and there's a profit if there's a need. No ifs in funerals—two million, one hundred thousand people each year meet their Maker. Give or take a few," he says.

"For whatever it's worth," Perry tells him, "I hope we all live forever."

"Uh-huh," Yackety says, in a tone that asks if Perry isn't being just a hair unrealistic in life's grand extravaganza. Yackety changes the subject. He's overdue asking how the missus is, and the kids, and Perry has given up explaining that he and Marcia have no children. It's the same question Yackety always asks, as he puts it, of that Charlie Sullivan upstairs on the third floor, who also has no kids—he and his wife, Dotty, want none. They say they've watched enough of their friends fuck up as parents and they've watched their parents fuck up as parents, too, so why believe that they'd handle the impossible any better? Dotty clipped out and gave to Marcia and Perry an article from *Time* showing that in a national survey of thirty thousand women, those without children were happier. "Ditzy women," Marcia said, burning the article in the sink. "Dumb and ditzy women."

Dotty is the manager of a fashionable women's shoe store at the Crystal Mall in Waterford, French and Italian shoes. She has no time for kids, she says, and she and Charlie don't intend to start socking away a single dollar for college tuitions. They're in their early thirties, and they plan to retire before fifty and then stay young traveling the world.

Charlie's dad owns a construction company, and it's through Charlie that Perry has landed the job for Roland Knudson—bull work at first, Charlie made clear—hauling cinder blocks and two-by-ten planks and buckets of mortar for the masons, wheelbarrow loads of pea stone. If he survives a couple of months of that, he graduates to building forms, rudimentary foundation work. There's the opportunity to move up quickly in the trade, Charlie said, all the way to brick archways and fancy fieldstone fireplaces and old-fashioned Dutch ovens. Charlie's a finish carpenter and cabinetmaker, reputedly the finest in the Mystic–New London area. Today is Roland's first day on the job.

"Mr. Yack," Perry says, "everything's squared away—we're moving back in tonight. The kids are cranky but fine; we're all fine in the household."

They both watch as the Mystic bookmobile noses into the driveway, then backs up and heads in the direction from which it came.

Even with his glasses on, Yackety says, "Pizza on Wheels," and Perry does not correct him. He says back, "Speaking of which—" "Kiddo, don't let me hold you up." Talkers are like that, Perry thinks, detaining you while telling you to make tracks. "We'll outlast the cockroaches," Yackety continues, making no move to get up, not until Perry offers to put the lawn chair in the trunk of his Olds 88. "That'd be nice," he says, "I wouldn't wanna forget it."

There's a BUY AMERICAN bumper sticker that Charlie Sullivan, back in April, doctored up, so it now reads, BUY AND DIE AMERICAN. Perry guesses that Gorman Yack probably likes the message. Yet his burden, like everyone else's, Perry reminds himself, and even says aloud sometimes, "So help me God," is to remain very much alive.

"Totally gross," Virtine says. "Gross to tarantula babies and globs of frog eggs and to anything that looks like poked-out eyeballs in jelly."

She's shot down, point-blank by her mother, who makes the claim that *all* babies in creation are both precious and beautiful, every last one. And the amended claim that, all right then, all *mammal* babies, by listing the following in what Virtine calls her totally gross-plus category: baby pink mice and featherless baby robins and baby anteaters and especially Virtine and J.J.'s baby cousin, Alex, whose face goes a long way toward redefining the words *baby* and *gross*.

"You've never even seen a baby anteater, or any other anteater," J.J., who's playing a TV video game called Sonic the Hedgehog, yells to her from Betty's bedroom.

Virtine, miffed and turning owly, her head cocked, decides to inflict on her younger brother an insult intended to shut him up and force him to close the door and mind his own stupid beeswax. She shouts in to him, "What do you know anyway about where I've been?" It's a lame assault, countered immediately by J.J. with a volley of high-pitched cackles. Perry, from where he's sitting, watches J.J. roll onto his back on the floor, knees drawn up and one hand covering his mouth, the other still pressing buttons to assist Sonic over or around or under or whatever's the object with the hedges. "If you can stand the honest truth," Virtine says, "you were a perfectly disgusting baby, too. You always had crud under your nose. Still do."

"Enough." Pauline's had it with the bickering, and as she begins to cough again, Betty says to the kids, loudly enough for J.J. to hear, "Now you two skedaddle and let the adults talk."

"Casino, Casino," J.J., galumphing into the living room, chants.

"I refuse to be seen anywhere with that blanko-brain dope," Virtine protests, pantomiming a gag as she aims her index finger into her open mouth. But she'll go; she's simply getting the last stab in, deflating this bag-of-wind brother of hers.

"My treat," Betty says, and Virtine, taking the five-dollar bill from her grandmother, inspects it as if she's been shortchanged.

"How much are cones?" she asks.

"Not nearly that much," Pauline makes clear. "You've got plenty."

"Don't even say it," Virtine instructs them all. "We're spoiled rotten—big deal, right?" Perry can see the allegiances have switched— now it's the two children lining up against the grown-ups.

"We already know what you're going to gossip about as soon as we leave, don't we, Virtine? It's no great secret."

She nods when he looks to her for confirmation. "Yep," she says, "Dad and his clay lay."

"The potter-snotter," J.J. adds, hopping on one foot to keep his balance while he stretches the back of his lime-green-and-purple Aqua-Sox over his heel.

"Go." It's Pauline, taut-jawed, who's ordered them to button up those lips and just go—and that means now!

They do, Virtine already lording it over J.J. that she's got the money, so he'd better just tag along without his stupid skateboard and concentrate for a change on not acting like a dork. This charade will all end when they get out the door, which Betty holds open, calling after them instructions to be home before dark—no more than forty-five minutes.

The new Pauline, as Perry thinks of her now, wears no makeup, and the silver half-moon earrings dangle and glint in the lamplight. Each sister is slouched against a padded arm at opposite ends of the couch, and each has a bare leg cocked on the cushion so that they are facing each other. Except for their identical smiles, though they are not smiling, Perry does not believe that anyone would peg them for twins, not anymore. Sisters, yes, and Pauline, larger hipbones and breasts, the older, by as many as four or five years.

"I just don't want to think about marriage as a life plan anymore," Pauline says, her bracelet sliding toward her elbow as she sits forward, straightening her spine and stretching both arms above her head. "Because it certainly is not. It was a twenty-year chunk of time in which I raised a family and tolerated a slob."

Betty objects to the name-calling. She says, "Pauline," trying to quiet her, but Pauline needs to let fly before she can decompress, and before the children return. She has in mind to bad-mouth Neil, and she turns on her mother, saying that one surefire way *not* to recover is to go all goosey in the lips and say nothing, just bottle all that anger up inside. "It's exactly the reason for my two root canals," she says, "all this grinding my teeth on tension every night. And popping painkillers, and night sweats. And these," she continues, reaching into her pocketbook and then holding up and shaking two tampons. "No periods all spring and now three in the past month. I feel lived in, and all achy and frowsy-looking and fidgety, and I refuse to treat myself like this anymore, or to excuse or stay silent about Neil—he's a first-class bastard. You don't see it, Mom, his meat-market mentality—but believe me, this isn't his first fling. God," she says, glancing first at Perry and then at Marcia, hoping to enlist their support against her mother's safety check on manners and restraint.

Perry likes the low neckline of Pauline's blouse and the way she slaps the tampons down on the coffee table as though they were cards, two aces, as though she is calling everybody's hand. She's not bluffing, she says. It's history with Neil, and if she refers to him as a bastard, it's not because she's taking a swipe; it's because it's true. At best, she says, the marriage was always marginal, right from the start. The trade-off? Simple—his money for her bod. And since he's the one who's flown the coop, her financial settlement will be substantial. As Pauline puts it, she's going to take him to the cleaners; she's going to hose him good.

It's Betty's predictable neutrality that has upset Pauline so much, and now she turns pure cynic. She says, "I suppose we could close the windows and lock the shutters and the doors and all go into mourning over the monstrousness of this terrible loss—that is, if anyone in this family really believes that, because I sure don't."

"I believe in repairing a broken rudder," Betty says, and Perry interjects to himself, Beam me the hell up, Scottie. And the moment turns as weird as any *Star Trek* when Basket, ignored and upset by the in-house quarreling, begins yipping at the TV screen for her kennel video. Perry has refused to play it during Betty's absence, a video Neil filmed a couple of years ago of his mother-in-law waving and saying, "Hi, Basket honey. Good, gorgeous dog, Basket, good angel sweetheart. Oh, look who's here to see you. Say hello to Marcia," who then steps into the frame and crouches, her rear end touching her heels, and opens her arms wide, as if Basket can now run through the chain link and be swooped up into the air and saved from her awful incarceration. There's actually a kennel in Stonington—so Betty claims—that shows home videos like this one to the owner's pet upon request.

"Don't, Mom, please," Marcia says. "Don't put Basket's movie on. Things are too crazy and strained right now. I'll take her for a walk. Let's both take her, okay?"

"Going, going, gone," Pauline says after Marcia and Betty and Basket leave. "Thank the god of burden and relief." Perry has misheard, believing she's said "bourbon and relief," and he gets up and pours them each a stiff one. He hands her drink to her over the back of the couch, then walks around and sits down next to her on the soft end cushion, and he says, "Cheers," and they clink glasses.

"To what?" she asks, and Perry says, "To something simple."

"Such as?"

"Oh, I don't know. How about to bulletproof dreams and endless days of bliss?"

"That about covers it," Pauline says, and nods, and it's not bottoms up, but not far from it; Perry exaggerates a grimace when he swallows. Pauline, a die-hard white wine drinker, begins to wheeze. Then they're laughing, Pauline admitting how pathetically stupid the whole situation's become and how paranoid and jumpy everybody's getting, especially she and Betty, who've been constantly at each other's throats. "Mom doesn't see it, but you can tell it's over, Perry—you know it is. I've told her again and again that we're not the Von Trapp family, but she refuses to listen. She's convinced we can cobble it back together. You know, 'Climb ev'ry mountain, ford ev'ry stream. . . .' And why not—Mom's always liked Neil. You've seen how he croons up to her, turning on the old charm. My God," she says, "I married a man who wears a pinkie ring!"

And a Rolex, Perry says to himself, and too much musk cologne, and always that goddamn shtick in his conversation, a chin like a pelican.

"What I need is a hot one-nighter—somebody with a steamy bedside manner. Got any wild and single beach-bungalow buddies? I'm ready," she says. "And preferably someone who can survive a double shift in the sack. A regular sex acrobat, if that sort of man even exists anymore. I'm bored by all of this, and horny, and as soon as the kids get back, I want you to take me for a ride on your Harley, a fast, curvy ride. I want you to scare me until I whimper."

Perry's smiling—they both are—and he says, "Okeydokey," and

as soon as Pauline leaves the room to change into some jeans and a sweatshirt, it dawns on Perry that no woman has ever ridden behind him on his bike, and the odometer about to flip over to ten thousand miles. Maybe it's the straight booze talking tough and sexy, but she's convinced Perry that she really is going to ditch that sorry sack-of-shit husband of hers for good.

If Perry were single, he'd be attracted big-time to Pauline tonight—there'd be a serious twang on his heartstrings for her—and if he were to have kids by her, he reasons and has reasoned, though not excessively, they would look almost identical to the children he and Marcia have been trying to have together. And here he is, sitting alone on a floral couch, wondering again if he's the only one who's entertained the notion of Pauline as a surrogate. He's read about zanier family arrangements—mothers bearing children for their daughters. But it seems too obviously a confession and alternative to what's missing in Marcia, what's defective inside her body. It's a subject he will never raise, but should it come up, the way the unspeakable sometimes does in the end, he knows he'll listen. And if he were to agree—and he realizes even thinking this way is pure craziness—he would insist it *not* be done through artificial insemination, but, rather, in a bedroom at night, just him and Pauline, and screw the logic that says that's too intimate, that it's all wrong.

Of course, it is, and this scenario he's just played out is typical of what's been going on lately in his head. He's been distracted by other women, courtesy, he guesses, of early middle age, and he has not been able to dismiss easily the pleasure he feels creating these fantasies. What's most troublesome is that he is not absolutely positive anymore that he won't act on them, despite the consequences. Had Angela Knudson kissed him in her driveway, he knows he would have kissed her back. He would have followed her inside, maybe stood with her a minute before turning down a lurid pink bedspread, then easing her down onto that bed. Because that didn't happen does not mean it couldn't have or that it won't sometime down the road, or that its equivalent in daydream and distraction is not damaging enough. It is, and Perry goes no further with this once the timer that Betty wound and set goes off in the kitchen. Perry finds the oven mitt on the counter and turns the stove off, then opens the door and slides out the Teflon cookie sheet—two dozen chocolate-chip cookies—and places it on the burners. Cookies for the grandkids to scarf down when they return. And just in case they decide not to sleep outside in the pup tent, Betty has already made their beds upstairs and turned down the Robin Hood sheets for J.J., the New Kids on the Block sheets for Virtine. Bob Benoit died when his daughters were twenty-two, but J.J. and Virtine are only little tykes, and Betty winces each time it's made clear to her that they'll be raised from now on without their dad. In her book, the dirt that Pauline's got on him is not dirty enough to compensate for that. The children, Betty argues. It's always the same rejoinder: "Reconcile," she says fitfully. "Please, you have to do that for the sake of those two children."

Because of her cough, Pauline, since midafternoon, has been taking hits of Robitussin right from the bottle, and this, mixed with the bourbon, has her flying pretty high. Perry can decipher only fragments of what she's been saying into the wind—something about not wasting any more of her life, and that what's upcoming for a change is fun, fun, fun, and Perry sings back over his shoulder, "Till her daddy takes the T-Bird away."

They've already crossed the railroad tracks onto Old North Road and have passed the tract of 1950s house trailers and the old bait shop on Masons Island and, in first gear, have continued into the rutted field beyond Quarry Road, stopping maybe ten yards from the edge of the river. Across and to the left, the lights of Noank. Upriver, Mystic's harbor. And above, the moon and the stars, and Pauline dismounting now, her hands on Perry's shoulders for balance. He has not exactly copped a feel, but Pauline's breasts pressing against him have sent tiny tremors along his spine. There's a distant buoy bell clanging, and Pauline, also listening to it, walks right down to the edge of the water. It's a sad music, reminding Perry of the widow's walks on so many of the house roofs that overlook the ocean and the river, and how those wives—"ghost women," he calls them—must have paced away the hours, waiting for their husbands, the buoy bells sounding more and more like funeral chimes. Which is contradictory to the mood he wants and she wants, but as he knows, whenever mood changes course, it's damn difficult to turn it back around. The bourbon in the saddlebag is not the answer, but when Pauline calls back for a nightcap, he reaches in and takes the bottle over. They interlock arms, like the first link in a two-person protest chain, and sit down shoulder-to-shoulder on the sand. She does not ask again for a drink; instead, she closes her eyes and leans her head against Perry's. Not to steady herself—the night has not yet spun out of kilter, and she's not about to get sick. Nor about to cry, nor drone on—blah, blah, blah—as the three women have done for hours at the beach house. She simply wants to get close, to nestle, and to speak softly back and forth, to be allowed to take a breather for a bit from the long, tedious, and nerve-racking day. And weeks, she says, and months, and, if the truth be known, the past twenty years.

"Perry," she says, "invent for me a mystery place where I can be happy and beautiful and sexy all the time, like those mystery places you make up for the kids whenever they gripe on about the world."

Perry doesn't hesitate. He says, "The intersection of Luck and Luck. That's mostly what it boils down to."

"Like dumb luck, you mean?"

"I guess, or like counting your lucky stars, or, like the people I see in my work every day, getting down on your luck, or finding yourself shit out of it. Or worse, believing each morning you wake up that your luck will change, that this, goddamn it, is going to be *your* lucky day. Lucky man," he says, "lucky woman."

"Lucky in love," Pauline adds, "which you and Marcia are, Perry."

Ah, he thinks, the hidden agenda surfacing, and he says, "We're not without our ups and downs."

"Of course you're not—nobody gets off scot-free, do they?"

Perry shakes his head. "Not in this life," he says, unscrewing the cap and taking a belt of the bourbon and passing the bottle to Pauline, who sets it down on a flat rock.

"And Marcia talks—she tells me things."

"Such as?"

"How she feels browbeaten by your moodiness sometimes, which she attributes to *her* infertility. And to other things, but especially that. Funny—I don't mean ha-ha funny; I mean ironic funny—that from the time we were little girls she used to talk about having kids, a great big family. Now she'd settle for one child."

"And she may never have that," Perry says a little too matter-of-factly.

"If not," Pauline says, "at least she has you." When Perry doesn't respond, Pauline asks, "Doesn't she?"

Perry picks up and tosses a stone and they both listen to it plunk into the river. Then Pauline stands suddenly and begins to undress, and Perry does nothing to stop her. He's leaning back on his hands when she bends naked to kiss him, smack on the lips, and then backs slowly away from him into the water.

He and Marcia used to skinny-dip plenty when they were first married. More often than not, with Perry standing chest-deep and facing the shore, Marcia would hike herself up onto him, her legs in a tight scissors hold around his waist, and in the buoyancy of the salt water, she'd feel almost weightless, he entering and balancing her against the slow and powerful swell of the waves.

"Coming in?" Pauline yells to him, a variation on a phrase Marcia used the first time they slept together. It was in Perry's dorm room, and she'd said to him, "Don't come inside me," but he did not pull out. They both worried for weeks, until her period finally came, unlike every other one to that point, five days late.

Perry wishes sometimes that Marcia had gotten pregnant back then—they'd have a teenager now, college-bound next month. But this other, drug-induced and desperate attempt to have kids this late is dueling with fate, and it cannot end well.

He remembers how they celebrated by dining out fancy and made resolution after resolution not to screw up like that again. And they never did. But of course that's all changed, and Perry has not bought condoms for years. Nor does he need one now, though it would be a lie to say he's not turned on by Pauline's striptease. No, not really a striptease— more like just getting loose and crazy and seducing the night.

Unlike with Angela, Perry's certain he can turn away from Pauline, which is exactly why he doesn't think to when, after ducking underwater, she bounces up sideways to him, her large, hard-nippled breasts silhouetted in the moonlight, which ripples and reflects across the surface, grainy black and white, 3-D.

She dries off with Perry's T-shirt, but not in front of him. She's revealed enough, and she's feeling good again, gushy and laughing and refreshed by the late-night swim. She bums a cigarette from Perry and sticks her panties into the pouch of his sweatshirt, and she says to him, "I'd rather *you* had taken them off me."

"With my teeth," he says back, smiling, and she kind of snorts a giggle and stands erect in front of him, her thumb out as he starts the Harley, and she asks if he's going her way.

Chapter 9

Betty has signed up for a senior citizens' class called Young at Art, which meets on Saturday mornings in downtown Mystic. She drives there in her Peugeot diesel wagon. Since its complete overhaul this past spring, it has developed a clatter somewhere in the underbelly, in the guts, as she explains the location of the noise. Perry has crawled underneath, but he can't locate it, nor can the mechanics at the dealership. Betty, the eternal optimist, remains confident that they have the expertise to figure such problems out. She refuses to fret over cars, over anything mechanical, saving that kind of energy and concentration for people—her children and grandchildren and sons-in-law. Soon to be singular, Perry now believes.

She's invested in a sketch pad and palette and brushes and a dozen or so silver tubes of acrylic paints. The art apron she wears says "Betty," stenciled in multicolored letters between the two big pockets. Already she's left for the Association, to learn today how to stretch canvas over a frame. She describes her instructor, Carl, as youngish and a touch kooky. She says he teaches there's no right or wrong in painting and that all art must trust the heart as a guide. She says mostly what Carl does is stay out of the way so as not to suffocate their creativity. Perry's always considered that kind of "anything goes" instruction as the sorriest, most simpleminded kind of teaching there is—sixties-vintage copout. But he refuses anymore to parlay such opinions into big-time bitches. There's no percentage in it. Each to his own, he thinks.

He suspects that Marcia, Pauline, and Virtine are right this instant cavorting around the mall, attempting to make feel-good purchases. There is little reassurance they will, given the effusive pitch at which they complain about the cruddy selections and outrageous prices each time they return from a day of shopping. Tourist markup, Marcia says, but they continue to go just the same.

Perry has volunteered to stay with J.J., and the two of them, after an hour of Parcheesi, have been horsing around on the beach, pretending to be limbo dancers, each taking turns holding out a fat red plastic Wiffle bat. J.J., once he's bent backward almost parallel to the sand, demonstrates the pelvic thrust he's got down pat, his arms straight out in front for balance. To make J.J. laugh, Perry is singing the "Limbo Rock," by Chubby Checker. The sexiest limbo Perry has ever watched was at a beach party at night, a bonfire blazing, and Marcia, in a bikini bottom and wet T-shirt and just drunk enough to shimmy her breasts a few seconds before arching upright on the other side of the bamboo pole, put everyone else to shame. As J.J. has done to Perry, whose spine is as brittle-feeling as old balsa wood. So they've switched to Frisbee, Perry catching the easy floaters between his teeth, like a dog. J.J. finds this hilarious, and he's been shouting, "Fetch it, Fido" each time Perry falls on all fours and wags his ass and barks and growls, then lolls his tongue, panting. Basket keeps glaring at him from the porch, giving her perfect imitation of a person, a balding, pinched-mouthed old hag.

✳ 104

Perry stays worried about the waves and the chop, which is why he and J.J. haven't yet taken the Jet Ski for a ride. But he could sure use a way to cool off now. The thunderclouds that earlier darkened the sky the color of prunes have passed on to the east, and the dazzle of sun is back, the weatherman predicting a heat wave for the next several days across the entire Eastern Seaboard.

Perry complains good-naturedly to J.J. that a guy could manufacture one heck of a hernia dragging this contraption across the beach. J.J. misses the joke and promises he'll push harder so as to prevent such a lousy accident from happening to his favorite uncle, and then he goes to straining against the bulk and weight of the machine, his toes curling under the sand, his face turning beet red.

"Whoa, all right already," Perry says. "Easy does it, pal, or *you'll* be the one with the hernia." But he's certain J.J.'s little nuts will stay firmly packed in place inside his scrotum. It's his own body breaking down that's got Perry nervous, the worries themselves symptoms of a condition he's unable to name, except to call it exactly that, a case of the worries. Recently, Marcia counted his gray hairs—not that there were all that many, but it's started, goddamn it, sure as shit. And the scarier part is that he's finding more hair each morning in his brush, and on the pillowcase, which maybe doesn't rate as a colossal setback in most people's books, but it's no limousine ride, either. Wayne says aging is like a blister on your ass—you keep trying to maneuver a way to sit down around it, and the only relief is when you're on the crapper, where most guys can't afford the luxury of parking their heinie for an entire day. But no sweat, he says, not until the mighty Moe goes permanently limp—when you can't achieve even half-mast anymore, Wayne says, *then* start the final countdown. In the meantime, for Christ's sake, stop punishing yourself.

The Jet Ski's called a Wave Runner, a one-person design that Perry picked up on a repo, and on a whim. He and Marcia both use it—

he more than she, and never together. But there's no problem squeezing somebody J.J.'s size on back.

"Fueled and ready to fly," Perry says, and J.J. hustles back to the porch for his life vest, which, when he returns, Perry checks carefully by pulling against the straps and buckle.

"It's on good, Uncle Perry," J.J. assures him, but Perry assumes his "I'm serious" tone: "We leave nothing whatsoever to chance," he says. "Not when we're out there we don't," and he points at the ocean, which is still much rougher than he'd like, the waves bashing against the red-and-white nose of the Jet Ski, shoving it sideways, the back eddies then straightening it out. Perry does not fight against this motion, and he's careful to keep his bare feet out from underneath.

J.J. stares at Perry, eyes deepwater blue—dominant Benoit genes—his nose freckled. He's a real lovey-dovey kid. Pauline claims the reason he's so affectionate, why he loves to be hugged and touched so much, is because beginning when he was only ten days old, she took him once a week for infant massages. Perry remembers holding him back then and how seldom J.J. ever cried, exactly the kind of little guy who makes people anxious to have babies, makes them instantly sorry that they do not. It was J.J.'s birth that convinced Marcia to get off the pill.

"What?" J.J. says, and Perry, without answering, winks and reaches out and rubs his fingers through J.J.'s hair. Then he turns the key in the ignition and it starts right up, emitting a single puff of bluish smoke, and the two of them hop on, Perry cranking the throttle, then backing off at the crest of the first wave so as not to go airborne, the sea spray cool on his face and chest before he turns on the slow diagonal toward the protected waters of Mumford Cove.

Although it's not that far, it's going to take them all day to get there at this speed, and J.J.'s already patting Perry on the shoulder as if to ask, What's the holdup, old man? It's not that J.J.'s unimpressed by anything short of aerial acrobatics; he's simply hoping for a mild breakthrough into the region of fun. That's the idea, isn't it, the two boys out on their own? The day's big bonus? So let 'er rip, and Perry does, dipping between the tubular swells and spewing up rooster tails behind them. "Hang on," Perry yells over the high-pitched whine of the two-stroke engine, the Jet Ski seeming to lift and skim now like a hydroplane, both Perry and J.J. whooping it up each time they *do* get some air, then splashing back down, heading out now into deeper water, heading almost straight away from the surf and the rocks and the channel the boats use motoring out of the lagoon.

And it's somewhere between where the channel edge begins and the cove that J.J., letting go for only a second, is thrown backward off the Jet Ski by Perry's sudden and slashing S-turn to avoid being swamped. "Hoooeee," he shouts, not noticing yet what has just happened in the riptide, not until he's finally through it and slowing way down and hooting over his shoulder some John Wayne ride 'em cowboy stuff. And it's right then, in the blurred periphery of his vision, that he knows, and more clearly than he has ever known it in his life before, terror. His hands and feet go instantly cold, then numb, and somehow he actually stands up on the sharply rocking seat and, keeping his balance, screams toward shore, where two people are crabbing between the huge rocks of the jetty, the one word that is never, ever misunderstood around water—he screams at the top of his lungs for help.

And circles, making wider and wider loops, uncertain if anyone has heard him or seen him flailing his arms. Inside the dips, Perry can see only water cresting above and around him, and blue sky, and even when he's able to ride the tops of the swells, the bottom quickly drops away and it's all he can do to keep the Jet Ski upright, fighting against the reverse chop and current, which keeps getting stronger and stronger the farther out he goes, the offshore wind ripping into the frothy gray face of the waves. And it's whipping Perry's face and hair, and he's afraid for himself now, too, wearing no life preserver, his panic submerged so far but beginning to rise through the entire tissue of his body.

Already he's gone hoarse and raw in the throat, and he can hardly make out his own voice anymore—"Jaaaaay J., Jaaaaay J.," until the only sound left is the distance and emptiness Perry first heard when his third-grade teacher, passing a brown-spotted seashell around the class, said, "I will now let you listen to an ocean. Where sailors disappear," she said, "or are buried." She said it was the very first, and would someday be again, years and years from today, the only sound on this earth. Perry believes that—he feels the enormous emptiness—and the trance he enters is a kind of shock or sleep, more severe by far this time than ever before, his mind so awash with blinding white light that he can survive it only by shutting his eyes and holding on to whatever he can and for however long it takes until someone finds and wakes him from this nightmare.

It's the thrashing *thwack, thwack, thwack* of the Coast Guard rescue copter he hears, then a man on a megaphone who knows Perry's name, and Perry whispers, without looking up, "Yes," as though his rescue depends on this. The Jet Ski bobs on its side, the motor stalled, and Perry, shivering badly, trembling really, has made no attempt to right and restart it. He's way past that. Nor has he any idea how far he's drifted, or for how long, and all he can think to do is acknowledge again that it is he. "Yes, I'm here," he says quietly, because this is indeed his name the man keeps calling, instructing Perry to hang on, to stay calm, that they'll have him out in a flash.

Although the voice is garbled by the wind and spumes thrown up from the funnel of the rotors, Perry has made out almost every word, but no mention of J.J. Perry cranes his neck and inhales the air he's sure he'll need in his lungs in order to be heard, and instead he swallows a mouthful of salt water and retches, and again and again through both his mouth and nose, until he can't even breathe, his eyes stinging and shut so tightly that he doesn't even see the diver who, in full blue wet suit, leaps from the rear door of the helicopter. A rope uncoils behind him, and at the end of the rope, a harness Perry is strapped into, the diver lifting each of Perry's arms through the straps, as though dressing him.

"J.J.," Perry is able to choke out. "Where's J.J.?"

"He's fine. He's okay; he's okay. Now don't talk anymore," he tells Perry. "You're a survivor, too. We're all home free if you listen and do what I say." The diver's face seems pinched inside his rubber headpiece, and Perry reads his lips more than he listens to the instructions to let go. Slowly, he opens his hands. The position he assumes is this: his body limp as a drowner's as he is airlifted out and away from the ocean, his arms flopped and hovering in a dead man's float. Suspended— and it does not seem either high or low, but only there—Perry's body rotates slowly left and then back again, hesitating, so that what he sees are the houses of Groton Long Point, and he counts down from the end one until he comes to Betty's, just a block shape in the distance beyond the surf that pounds the sand and pebbles and the bone-bleached fragments of shells. Then dizziness, and what follows is a kind of stop time, the odd images of his motorcycle and Bob Benoit's golf cart parked side by side in the garage, the double stroller and a piece of Peg-Board on the wall that has hung empty for years, except for a calendar nobody has touched since Bob flipped it to the month he died. Perry does not remember the death day—it isn't circled. Late October something. But it is that same feeling of a life lost that Perry bows his head to, and he folds his hands and prays to God to protect the children beyond this day, and by name he begins with J.J. First and last names—J.J Schwerk, Virtine Schwerk, baby Corey Knudson— the litany growing as he dangles and is warmed finally by the thought of each of them and by the sun on his back and shoulders, the old fear beginning again to perish.

* * *

Perry suffers no hypothermia, and he unwraps the gray military-issue blanket from around his shoulders, the chopper still several minutes from landing on the strip of lawn at the Coast Guard station in New London. The Jet Ski does not hang by a cable between the sponsons like something out of *Apocalypse Now*. It floats to who knows where.

The diver, sitting opposite Perry, has already pulled off his headpiece and flippers and unzipped his wet suit, and he licks his thumb and forefinger, instant energy from the Devil Dog Perry's refused. He will also refuse further medical attention, and, already having made this clear, he sounds thankless, his follow-up refusal to talk a defection. Perry doesn't care. He wants only to get home to J.J., who, as the rescue swimmer explained, was not caught in the rip, but, instead, carried harmlessly back to shore by the waves. J.J.'s the one, running down the beach, who sounded the alert, the one, the pilot adds, "who saved your seafaring ass." His southern accent disorients Perry, as though this entire miserable episode has taken place off the coast of Georgia or South Carolina and not in the local waters outside Betty's picture window. Casting off on a toy with a kid on back, which is what the pilot calls it, "a water toy." Perry has never heard the words *deep shit* spoken so nasally, pronounced with so damn many *e*'s. "Yessir, that's where you'da been floating in another fifteen minutes, in real deep shit."

The oldest of the three is maybe nineteen or twenty. The copilot, a grinner, glances back to see how Perry's handling this, Mission Accomplished suddenly transformed into Project Insult. For this, Perry is actually grateful—at least it signals that he's out of danger. Less dramatic than being sprawled unconscious on the floor, receiving mouth-to-mouth, the pilot on red alert and heading full tilt back to the base. He's radioed instead: "Repeat, this is a no-distress situation." And as

✳ 110

much as anything, this has consoled Perry, the dumb prick who's come, as the pilot described it, within a c-hair of joining the recently departed, and who has just cost the taxpayers in the thousands. "We gather here . . ." et cetera, et cetera, and Perry raises one hand and nods in agreement, a full surrender to his stupidity. And what happens next is not rare among men who respect their jobs—they give Perry the silence his gesture has asked for, and he hunches forward then, his face in his hands. He does not believe the women will grant him this— it's not in them. They'll not mean to, but they'll ignore however bad he feels, going at him instead with the kind of blow-by-blow interrogation that can only leave them crying and hysterical and blaming him for the tragedy that might have been.

No forms to fill out, thank God. They simply log Perry's name for the record, loan him two quarters, then let him go barefoot and bare-chested down the hall to use the pay phone.

J.J. answers on the first ring, and that voice saying hello is all Perry needs to hear, what adrenaline he's been riding on sapped so completely that he's not at all certain he can even respond. "Hello," J.J. says again, just as softly. "Is that you, Uncle Perry? Are you all right?"

Perry presses his forehead against the cool wall tiles, the receiver feeling like a fifty-pound dumbbell in his hand; he's afraid he's going to drop it if he doesn't lower it immediately. He blurts into the mouth-piece, "I love you, pal. Wait there for me, hmm? Listen, listen to me, I gotta go. I can't talk now," and he hangs up, using both hands, and finds his way to the water cooler, where he presses on the foot pedal and drinks. And from there to the bathroom, where he locks the door and, leaning over the sink, stares close-up at himself in the bright light of the mirror. Adrift at sea is right—he's salty and bleary-eyed and as scruffy as the losers he's seen stagger some mornings from the drunk tank, guys a long time on the skids, and this likeness infuriates Perry. He needs a shower and a shave and some clean clothes. He needs a cigarette, and most of all he needs a ride home. Wayne has no car, and Perry refuses to call Betty at the Association. He simply couldn't handle that.

He considers Steve Hazelton, a longtime New London attorney who minces no words in the courtroom—he believes leniency is equivalent to weakness, and he rails against the wrist-slap sentencing by too many judges these days. Don't adjust the punishment to fit the crime, he says, make the punishment worse. Use your noggin to outsmart these punks, then outhurt them. That's how you make good on your promise to uphold the law. Piss salt, he says, into the wounds of the bleeding hearts who defend the deviates. He advocates tying them all to the pylons on Sunday mornings and watching the water rise.

Maybe once a week, Perry eats lunch with Steve. They walk downhill together from the courthouse, past the thrift store and Sarge's Comics, to Thames Landing. Perry has stopped ordering coffee around Steve because of his habit of flipping the metal creamer lid up and down with his thumb as he talks. Otherwise, away from the job, he's pleasant company, smart and funny, a man in his early fifties who's devoted to family and to the restoration of antique Chris-Crafts and Garwoods, and who would drop his sanding or varnishing in a second to come bail Perry out. And Perry begins to dial, then rejects the idea, unwilling suddenly to be seen looking like this by the people he works with. Which includes the cops, so Perry does not call the dispatcher, either, to check if there's a cruiser out his way, possibly Tony Frye or Gordon Butterbaugh, guys who'd gladly help him out, but who'd also mouth it up afterward around the precinct that our esteemed Officer Lafond was apprehended by the U.S. Coast Guard while trying to flee on a Jet Ski to China.

These are not good-enough reasons for calling Angela, who should be not a last option, but no option. Perry understands it's a nitwit impulse, a married man phoning a married woman when he knows her husband's away. Roland is working a six-day week. Because his driver's license has been revoked, he's over in Ledyard without his truck. He's arranged for a lift each morning from Kenny Delany, one of the carpenters, and they're splitting the cost of the gas and working together on a new condo complex. It's Roland's assumption, and it's correct, that Perry needs to know these kinds of details until Roland can prove all over again that he's trustworthy, and that will take some time. He's thanked Perry for getting him the job and, according to Charlie Sullivan, Sr., he's been working like a demon. This does not surprise Perry; he has always prided himself on the accuracy with which he judges other people. It's a sense he has, and a gift he's convinced is rare these days, when everybody and his brother is running a scam from some secret chamber in their hearts.

Perry drops the coin in, listens for the dial tone, then punches in the numbers, half hoping that Angela doesn't answer. When she does, Perry lies to her, saying he's tried everyone else he knows. He says, "I'm sorry," and part of him is, and resentful that the events of the day have boxed him into this corner—no money, no car, no clothes, no dignified solution, he tells her, to an absolutely horrible day.

She's just gotten in from signing up for summer classes at Mitchell College, and she agrees to come get Perry and drive him to Mystic before she picks up baby Corey at day care. He feels a lightness in his chest, and he says to her, "Please, come right away."

She pulls up within fifteen minutes, Perry walking out in his bathing suit to meet her in the parking lot. He barely resembles Mr. Lafond, the man with the air-conditioned office who troubleshoots and smooths things over between the jailbirds and their wives, the man with the gentle demeanor, the almost innocent charm. He makes his way gingerly across the gravel to the truck, which idles roughly, Angela heavy on the accelerator each time it's about to stall out. Perry opens the passenger door and climbs in. Immediately, he can feel the heat from the engine on the balls of his feet.

"Thanks," he says, "thanks a lot for coming," and she hands him a shirt of Roland's. "Something he won't miss," she says, which is all there is to recommend it—country-western-style, pearl snaps down the front and across the pocket flaps. All he needs are Wayne's red-heeled cowboy boots and he could pass for a rodeo clown, win a goddamn stare-down with a Brahma bull named Butterbean or Diablo. But these are intentions far from a man who almost drowned. What Perry would honest to God like to do is sweep the debris of toys from the seat between him and Angela, then lower his head onto her lap and sleep. Perry has heard Betty say, on more than one occasion, that there is no pillow as soft as a clear conscience, but he's distracted by the way Angela's white cotton skirt is bunched up under her knees, and by the dim outline of her thighs against that fabric. She's barefoot, too, and one extra button of her blouse is undone, as though Perry's distress phone call interrupted her just as she'd begun to undress and she'd hurried out to him. All he's been willing to admit to her is fatigue. He does so by breathing deeply and combing his hair back with his fingers, and by clearing his throat.

"Calm down," she says. "Here, hold my hand, come on. Now squeeze it, squeeze hard."

He hasn't the strength, but the effort is enough to help take his mind off what he's been struggling to say to her—that after his near-death experience he's ready to take this thing between them further if she is. It rings of evangelist TV lingo, the fucking sage on the stage. Saved and shown the light—all second-chance, born-again bullshit that Perry knows inevitably boils down to apologies for fucking up first time out of the chute. So far, he's not had to do that, certainly not because of another affair, and he does not resist letting go of her hand when Angela tells him they have to move, that they need some air. There are beads of perspiration above her upper lip and at the four corners of her eyes. "Unless you want to expire right here," she says, and smiles, and Perry shakes his head no. If this were Marcia's car, Perry would blot out the early-afternoon glare with the cardboard sun shield and turn on the air conditioner, and they could discuss this as adults in a civilized temperate zone of comfort. They could recline the seats and relax, allow what each of them had to say to the other to sink in.

Angela has asked Perry, "Which way?" They're heading across Eugene O'Neill Avenue and toward the Gold Star Bridge. The pickup's cab is like a grimy sweat bath, the windows open but the heavy air stale and toxic-smelling, like exhaust. Perry, slouched in the seat, could be accused of intentionally ducking down, afraid of being seen in this hot rod in the center of downtown, and now even on the outskirts. He would neither deny nor confirm the charge—nolo contendere. A man without a defense. "Do you swear to . . ." and he'd say no, because he's convinced he can no longer distinguish between the truth and the lies, the why and the why not of things. Not that a sharp-minded prosecutor like Steve Hazelton couldn't put it all into clear and ruthless perspective, first the indiscretions—a word or a casual touch, forgivable, he'd say, once or twice, given the circumstances—but then the conscious infidelities.

"It's not a crime for me to drive you home," Angela says, as though coming to his defense. "And it makes me feel pretty lousy that you'd call for a ride and then think you need to hide. We've done nothing wrong yet, have we?" When Perry doesn't answer, she adds, "Do you want to so badly?"

"I want it to happen," Perry says, "but I don't want it to be wrong." A self-righteous, chickenshit response.

"How can it not be?" she asks him, raising her voice, then hitting the blinker and checking behind in the rearview mirror as she turns onto Chrystal, and Perry has no answer for this. Roland's shirt sticks to his back as he sits up, the sun glinting off the hood and the windshield, so that when he squints, everything they pass becomes a blur—the party store and the parked cars and the houses, the green-and-white highway markers for I-95. "I'm sorry about what happened to you out there today," she says, slowing for the entrance ramp, "I truly am—that's awful, a scare like that, my God, but it in no way justifies a fling between us. Can I use that word? Because that's what we'd be guilty of, a fling. And why me, for what?"

"It's not a fling; it's not that at all—not at all."

"Then what is it? What is any of this based on?"

"A feeling," Perry says.

"What feeling? Explain it to me."

He turns away, the air suddenly cooler midway across the bridge. Hundreds of feet below, on the Groton side, General Dynamics, where Perry has taken J.J. to see—yep, he told him, that's right—real live war subs. Followed by a trip to the video store for *The Hunt for Red October*. Perry's mind is a tangent—from J.J. to submarines to how, as a probation officer, his track record had been exemplary until a week ago when he first tried, while on the job, to ad-lib his way into a woman's pants. That's correct, her husband in jail and Perry sniffing around, and these are the terms he keeps thinking in since Angela used the word *fling*. He thinks about Marcia signing on for whatever it takes to lure the stork, and himself riding in a jacked-up truck with this pregnant woman he'd like to bed down, or imagines he would, and she says ha, in so many words. She says, "Roland likes his job. He feels like a winner for once. And he's changed his mind—he wants me to have the baby after all. And the name for all this is hope, something I haven't had much of until you helped us out. I owe you everything for that, and I'm tempted still, believe me I am, but this thing between us—it's best that it didn't happen, and it can't now. Please," she says. "Please understand what I mean," and for the first time she calls him Perry instead of Mr. Lafond.

She's wearing a sleeveless blouse, a wristwatch on her left wrist. Up ahead, though it's Saturday, yellow caution lights blink alternately on and off where the traffic has slowed into the funnel of a single lane. Angela brakes and glances over at the man in shorts behind the jackhammer, his tanned triceps vibrating against the shock of cement. Perry rolls up the window, then rolls it down again once they're beyond the dust of the construction, and he flashes on Roland hauling cinder blocks overtime in this heat, not only for the money but to prove he's finally gotten a goddamn fix on his life. And Jesus Christ, Perry says to himself, get a look at me. That's the issue in a nutshell, isn't it, to get a good fucking close-up look at what has happened to me?

"Swing right and take U.S. One," Perry says as they cross the bridge, not because it's longer and will give them more time to talk, but because he's positive Marcia won't drive home this way. She'll stick to the expressway, exceeding the speed limit as always, and Perry is not willing to risk that she won't pass them.

"Okay," Angela says, "that's fine, but it's going to take twice as long, and I have to pick up Corey and groceries for tonight and tomorrow. And you should stop with the cold-shoulder treatment— it makes me sad."

"Virtue's a sad business sometimes," Perry says, but it's a nasty dig and he apologizes. "I didn't mean that."

"Some men never do," she says. "My father never did—he never meant it—at least that's what my mother said whenever he hurt her, or me. He was in the lumber business—he owned a sawmill—and I was a bit of a tomboy back then, and one day he welded a basketball hoop to this huge round saw blade, and that was the backboard. All those rusty carbide teeth. Only a man could think of that.

117 ✳

"Some evenings, he'd drink vodka, and then he'd force me to play and he'd guard me way too close—he'd have his hands all over me. His left one—it looked like a craw because he'd cut off two fingers.

"Then he'd get the ball and I'd have to try to defend against him, not just outside in the yard but later on in my bedroom, too, and of course I couldn't. I was thirteen when it started, and it was Roland who later got me out of that house. And later still, the one who served time, not my father. You know the history of Roland's growing up, don't you? Now you know something about mine. It's not all that different. No. I'm not virtuous, but I do get sad, like you do, though for different reasons, I guess. You're a good man," she says. "Industrial-strength good, and I honest to God need you to be my friend. And Roland's friend, too, and that's why I have to resist reaching over to touch you."

Perry stares at her. He makes calipers of his thumb and forefinger and massages his temples and understands exactly what Nietzsche meant by one's "loneliest loneliness." The day has beaten Perry up and there's no place to flee. This detour will still take him home, past all these houses where who knows what kind of cruelty goes on inside. Yes, even in the homes of the rich, where the madness is oftentimes better disguised. Perry simply wants to close his eyes for a while. And that's what he says: "I'm so damn tired."

Enough said, and they both stay silent until the pickup crosses Allyn Street, and Perry says, "Next left." He has no key to get into his apartment, but he says, "Here's good," and Angela pulls up to the curb out front.

"Don't sit here," she says.

Perry nods and gets out and crosses in front of the truck, looking both ways, but not back at Angela. He's certain that Betty is home with J.J. by now and that Marcia and Pauline and Virtine are probably not. He wonders if anyone from the neighborhood would even recognize him like this, back from the wars, so to speak, and needing a little time and space to return to himself, to make the proper adjustments.

Perry presses his forehead to one of the four windowpanes, his hands cupped like blinders around his eyes, as though he's waiting for someone, a ghost perhaps, to answer his knock. He aches everywhere and has no energy whatsoever even to turn around and climb back down the stairs for a brick or a rock, or for a glove or rag from the garage to cover his fist, so he simply draws back and punches through the glass. He flips the lock up and turns the doorknob from the inside and the door opens.

Plus the obvious, he's lacerated himself behind the first knuckle and deep into the meaty muscle of the palm below his thumb. "Fucking shit," he says, and squeezes his wrist hard with the other hand, keeping the pressure on like a tourniquet. He's light-headed and almost steps barefoot onto the shards and slivers of glass scattered across the floor. There's nothing around that he can use as a broom, nothing at all. Except, of course, what he's wearing, and since that doesn't include a jockstrap, he's bare-assed on the landing when he takes off his bathing suit, the bloodstain opening and spreading out on Roland's shirt where Perry's been pressing the gashed fist against his heart. "Good mother of God," he says, and drops the trunks and sweeps back and forth with his foot, clearing a safe and usable path to the kitchen sink.

He allows for the cold water to run, medium pressure, and then turns his head sideways while bending lower so he can drink right from the tap. What Marcia refers to good-naturedly as his low-class liquor stash is the narrow space in the cupboard next to the peppercorns and parsley flakes and the box of toothpicks and the Tabasco. At best, two or three shots of Wild Turkey are left in the fifth, and Perry twists off the cap between his teeth and spits it onto the countertop. "Dumb," he says aloud. "You dumb, ignorant, simpleton bastard," talking as much to the pain as anything, though he knows damn good and well he's confronting every part of his life on this day. His first pull empties the bottle, the whiskey burning his throat and high up in his chest, but that's exactly what it takes for him to spread his fingers wide apart and then to lower his hand under the running water. "Jesus Christ Almighty," he says. "Good Lord," and he tightens his jaw and sucks the air in long breaths as he turns his hand over and slowly back, the water red as it splashes onto the stainless steel. After a few minutes, the bleeding slows, the white skin flaps puffy and jagged.

He can barely reach the wall phone from where he stands, but he can reach it. And he does, the whiskey, he thinks, evaporating all at once into his frontal lobe, so he's not surprised by the croupy, distant ring in his voice and by the utter and complete concentration it takes to explain to Betty his whereabouts—how he's ended up back at the apartment, and in what state of mind after such an ordeal. The bottom line: he's exhausted but alive. After asking about J.J. again, he says good-bye and hangs up.

What's clear to Perry is that he'll need to invent a story to cover his tracks. In the bathroom, he bandages his hand by doubling over the squares of gauze and wrapping them with the wide roll of adhesive, a real hack job in place of the stitches he needs. "Here," he says to himself, and pops two ibuprofen, then pinches open each fake pearl snap down the front of the cowboy shirt, which he uses to wipe away the blood trail from the sink all the way back to the door. Now the evidence from the cleanup—first he balls up this gaudy shirt and stuffs it inside an empty grocery bag, then shoves that bag to the bottom of the wastebasket. So far so good. Then the broken glass so nobody else gets cut. He finds one piece on the edge of the living room rug and vacuums the entire area, the bad hand held against him as if held by an invisible sling.

There's actually a cool breeze through the screens on the street side of the house, and the smell of insecticide, he notices, has almost completely vanished. It's quiet here and it feels very good finally to collapse naked and alone midday on his and Marcia's bed. His premonition, the instant before sleep, is that she'll tiptoe in and lie down next to him and kiss his hand. And true or not, it's the least painful image he can concoct, and he holds on to it as he goes under.

Chapter 10

It might not have been as life-threatening as falling into deep sleep outside in snow country—northern Michigan in January or February—but had Marcia not awakened Perry and helped dress him and rush him to the emergency room at Pequonock Bridge—well, as Perry knows, complications develop. To the tune, in this case, of twenty-five stitches to repair the severed radial artery and to close the two wounds. He has a lot of explaining to do, but it's early Sunday morning, still too soon to be hit with the third degree, thin feathers of sunlight just beginning to filter through the leaves and through the screens of the bedroom windows. There's been a rain shower during the night—Perry smells it as he watches the numbers on the clock radio snap over to 8:00 A.M. He doesn't hear any traffic, nor a single sound from anywhere in the apartment.

It's clear to him that Marcia has injected herself with the Pergonal, an act unannounced and, he thinks, akin to him claustrophobically lowering himself down a well, a desperate gesture aimed at meeting the demon head-on, at neutering the goddamn son of a bitch.

Although Perry has waited in bed for Marcia to return, she hasn't, except when she tiptoed in to get a syringe from the tennis ball can and then tiptoed out again. Perry, staring at his bandaged hand, turned and resting palm up on Marcia's pillow, recalls that there are two schools of thought regarding fertility drugs: one, that intercourse during ovulation should occur only once each day so that the sperm count stays high; the other—the one they've subscribed to until now—to get on it like rabbits. In layman's terms—no pun intended, Perry had said as he and Marcia walked out of the obstetrician's office—it boils down to the difference between quality screwing and volume screwing. It was during that same visit that Dr. Moska gave Perry a testicle check, then advised him to switch from jockey shorts to boxers, thus preventing his balls from getting too hot. Perry was tempted to inquire of the doc if he preferred Perry buy Hanes or Fruit of the Loom. Fucking unbelievable. Followed the very next day, Marcia told him, by Lucy Harrington's proclamation in the teacher's lounge that the sex of any unborn child is determined better by Madame Sarah, New London's most famous fortune-teller, than by any OB-GYN. Lucy, three years younger than Marcia, had just returned from two months maternity leave, and this her fourth and, as she made public, final child—regrettably, all boys, exactly as Madame Sarah had prophesied, and the amniocentesis, the test botched, had not. "Which all goes to show—" Perry had started in, but Marcia cut him up short. "Stop," she said. "Perry, stop grousing about it. We've made the commitment to do everything in our power to have me conceive, so get used to the 'body carnival,' as you call it, and comply. Otherwise, the entire ordeal will be too awful. You have to stop smarting off all the time and decide you're really going to help me."

The antibiotics he's supposed to take every six hours will only weaken his sperm, as will the painkillers, which makes the throbbing an odd kind of pleasure, a statement, and for once without the wisecrack edge to it that Marcia hates. He certainly won't toss the pills—that's overkill—but he promises himself not to take any.

As soon as he hears Marcia leave to go get the Sunday papers, he gets out of bed and out of his pajama bottoms, then showers with a plastic bag over his right hand. There's no reflex whatsoever in the thumb and the first two fingers, and no way in hell, after drying off, that he's even going to try sliding that hand through a shirtsleeve.

The spaz act of brushing his teeth left-handed makes apparent how impossible these next few days are going to be. Marcia will play nursemaid up to a point, and that point depends entirely on how pissed off she's gotten already, and to what degree he can disarm her. The smart move is to demonstrate remorse and not to play for her sympathy—she'll offer plenty of that on her own, but not without asking her share of questions. Perry knows, unless you're in a coma, a woman as intelligent as Marcia will demand, and rightly so, some degree of accountability. Since finding him on the bed late yesterday afternoon, she has accepted his silence, it-self an explanation, though short-lived, of course, in the wake of any healing.

Which there's been overnight, though painful during stretches of sleeplessness. That pain must show in his eyes, because the first thing Marcia does after Perry sits down opposite her at the kitchen table is to line up the tiny white arrow and the plastic dot, then pop off the childproof cap of his codeine prescription with her thumb. "Here," she says, "take one of these."

"I . . . I'd rather a cup of coffee," he says. He says, "Listen, I don't want to louse up anything else—the big stuff," but even that admits too much guilt, and he starts to backpedal. "What I mean—" he says, but Marcia stops him.

"That time has already passed for this month. It's happened or it hasn't. You know damn good and well that this morning was the final injection, and I needed you to help me, Perry, like you're supposed to." Then she pauses and takes a deep breath and, in a softer voice, asks, "How's your hand?"

✻ 124

"It's felt a whole lot better."

Marcia shakes her head, pushes her chair back, and gets up to pour Perry his coffee, plus a glass of orange juice. He does not reach for the sports page that Marcia has set aside for him out of habit.

"Your stomach's growling," she says. "You need to eat something. I'll cut you up a slice of cantaloupe—something light to start. How does that sound?"

The aperture of hunger opens suddenly now that Perry's forced to think about food, something he hasn't done since this time yesterday. Yes, he'd like to eat, but he winces instead when Marcia drops the scooped-out rind into the wastebasket, on top of the bag concealing Roland's bloody cowboy shirt. Perry's almost certain nobody saw Angela drop him off, so he says, "By taxi" in response to Marcia's initial probing. Her profile stays rigid as she shakes the Reddi Whip can, the spritzing sound loud under the pressure of her finger.

"You took a cab all the way home? How did you pay if your wallet was at Mom's?" she asks, lowering the fruit bowl in front of him, then sitting back down. She's concentrating hard for his response, and he doesn't hesitate to answer. This is exactly the track he wants her sniffing down. "That's why I broke in," he says. "Charlie and Dotty were out—I tried them—and the cabbie hit his horn for the third time and I just freaked. I don't know—I was all disoriented and miserable and wanted the guy gone so I could lie down. I paid him out of the cash stash. Go check if you don't believe me." He hopes he hasn't sounded too eager for her to do this.

"It's a question, Perry, not an accusation. This is all just so incredible, so . . . so frightening. You're almost washed out to sea, and poor J.J., he gets this panic phone call from you and then you disappear again. He thinks you blame him, for God's sake. Do you have any idea how upset he is, how upset we all are?"

"I'm sorry."

"You're sorry! How convenient. And how stupid this whole

thing—going out in that weather. None of it makes the slightest bit of sense."

He's too far into the lie already to back out, so he rides with it. The cash stash is what he and Marcia call the emergency fund they keep hidden in an envelope folded over in Marcia's underwear drawer—Perry's suggestion of a hiding spot. There's blood on the envelope now, and there's money gone, transferred yesterday into a new secret account yet to be named—the cover-up or deceit account. His entire alibi rests on this single detail, and on the permanent disappearance of Roland's shirt. Marcia isn't one to sort through trash, but if suspicious enough, she'll check out the envelope once Perry leaves the house. Since Wayne's within easy walking distance, that's the plan, the route all downhill until West Main flattens into the center of town, crosses the drawbridge, and continues winding on toward Stonington and beyond. Already he's stuffed the pilfered, wadded-up bills into his left pants pocket. This image of himself steals his appetite again, and Perry slowly lowers his spoonful of cantaloupe back into the bowl. Sweet Jesus, he thinks, flattening the palm of his good hand onto the table, fingers splayed out, and Marcia reaches over and begins to squeeze each knuckle joint, from thumb to pinkie and back again as she talks, Perry's eyes closed and his good sense screaming at him to keep his stupid mouth shut. She mentions death wishes and the early signs of suicide and how she's sure Perry has none of those, but his moodiness is enough, if she *were* to get pregnant, to make her miscarry. She wants her husband back. "I can't take it anymore," she says, "I swear to God I can't. And listen to me, listen closely, because I mean this—don't you ever deceive me. You owe me at least that," she says, and Perry nods in agreement, frightened by the trembling in her voice.

And by not knowing anymore—"Do I, Mr. Nietzsche?"—if he really "will be able to converse well with this woman into [his] old age." Maybe Wayne's onto something when he argues the common language between the sexes is silence—it's quickly filling the kitchen and Perry's got to get out of here. If he doesn't, he's going to scream.

Marcia shows only momentary alarm when Perry explains the fresh air will do him some good on his way to Wayne's world, and he doesn't mean the movie.

"Tell him for me that I'm depending on him to cheer you up." And only then does she agree to help Perry on with his socks and shoes and shirt, and before he leaves, she says, "Okay, but first you have to call J.J."

"That's item number one on my list," Perry says, sounding as though he's actually begun what Marcia calls "the linear process of unburdening." What he doesn't tell her is that it's the *single* item on his list.

"He's only eight years old, Perry. Eight years old."

How old? Perry almost asks. Could we hear that once more, please, just to be absolutely certain? Or better yet, how about a show of hands? Question: Who among us still needs to be reminded of what can happen to a little kid besieged by guilt when he feels suddenly abandoned by those he loves? Anybody here, per chance? You with the bad hand. You, Perry Lafond, of those child-induced incubus nightmares? Perhaps you've forgotten what it's like.

Perry involuntarily shakes his head, and Marcia, leaning toward him from across the kitchen table, asks, "No what?"

"No nothing," Perry says.

"I'd feel a lot more comforted if your nothings were nods," she says, and she gets up and walks behind Perry, gently cupping one of her palms around his chin, her other hand, fingers splayed out, pressing on his forehead. "Like so," she says, but even the slow up and down motion makes Perry woozy and slightly nauseous. "Think positive thoughts, Perry. Think in yesses for a change. I'm tired—really, really tired—and bored and frustrated and beaten down by your Grim Reaper routine. It's too depressing. Look what it's done to you," but there's no mirror handy, and Perry's eyes are closed anyway, and although he whispers, Yes, yes, yes to himself, he simply doesn't believe it.

Nor does J.J. completely buy in when Perry tells him, "No, it can't be today, but soon, I promise."

"Soon when?" J.J. asks. "I hate soon, 'cause it never is when grown-ups say it."

"Hey, this is your uncle Perry you're talking to, and I'm not exactly overjoyed about being out of commission, either. But the hand's pretty bad, pal, so I've got no choice. I've gotta take it easy for a day or two and let things inside there heal. Make sense?"

"I guess," J.J. says, "but things could heal here just as good, and we could start the Parcheesi game over so I wouldn't already be ahead."

Perry can hear J.J. rattling dice in the cardboard cylinder, and he can also hear what sounds like waves pounding the beach.

"We'll finish the one we started first," Perry says. "I don't want anyone feeling sorry for me, if you know what I mean."

"You're not coming over is what you mean."

"Yes," Perry says, "but not because I don't want to, and I need you to understand why. If you don't, I'm gonna feel lousy, and I don't feel so red-hot to begin with."

"Virtine said people can drown in an inch of water and that she doesn't know how a dope like me survived a whole ocean. She said I should've held on tight like I was supposed to and none of this would've happened."

"No way," Perry says. "Those waves were simply more than we bargained for. Lousy judgment on my part to go out there in the first place, so if anybody's at fault, it's me, not you."

"Uncle Perry?"

"I'm right here."

"When bad stuff happens, does somebody always get blamed? Does somebody have to?"

"Don't know," Perry says. "Doesn't seem quite fair, though, does it?"

"Only if it's, like, short blame. That's enough to learn a lesson, and I don't think you learn it any more good after a long time. Maybe you learn it even worse."

"Exactly right," Perry says. It's so simple and clear that for several seconds after he says good-bye to J.J. and hangs up the phone, Perry *does* nod.

"That's more like it," Marcia says as he turns slowly around. "See how easy?" But ringing in Perry's ears is what J.J. said about short blame, and like magic, when Marcia kisses him on the neck and cheek and lips, it appears as though she's truly ready to forgive. "There," she says, "how's that?"

"It's better," Perry says. "It's good."

"It's a start anyway," Marcia says, "and if we concentrate on getting our lives back in order, we will. Second thing on the list—an emergency leave from your job. *Emotional-medical*: that's the term at school for a nervous breakdown, which you're on the edge of, Perry, and I'm convinced that working day in and day out with those people of no hope has contributed to this. I don't mean that as a criticism of anyone— you know that. I'm simply trying to reinforce the notion that you need to devote your energy to me, to us."

Perry suppresses the urge to say he's not sure how to anymore, and that reason and temptation have gotten all screwed around in his mind. And she can believe it or not, but he loves her more than he ever has—much more—so how can it figure that lately he's felt closer in spirit to "those people," and in particular Angela Knudson? How does anyone confess something like that without fear of recrimination,

129 ✳

without fear of the long-term blame even J.J. feels in his heart is a killer?

"Eight years old," Perry says. "It's too young."

"He'll be fine now," Marcia assures him, completely missing that Perry is talking about himself.

By the time he arrives at the houseboat, Wayne has already won a case of Mellow Yellow for being the first person to call in with the correct title and name of the group—"Ninety-Six Tears," by ? and the Mysterians. It's a Sunday-morning radio show called "The Sixties: The Music That Saved Us." Perry only vaguely remembers most of those songs. Except for Janis Joplin and Jimi Hendrix and a few others, he's in the dark, without any prizes. In the past year alone, Wayne has won Pizza Express pizzas and subs, a membership to the Body Shop gym—state-of-the-art Nautilus—which he tried to cash in and couldn't, a "Best of" CD by the Blues Magoos, and a dinner for two at the gourmet restaurant in downtown Mystic, the Bravo Bravo. He hasn't used the gift certificate, which he digs out of an unlocked metal strongbox. "Here," he says, "you use it—use it with Marcia. If it doesn't help clear your head, at least the chow'll be good. It doesn't appear likely I'll have the opportunity to dine out with the ex for a while yet."

"The ex" is in reference to an old girlfriend and, Perry believes, a fabrication of Wayne's—if not totally, then at least partially made up. The real ones Wayne brings home are all one-nighters, and there have been plenty. He refers to them as "coyote dates," meaning he'd rather chew off his arm than wake the woman whose head is resting on it in the morning. Let weakness abound, he says, while he waits for his ex to return from finding herself—Europe first, followed by postcards from Morocco and Tangiers and Budapest. And, more recently, the postmark from Springfield, Massachusetts, a letter explaining she's living with her fiancé, who's employed by Smith & Wesson.

"She sounds dangerous," Perry says.

"They're all dangerous," Wayne says back, "and we're dangerous to them, too—that's life's crazy denominator, all of us dangerous people trying hard to stay alive long enough to fall in love and get happy with somebody else."

"And then we die, right?" Perry says.

"We do indeed do that, and I don't mean to be profound, only accurate on a subject I know more than a little about." Wayne has never visited the Vietnam Veterans Memorial in D.C., but he can rattle off his share of the names engraved in that dark marble, guys like him, but they didn't survive to come home and hole up for twenty years on a houseboat to try and figure that war out. "Steppenwolf," he says after only the first couple of notes, "Born to Be Wild," and on the chorus, he sings along.

Perry admits to the spirit of that tune but wonders if it's possible in the 1990s. The newer anthem? Born to grow timid and ponderous by early middle age, less than a decade before the end of the century, when Perry will turn forty-seven, maybe a father by then and maybe not, entrenched even deeper into the bunkers of the middle class.

"You're fighting against the person you're afraid you've become," Wayne offers up. "Tiptoeing all these years through the booby traps to get to a safe middle ground—good pension plan, medical benefits, a stylish home in the suburbs if you so desire. Two cars and no more problematic sex now that you've discovered at least three positions guaranteed to work up a muffled grunt or moan. Splashy plans down the road. But there, staring you in the kisser, the fucking enemy himself, boorish and smiling and patting you on the back to welcome you. 'Sweet victory,' he says, and you think, Sweet Jesus, what have I been defending all this time with my life?"

Without asking if he wants one, Wayne pours Perry a shot of rum. "I admit it," Perry says, "morale is pretty low on the old home front. I'm fucking up, Wayne. I'm losing it."

The disc jockey announces there's just enough sixties time left for one final cut. "Classic hippie," he says. "'A get out your sandals and beads and crank up the dB's' kinda tune," and it's a song Perry does remember, Hendrix belting out "Foxy Lady."

"All right!" Wayne says, pouring himself a drink, too. "To foxy ladies," and he toasts this final blast from the past, the straight rum exactly what he and Perry need to clear their heads at midday.

Followed immediately by the ritual noontime joint. Even without Marcia around, Wayne does not offer Perry a single toke, but he has placed the Bacardi bottle on the floor by his friend's feet, and he's switched off the radio. Except for this weekly three-hour broadcast, Wayne says the music and the DJs are all limp-dick failures.

As always, it's cool inside the houseboat, and still dark because the sun has not yet burned through the haze. When he listens for it, Perry can hear the foghorn, and now and then a boat motoring slowly up or down the river.

"Let me get this straight," Wayne begins. "You tossed the bait on the water, but your errand girl didn't bite. Or did bite, but you didn't set the hook."

Had Perry referred to her as Angela instead of "this woman I met," Wayne might have called her, as she deserves to be called, by her name. But nameless, they both know that the "almost" affair has nothing to do with love, and maybe that's all Wayne's attempting to make clear. And he continues: "So you try again, but this time she sends you packing—she plays hard to get and you freak and mangle a perfectly good hand. Nice work. Very touching. You want my professional advice? Holster the wiener, cowboy. You've got some mystery to solve—the clues ain't buried in some strange woman's pants. You asked, and that's my honest opinion."

He's got lots of opinions, and limitless range. The best motor oil? Shell Fire and Ice. The best dope? It's a tie between Humboldt County sensemilla and Maui Wowie. Acapulco Gold is overrated because it leaves this tarry mucilage in the water pipe. The best actor? Rip Torn, of course. Family outings are potlucks from hell, anemones the most beautiful of the sea creatures, and by far the most sensual.

Wayne has spoken like this, confident and freewheeling, from the first time he and Perry met, right here on the houseboat. A guy named Vincent Sisco, or, as Wayne called him, "the Sisco Kid," a first offender, was arrested and arraigned and pleaded guilty to pirating lobster pots, most of them Wayne's. Under the Victim's Rights Law, Perry was obligated to contact Wayne for his version of the crime, to get his feelings about a just punishment, and to assess his losses, the appropriate restitution, the crime's impact on the victim, and how he could be made whole again.

"Made whole again?" Wayne said, cracking a pop top on a can of Bud, beads of foam sweating out. "That's a tall order. I give up," he said. "Give me a hint," and he smiled, taking a sip of his beer. "Excuse my manners," Wayne said, "you thirsty? You got time for a cold one?"

The time, yes. The beer, he'd have to pass. Wayne talked at some length about the lawlessness of Mother Nature, who'd stolen a third of his pots—eighty-two to be exact—in a single storm. "Some guys take their cues from her, I guess. At forty bucks apiece," he said, "figure it out. It's a little like grand theft auto. But this Sisco Kid, that's punk potatoes. Sooner or later, I'da found 'em and straightened it all out—high-seas justice, if you get my drift. That part's the romance—just boats instead of horses, but not unlike the Wild West."

"Without the guns," Perry said.

"Whatever you say, Sheriff," and Perry glanced down at Wayne's cowboy boots, and Wayne continued. He said, "Don't go poring over too many legal documents on my account. Believe me, the guy ain't worth that."

133　✳

"What do you see as a realistic punishment?" Perry asked in his official, new-job manner.

"Listen," Wayne said, "I don't give a shit if he stabs and bags trash along the highway for the rest of his unnatural life or doesn't, so long as he baits and resets that line of pots he dragged away. Had he raped my wife, assuming I had a wife, or touched my kids—same assumption—yeah, well, you get the picture. Sisco, he's just blowing smoke, a brainless juke-joint rustler. A hanger-on. Maybe I should settle with him, double or nothing on a single game of pool."

Not exactly what's referred to in the probation business as "victim-perpetrator therapy," where the officer brings both together, face-to-face, to see each other as human—the victim an ordinary Joe struggling like everybody to get by, the perpetrator a lost soul stuck behind the eight ball. Defuse bitter feelings on both sides, thereby creating a noncombative atmosphere in which the details of restitution can be calmly and fairly arrived at. Good theory, but rarely did it happen that way, and Wayne represented a refreshing change from the vindictiveness by victims of even petty crimes, bloodthirsty and screaming holy murder for maximum incarceration. Consider one Gus M. Sizek, a tactless and pit-faced used-car dealer whose toolshed at home was used one afternoon by fifteen-year-old Cassie Shellito to hide, she alleged, from her drunken father. She smoked cigarettes and she peed in there, then cried hysterically and banged her fists on the inside of the door when Gus padlocked it shut and called the cops and pressed charges—trespassing and unlawful entry and destruction of personal property. Perry suggested she square things by mowing his lawn or raking under the hedges, but Gus said, "And teach her what?" He said, "Lafond, do you have any idea how long it takes to get rid of the smell of a woman's urine in a windowless shed? In this heat? And by the way," and he explained how he'd sold Joe Shellito a Buick Skylark and knew him as a neighbor and a customer to be a decent and sensible man, and goddang these little tramps who try to finger and shame their fathers. Perry said it sounded more like the other way around, but Cassie never actually made that charge, not even off the record to Perry, and Gus later said to him, "You won't last at this."

Maybe he was right. It's beginning to feel that way. Cassie Shellito would be about Angela's age right now, mid-twenties. More than once, Perry has punched Cassie's name into the computer, but the screen, always green and blank, is a field he imagines her fleeing across. And occasionally, he still considers guzzling beer and sneaking into Gus Sizek's toolshed and lighting up and pissing like a racehorse.

"You're a bad man, Perry Lafond, old Frenchman, a very bad man, which is why I've always liked you." Wayne's slouched down on the futon, the roach and the roach clip in the ashtray beside him. This is the only day of the week he doesn't haul pots, the only day he dopes up this early and crashes for a couple of hours, as he says, to claim his righteous share of the world's precious z's.

Perry watches him not so much fall asleep as go out like a light, a trick, he told Perry, that he learned in Vietnam, where you had no time to mess around tossing and turning and wondering who back home was jumping your girl or your wife or your kid sister. He said he had a buddy over there, this kid with a giant Adam's apple, who, each time he closed his eyes, came screaming awake with the same nightmare about flash floods, his father's cows trapped and bawling in slow motion in a barn filling with water. Bawling to beat hell, and hay bales floating and bobbing just under the roof rafters. A very American nightmare, Wayne said, as opposed to Delmer Primrose's about leading a VC sing-along. It was his major worry, how a hick from Lazarus, Tennessee, a high school–casualty dropout, could possibly be privy to all those goddamn gook words. He talked while he ate, worrying aloud in his backwoods accent. And he worried aloud behind his mask while cleaning latrines back at base. Same deal while out on

135 ✳

patrol or staring into the entrance of a VC tunnel. He died instantly one morning under a bright blue sky, while walking right next to Wayne—a single round of sniper fire, the bullet entering straight into Delmer's open mouth.

Which was no weirder than anything else, Wayne said to Perry during the early days of their friendship, when he was still talking a lot about the war. He doesn't much anymore. And it's the same with shooting pool at John's Tavern, just across the drawbridge and around the corner on Cottrell Street. Perry can't remember how the subject of pool came up during that first visit to the houseboat, but it did, and he could tell by the way Wayne slapped down his quarter and chalked his cue after they'd walked over there together that same night that he was better than good. Very first game, he ran the table on the break—cross-side, multiple combinations, the cue ball spinning backward across the bright green felt with more English than Perry had ever seen. Perfect placement, and that sound—the kiss-kiss the balls made, each falling dead center into the pouch of whichever leather pocket he'd called. Something right out of *The Hustler* or *The Color of Money*. Except for the stakes—loser sprung for the fifty-cent drafts.

Perry figures that Wayne was looking for a male friend back then, somebody who'd settled down here from parts unknown, but not *too* settled down. Somebody outside the tight cliques of this cliquey town, a guy who made no stand anymore about having gone or not gone to fight in Vietnam. And certainly nobody who'd been over there and returned with only part of his innards, and whom the bank had shot down on a car loan after a quick credit check. And without a set of wheels, how the fuck was it possible to get your sweetheart back, the one who in 1969 or 1970 pressed her immaculate breasts against the static of the console TV screen, closed her eyes, and listened to the death count? It's that erotic image that kept him alive, that "kept all of us alive," Wayne said, "who listened to guys actually read those kinds of love letters out loud. And later destroyed us, those same young

and beautiful women unaroused by a bunch of shell-shocked vets."
Had he enlisted in the Peace Corps instead of the war corps, Wayne
estimates by now he'd be a father of three or four. A real close family.
His wife—he can describe her to a tee—an ex–Ice Capader with
auburn hair and perfect legs who skated for a year as Minnie Mouse
for Walt Disney. But other times, the eyes are hazel or dark brown.
"Never mind that," he'd say if Perry pointed out the contradictions.
He'd say, "Perry fucking Mason," and he'd repeat, "Never you mind,"
and the next set of details, however different, would be as exact as the
last, right down to the sharpness of the chrome blades.

Bit by bit over the years, Perry has attempted to piece Wayne's
past together. A sister he grudgingly admits to who lives in Santa Fe
or Atlanta or Princeton, New Jersey. Or elsewhere, of course, K.C.,
D.C., L.A. Married to some wheeler-dealer property investor, "Probably in cahoots with the whatchamacallit bank scandal," Wayne said,
meaning the S&L, "that government-protected gang of criminals. Mil-
lionaire bank robbers," he said, "and the judges still equating petty
theft with mass murder for the rest of us peons scrimping to stay
aboveboard."

Perry believes the sentiment, but not the reality—Wayne's got
some money, from where remains a mystery. Unlike most of the
other small-operation lobstermen, Wayne doesn't have a second job
at General Dynamics or working on the *Seawolf* at Electric Boat, nor
is he moonlighting or selling dope. If he were, Perry would know
about it—it wouldn't be the sort of secret Wayne would keep from
him. He might even ask Perry to run a computer check—insider
connections and all that—to make sure there was no surveillance going
on, no chance of him getting busted. And Perry would do it through
Gordon Butterbaugh with one quick phone call.

It's possible Wayne inherited money. Both his parents are dead,
not uncommon, Perry thinks, among the sons and daughters heading
toward fifty. Perry doubts his mom will be around for long after he

hits forty, and in this context, forty seems much too young. Not that children any age expect their parents to outlive them, nor would anyone want it that way.

Perry seldom goes home to Michigan, despite Marcia's urging him to do so, especially since his mom's stroke. It's borderline impossible, he tells Marcia, but she insists if he waits too long, he'll forever regret it. She's not anxious, though, to travel with him to "Doomland," as Perry's brother, Hank, calls it, and without her, the visits are simply too oppressive. His dad skulks around the house and the barn from the time he gets up, leaving Perry to sit in the living room with his mom, who turns bossy and demanding whenever her eyes are not glued to the TV. Sometimes to get her attention, Perry actually has to get up from the couch and switch the set off, then take the remote from his mom's left hand, her good hand. It's the only way she'll hear what he's saying, that he'll be back in an hour or two, that he's going to run a few errands in town. It literally takes Perry weeks to regain his equilibrium after each trip out there.

And that morose feeling is not unlike what he's feeling now, as though he's gradually inherited both his mom's paralysis and his dad's untreatable and monstrous resign. It scares Marcia and it scares Perry and he has no idea in the world how to begin to talk about it, except to Wayne, and he's passed out. But not before he said that what matters isn't how often or how far down you go, only how much of yourself you can eventually coax back to solid ground. For the moment for Perry, very little, the reason he pours himself another stiff hit of rum, and because it helps to numb the terrible throbbing in his hand.

Perry's half in the bag when the phone rings. "It's Marcia," Wayne says, scratching the back of his head and then yawning. "Hey," he adds when Perry nods but makes no attempt to get up, "it's for you."

✳ 138

Perry's light-headed and he's afraid he's going to slur his words, but so what? In Marcia's book, there's nobody alive more blameworthy than Wayne. She maintains that *he's* the problem, the instigator. Even if Perry is a willing participant, as he insists he is, getting so blitzed, as Marcia has often pointed out, is not a natural penchant of his.

From the start, Wayne has shamelessly accepted this as a condition of their friendship, and "Perry the innocent," as Wayne has called him, has long ago stopped apologizing for his wife's refusal to hold him accountable, too. Wayne has never had to say to Perry, "Blame it on me," because Marcia absolutely will. "No," she said after the first few nights Perry stumbled in blitzed from Wayne's, "he doesn't twist your arm, he twists your brain."

"Hello," Perry says. Wayne is preoccupied, struggling through yet another marathon yawn.

"Are you ready for this? A woman—her name is Alethea Papendick, I'm not kidding—found the Jet Ski washed up on her beach at Montauk. Isn't that unreal? She phoned the police and they traced the registration numbers back to us. She says it looks fine to her, and that the key is still in the ignition."

"Good. Call her back and tell her it's hers. Tell her to keep it," Perry says.

"No," Marcia says, "I most certainly won't do that—it makes absolutely no sense, which is what you're talking again, nonsense. At least we can go get it and then put it up for sale at Palmer's. We can salvage that much from all of this, don't you think?"

She's decided to push; her informative and practical tone says so. It says, Why can't you work just a trifle harder at blotting yesterday's cruddy memories out of your head? Or is the fifteen hundred dollars' worth of Jet Ski the price of self-pity these days? The practical talk Perry's learned and practiced in his work is no match for Marcia's all-out offensive. He imagines her gnashing her teeth as he says, "How?

Drive seven hours to get four miles?" which is what it takes looping around through New Haven and New York City, then all the way out to the tip of Long Island.

"You're approximating the ridiculous," Marcia says. "Think, will you? The puzzle's much simpler, Perry. Who's talking about driving there? Maybe you should just stay out of this. Obviously you're in no shape physically *or* emotionally to be of any help anyway, so put Wayne on. And please don't argue about it—I'm not in the mood."

Nor is he, and when Wayne draws open the window shades, Perry winces. He belongs in his bed, asleep, his medication and a glass of water beside him on the bed table. In the momentary silence, he succumbs to that vision and actually closes his eyes and tilts his head, as if toward a pillow. And the instant he begins to fall, Wayne is there, holding Perry under both armpits, then lowering him carefully onto his back on the carpet. The receiver has landed only a couple of feet from Perry's ear, and he can hear what still sounds like Marcia's voice, though now it seems dream-muffled. "Hello?" she says. "Perry? Hello? Is anybody there?" But all he can do is lie still and breathe hard into the dizziness of the booze so that he doesn't completely pass out. He's protecting his bad hand by covering it with the other one on the top of his chest. "Perry, answer me if you're there." But even if he wanted to, he can't.

Wayne, returning with a cold washcloth doubled over and now pressed to Perry's forehead, reaches over and quietly hangs up. "Is she onto you?" he asks, but Perry is too woozy-feeling to even shake his head yes or no, and when the phone rings again, Wayne says, "Sorry for the screwy connection. Nah," he says, "the aftereffects of yesterday's overdose. No," he says, "uh-uh." He tells her it'll do Perry a world of good to hang out on the houseboat for the afternoon. "It's premature to call in the coroner," Wayne jokes. "He'll bounce back." This is followed by a long pause while Marcia talks. "No again," Wayne says. He says, "Marcia, he'll call if he needs a ride later on," and the conversation turns to the business of embarking on Jet Ski rescue plans.

Perry's mind keeps slipping in and out of the moment, and Wayne, on the floor now on his knees, flashes Perry the peace sign. Perry's eyes are slits, and he can't hear a word that's being said anymore, so he shuts his eyes. And the very last thing he feels before sleep is Wayne patting him softly on his leg, as he might have twenty years ago to comfort a frightened and badly wounded soldier.

Chapter 11

Marcia says she certainly *can* stand to look at him, and she demonstrates by averting her eyes from the TV screen and staring over at Perry. She's sitting cross-legged on the floor, a glass of lemonade on a coaster beside her. Perry's on the love seat, a pillow on his lap and his hand resting on top of that. The painkillers have helped, as have the four or five hours of deep sleep at Wayne's and the chicken tenders and fresh asparagus Marcia fixed him for dinner.

It's she who suggested they relax with a movie. While she's been at the video store, Perry's been on the phone with Cal Hyde, his field supervisor. "All's well that ends well," Cal said, reassuring Perry that his appointments are covered for the next three days. "What, are the rest of us amateurs? Relax," he said, "these things happen. It's nobody's fault."

But the argument that's brewing kind of is—it's Marcia's doing. "Your choice," she'd said, and he asked her to pick up *Truly Madly Deeply*, but she returned with *Havana*, and with what Perry believed was a wiseass answer.

"Havana's foreign enough," she said, and Perry's been telling himself that Redford's fine. At least she hasn't come back empty-handed in favor of watching *Mystic Pizza* again. He imagines her putting it on, then stopping it and saying, "Remember her, that woman in the background in midstride, that woman you married? That's Main Street, where you were today, that she's walking down." And, after fast-forwarding, as she does sometimes, she'd say, "Look, there's the drawbridge opening, and the Seaport upriver and, on the periphery of each frame, the images that surround our life together. This is where we live, you and me, by choice."

Now, watching *Havana*, she says, "So what's wrong, Perry? What on earth is it that you need to tell me?"

A lot, he thinks, too much, but it's exactly that kind of inexactness that keeps frustrating Marcia, so he blurts out, "The whole J.J. episode—Jesus. Marcia, turn the movie off if you want to talk."

There's nothing halfhearted about the way she scrambles over on her hands and knees and presses the stop, eject, and power buttons, in that order and all with her index finger. Then the sound of the set, and then she turns and faces him, the blank screen behind her head. It's as though he's about to talk to her on a monitor, and he says, "It would help if you'd move closer."

"It would help if you'd *let* me," she says. "You flinch every time I try, or you fly off the handle, or, worse, you just clam up. Perry, if this is all preliminary to what I hope it's not, you have to tell me. You have to come clean. I hope to God I'm wrong, but if there's another woman in the picture, let's begin with her."

In the picture—he hates that phrase. "No," he says, "not like you mean."

"Outside the picture, then—someone you're attracted to?"

"I'm attracted to Pauline, for God's sake. I'm attracted to strange women holding babies because they're *not* mine, babies I can walk away from without being frightened every second about what's going to hurt them. Jesus, my own sister drowned in our driveway. I mean, what'd you expect? That I'd miraculously loosen up on this parental thing? It keeps getting worse is what it does."

"The miracle *is* having children," Marcia says, "and people *do* relax once they have their own—ask anyone—and being a father is precisely what you need to get over all these awful fears. They're making you crazy—they're making me crazy. J.J. didn't almost drown—you almost did. You protected him with a life preserver. He told us that, how you tugged on the straps, but that you didn't wear one yourself. You're the one I worry about losing, not any children we might have. You'll see, it'll be the children who save us, who make us happy again."

"When? When am I going to see, Marcia? We're almost forty. A year's not just a year anymore. It's not like going from twenty-five to twenty-six. Age is the real culprit here, and it's irresponsible as hell after awhile to keep at this."

Perry glances over at the window as a June bug pings the screen. There's a breeze in the curtains and it's completely dark outside, and he knows Marcia wants to see his eyes when she speaks again, so he turns back to her and doesn't blink. She waits a few more seconds and then she says, and calmly, "I have a doctor's appointment on Wednesday. What should I tell him?"

"You mean a swami appointment, don't you? Tell him this—tell him he's an opportunistic motherfucker, and ask him for me how badly he was beaten as a child to want to put people through this shit. Tell him in my business we're always curious about the revenge factor."

"And you've decided to take yours out on me," Marcia says. "After all this time together, to end up here in this pitiful conversation. Do you have any idea how much it hurts to hear you say you're attracted to my sister? And worse, to strange women holding babies? Can you possibly imagine in that male brain of yours what that says about me?"

"You're mixing up motherhood with womanhood," Perry says,

and he realizes immediately how smug and presumptuous and uninspired that sounds, but he doesn't apologize.

"Who's that muscled nitwit you like on big-time wrestling? The Macho Man, isn't that his name? Well, that's what this is all about, the macho factor, a case of frustrated sperm. You can't have it both ways, Perry, disappointed that I can't conceive and afraid I just might. That's really terrific, and you can use it all as an excuse to go sniffing poontang—isn't that what macho men call it? Or muff? Or beaver? Though you won't admit to it, that's probably where all this is headed, you knocking up some twenty-five- or twenty-six-year-old. I haven't mixed up anything, except what I expected from you, from a husband. All of a sudden, it seems like so much is missing. Too much," she says.

"Meaning what, exactly?"

"You tell me, why don't you?" she says. "Why don't you tell me?" She's crying hard, getting up and running by him out of the living room. He doesn't call or follow her, not even when the door slams, followed by the thudding of her bare feet down the stairs. Perry concentrates instead on the blank TV screen, and he imagines those behemoths Marcia's always been disgusted by, each one outrageously outfitted and entering the ring with two-by-fours and live snakes and chains and Viking swords, with electric shock guns and managers with names like Bobby the Brain and Mr. Fuji. Perry watches because of the elaborate farce of each match, the ferocious yet harmless pile drivers and reverse body slams and karate chops to the throat, all of it carefully choreographed so that nobody gets injured. A world of fake violence, the good guys against the bad guys. Then presto, and no matter who's been groaning and bear-hugged and flattened by six hundred–plus pounds of the Earthquake, he'll be fine. Recovery time? As long as it takes to get out of sight of the screaming fans and safely into the dressing room.

Bouncing back from even the smallest domestic spats does not go anything like that. The attacks are real, and real pain the price of admission, and Perry knows that both he and Marcia have paid tonight.

He hears her car start; then he sees what he knows is her left high beam aiming up and reflecting off the undersides of the leaves outside the window. If he wanted to, he could manage with some difficulty to start the Subaru and steer and shift with his left hand. Or he could more easily have chased after her on foot, calling from the stoop for a truce.

Maybe it *is* the macho factor that's stopped him from doing that, too. He promises himself he won't call over to his mother-in-law's. Marcia's bailed before, but this time he'll wait her out, tough guy all the way. He begins with a dare to himself to try to flex his fingers, to curl them into a slow fist of disdain. It feels as though the stitches are about to split, and he breathes in and holds his breath, his eyes squeezed so tightly that they begin to water, and finally one stitch does pop under the bandages before he stops.

It's not Marcia who walks into the apartment midmorning; it's Pauline. She checks first in both bedrooms and, not finding him there, calls Perry's name. He doesn't answer, and when she finds him, she says, "Whoops," as though she's discovered Perry sitting next to some half-naked bimbo on the love seat. It's obvious from his puffy face and slouched shoulders that he's been there most of the night, *The Portable Nietzsche* open on his lap: "Nausea, nausea, nausea—woe unto me!"

Great choice for a depressive, Marcia told him the day before yesterday. Read Thoreau, she said, or Hegel or Teilhard de Chardin. And she held out a bottle of vitamin B_6 and said, "Take two of these—they reduce stress."

He didn't even look up at her.

And there's nothing depressing or stressful about the passage he's been reading and wants to believe: "Everything breaks, everything is joined anew. . . . Everything parts, everything greets every other thing again; eternally the ring of being remains faithful to itself."

And to what's right, Perry thinks, and he hopes he can figure out what that is before the bottom caves in.

"Hey, don't frown so much," Pauline says, "it'll give you creases in your forehead."

Pauline, a longtime sun worshiper, has crow's-feet at the corners of her eyes and they deepen as she smiles.

"You the emissary?" Perry asks.

"Winds out of the east at twelve to eighteen knots," she says.

"That a message or a code?"

"I've only ever known my sister to take the direct approach—it's a message. She and your friend Wayne are this very minute on their way to Long Island on his lobster boat."

"You make it sound like they're running off together."

"Well, I wouldn't blame her," Pauline says. "He's a nice guy. Nice-looking, too. I met him when I dropped Marcia off. He had all these nautical maps spread out on his table, and coffee made, and a lunch packed, beer on ice. I wish I were going instead of Marcia. I could use a fun voyage about now. To almost anyplace."

"Yup," Perry agrees, and Pauline tilts her head back, a sexy little maneuver to show how she might work some magic on a loner like Wayne. She shrugs at Perry's dull insistence that he's not her type. "I'm serious, he's not."

"I like you a lot better when you're not," she says. "Like the other night. Be honest, didn't that feel good to be on the loose for a couple of hours? We're entitled to that, aren't we? At least that's what I was hoping for, coming back here to stay at Mom's, but I'm ready to leave right now. It's turned into—I don't know what—a lonely hearts club or something, and Mom yacking about how now's the time to invest in eternity. Whenever she walks into the room, I half expect to see her flanked by angels. She's gotten worse. Apparently, it all goes right by Marcia, either that or she's more forgiving than I am, but the whole thing's driving me bananas."

"The kids holding up?"

"Virtine's in a snit, accusing us all of being demented. She says it's been the crummiest summer ever, but she's got a friend down the street, the Pampoos' daughter, and according to Virtine, that family's fun at least. She said people in that family aren't crying and arguing all the time. She's over there from morning till night. J.J.—he's so confused. He asks about his father all the time, and about you. He says he hates being the only boy in the house, and who can blame him? That's partly why I stopped, to see if you'd drive over with me—it doesn't have to be for long. I warned J.J. no roughhousing. And Marcia won't be back until suppertime."

"And the other reason?"

"To see how you're doing."

Perry lifts and turns his hand over. A star of blood has soaked through, the thumb and forefinger swollen black and blue.

"The bandages need to be changed," he says, pushing himself up from the love seat, "and I need some coffee and breakfast for starters." He pauses. "How *is* Marcia?"

"How do you think?" Pauline says. "And that's the other reason I want to leave, because I can't stand to see the two of you like this."

"Me, either," Perry says.

"Then why don't you fix whatever's the matter?"

"Why didn't you?" Perry says, and Pauline hesitates a few seconds before following him as far as the bedroom. The bed's still made, and that's where Perry tosses the gauze and salve and the wide roll of perforated tape, then the sharply angled surgical scissors.

"Ever done this?" Perry says, and Pauline answers, "You wish."

He sits on the edge of the bed as she walks toward him, theatrically holding her stomach. But the queasy act is short-lived. "Let's have a peek," she says, and Perry notices for the first time a small V-shaped scar on her left knee, and that's where he concentrates as she stands over him.

"Tell me when I'm hurting you," she says, as though she intends to, and begins cutting along the inside of his wrist and across the palm. She puts the scissors down and peels open the bandages and says, "Wow!" Then adds, "Thank God something this ugly isn't contagious."

Mostly, it doesn't hurt—a twinge or two—and Perry starts calling her Doc Pauline. He's never had a woman doctor, nor has Marcia. Even when the bedroom door slams shut from a sudden wind, she doesn't flinch.

She's much better at this than Marcia—all the practice with scrapes and abrasions required of motherhood, plus those two semesters in nursing school. And she's not at all embarrassed by Perry in his underwear and pajama top, though he is, a little, holding out a disfigured hand that a few nights ago might have tried to steer Pauline underneath him by the river. He also knows, had he tried, that she would have known exactly where to stop. As Angela knew, and he wonders if all women in shaky marriages have some kind of built-in transmitter that bleeps an adult warning against such folly, some impenetrable, ironclad instinct that's evolved slowly into the very hub of their existence—a polite "Fuck you, Jack, I'm no home-wrecker."

Perry showers but doesn't shave. "I like the scruffy look," Pauline says. "Maybe you should grow a beard." She helps Perry with buttons and shoelaces and belt buckle, the whole time prattling on about this bearded anatomy professor she adored at BU. "A short blond beard," she says. "And he'd wear these expensive linen sport coats, but underneath, a Slim Goodbody T-shirt diagramming life-scale body parts—heart, lungs, liver, globby intestines. He'd pull open his lapels and breathe in and out to demonstrate the movement of the diaphragm, and to watch the young coeds come unglued—which they did. He had gray eyes and the most passionate disdain for late-arriving students I've ever seen. He'd point to his heart and shut his eyes for up to ten minutes. A true dilettante, but fun to stare at.''

And so is their waitress at Food & Company. Her collar's up on her Izod shirt, and she's got a bouncy ponytail. She recommends the Polish soul-food special that's hot and hot, meaning, she says, spicy and delicious. Perry orders it, Pauline opting for the eggs Florentine with chopped chives. There's nobody in the restaurant Perry recognizes—all tourist eaters, chins down, forks ablaze so they can make the noontime show at Seaworld.

Perry's said fine, for time's sake, to taking the nonsmoking table in the corner. Next to them, a woman in a paisley maternity dress listens, with all the concentrated nervousness of first-time mothers, to another, slightly older woman deliver an impassioned soliloquy on Jane Fonda's *Pregnancy, Birth and Recovery* workout tape. Pauline raises her eyebrows, then takes a slow sip of ice water.

The waitress returns and pours from two different pots—decaf for Pauline, real coffee, as Perry calls it, for himself. The waitress, seeing Perry's hand, says, "Ouch, what happened?"

"Disagreement with a window," Perry says.

"Looks like you lost."

"It happens," he says, not having the heart to tell someone so young that he's lost every bout he's ever fought against depression. There's no muscling in—you learn to keep it at arm's length, or you get hammered. And recover slowly, which is what he and Pauline are doing here. And they're doing okay so far. The waitress leaves and, the next time by, drops a handful of jelly and marmalade packets onto the table. She says their breakfasts are coming right up.

The walls of the restaurant, the renovated end section of a thimble factory, are sandblasted brick, the old square-headed nails still dotting the floorboards. A tin-plated ceiling. It's a place Marcia likes, the ambience bohemian posh. Even the busboy appears college-bound in his Top-Siders and Guess? jeans, the cuffs rolled. Low man on the totem pole, he's nobody's whipping boy. Not here, where a crustacean omelette is standard on the menu—as opposed to the heartburn luncheonettes in New London where Perry also eats, the counter grills sizzling with midmorning burgers. No specials on a blackboard, just the same plastic-covered single-page menus of a million fingerprints—some of them Perry's parolees and probationers, some of them his.

This morning, he prefers Food & Company, the waitresses wearing shorts. Because the kitchen is upstairs, Perry has a perfect view of their tanned legs climbing and descending, a workout for young women spurred on by generous summer tips.

"I'd last all of about one shift," Pauline says, "and spend the whole night waking up with charley horses." Her arms are crossed, both elbows on the table. "Unless, of course, I had someone to massage them."

Perry holds up his bad hand, a smart-ass offer, and then he winks. The food arrives and Perry and Pauline eat while they listen to that same woman denounce holy matrimony as a female prison. "You've lived with him how long?" she asks. "And happily during much of that time? Ingrid," she says, "a relationship isn't half the bother a marriage is. All marriage does is make what you're doing now legal, and encourages domestic rape. Believe me, I speak from experience. A baby and a beau is head and shoulders more glamorous these days than a baby and a husband—that's on its way out, as far as I'm concerned, like breast implants and low hemlines and aggressive men. Show some gratitude for what you have and for who you are."

Perry's growing impatient for Ms. Pregnant to speak up—if she's old enough to have a kid, she's sure the hell old enough to voice her opinion on all this nonsense. Pauline stops buttering her toast, a pause to show she's considering what she's just heard, and she shakes her head no when the waitress asks if she can bring them anything else. A gag, Perry almost says, and he'd like to help tighten it around the mouth of old marriage basher, her hair dyed the color of a shiny new penny. She's wearing stretch pants, oversized shoulder pads in her black silk blouse. She's got a face like a greyhound, lips pursed like an angry nun.

"Can I have a bite?" Pauline asks. Perry has pushed to one side of his plate a half dozen ovals of sausage. He nods and lifts one between his thumb and forefinger and places it like a Host on her tongue. She closes her eyes and chews slowly and says, "Yum."

Perry remembers receiving communion during the church service at Hank's wedding in Grand Rapids, and how the guests shouted and squealed and flung handfuls of rice above the bride and groom as they departed down the stairs of Blessed Sacrament, the photographer snapping away as he walked hunched and backward in front of them. At the reception, it was Marcia who caught the bouquet, then held on to it all afternoon as she and Perry danced to the music of Newt and the Salamanders. And ignored the bridal registry at Hudson's in favor of buying Hank and Connie a basset hound puppy they named Necco, after the brown and white and black wafers. None of which gives Perry the right to lean over and excuse himself for interrupting, but he couldn't help overhearing, and he just wants to cast his vote for tying the knot. "No offense," he says, "but anything less is bogus, bogus and chickenshit."

Pauline, acting the agreeable and loving wife, nods and smiles, and as soon as the two women get up and leave without a word, she bends forward and says to Perry, "You nincompoop. What, are you all of a sudden the nuptial spokesman for Mystic?"

"Did I sound inspired?"

"You sounded fussy and Republican. You sounded like an ass."

"And Brunhild there didn't? Fair's fair, c'mon, Pauline." Perry's got her riled now and he's enjoying it. He glances around to see if it's their turn to be eavesdropped on, but nobody seems the slightest bit interested.

"What's so fair about marriage, anyway?"

"Personally or philosophically?"

"It's a ridiculous distinction," Pauline contends, puncturing another piece of sausage with the end tine of her three-tined fork.

"All I'm saying is let Ingrid get hitched and retain her maiden name if she needs to make a statement. I'm all for that."

"Now you're sounding like Dan Quayle," she says, and she and Perry trade plates so she doesn't have to keep reaching across the table.

"How about the guy's part in this? That's all I'm defending. Unless I'm mistaken, he just got devoured over breakfast, didn't he? Gives the word *lady-killer* a whole new meaning."

Pauline looks over at the two half-empty glasses of iced tea, the muffin crumbs on the tablecloth. "It's none of your business—you have no right to interfere in their conversation, to pester people and to make these public judgments."

"They *made* it my business by being so loud and obnoxious—they wanted us to hear."

"This is getting stupider by the second," Pauline says, raising one finger to signal for the check, and when it arrives, she insists on paying. No argument from Perry. He doesn't even offer to put down the tip, and as Pauline does, he says, "Don't be so cheap."

"What?" she says. "That's almost thirty percent."

Perry, already standing and pushing his chair in, says, "So? What's another couple bucks if it helps her to remember me?"

Pauline's sarcastic *ha-ha* warns Perry he's on thin ice, joke or no joke, which he acknowledges with an innocent shrug on their way out to the car, his arm around her shoulder.

153 ✳

J.J. says he's not sure what he's going to do yet with the six silver pinballs. For right now, he's clicking two of them together as Perry explains what flippers are, and bumpers and tilt. J.J. has never played pinball, just as Perry has never played the arcade video games that J.J. rattles off: Wacky Gator and Lightning Fighters and Jungle Jive. Perry and J.J. have killed the afternoon cruising garage and yard sales, and have stopped at Burger King's drive-thru for a couple of Cokes and some Famous Amos chocolate-chip cookies. Next to J.J., an Aqua-Rocket and a Slinky, and in the far back of Pauline's new Ford Explorer, a green beanbag chair, a five-dollar purchase. Perry hasn't seen one of these dinosaurs since the early seventies. His college roommate, a beefy psychology major whose forearms bulged from consecutive semesters of squeezing a hard rubber ball, studied in a chair identical to this one. Studied and squeezed. "Squeezed and studied," Perry says, "and every single night before bed, he'd curl forty-pound dumbbells, a hundred curls total for each arm. Yeah, and that year he won an arm-wrestling competition at a bar over in Ypsilanti."

J.J's slumped low in the seat so that the sun reflecting off the windshields of oncoming cars isn't blinding him. They're on Green-manville Avenue and the traffic is heavy.

"What prize did he win, Uncle Perry?"

"Oh, a trophy, I think," and Perry laughs and says, "plus all the beer he could drink—nothing too great. After that, we started calling him Roger the Brusco."

J.J. scrunches up his face. "I don't get it," he says. "What's that mean, Roger the Brusco?"

"Well, that was really his name—Roger Brusco. Adding the word *the* kind of turned it into a tough-guy name. You know, like Dick the Bruiser or Andre the Giant or J.J. the Terrible." Perry winks down at J.J., who smiles back.

They pass the cemetery, the shadiest place in Mystic. Giant syca-
mores. Cemeteries do not remind Perry of his grandparents, all four
of them buried in northern Michigan, where his parents will also be
buried someday. It's where Janine, whom he always *is* reminded of, is
buried, too. Janine Marie Lafond. He has often imagined the stonecutter
engraving those dates: June 10, 1959–July 17, 1964. Born and died.
Those are the tombstones that stop you, Perry thinks, more so than
the infant deaths. Children who lived long enough to make your
palms go damp now, as Perry's do, just driving past these graves.
Kindergartners, nursery schoolers, even preschoolers who stay home,
where, as Betty said to Perry once, "a mother's heart is the classroom
of learning." And a father's heart, Perry wanted to add, but said nothing,
remembering Janine riding on their father's shoulders at the state fair,
his hands around her ankles, cotton candy stuck in his hair. And how,
from up there with an overhead toss, the ring bounced and landed
around the neck of the bottle everybody else was aiming for and
couldn't hit, the one for which the prize was that giant pink stuffed
bear, itself a sale item on the collapsible table a few years later, Perry
the one who took the money and placed it inside the White Owl cigar
box and did not say thank you. As soon as the customers drove away,
he carried the folding chair to the back wall of the garage and sat down
and cried.

That is what J.J. says Aunt Marcia did last night. "A real lot," he
says. "I was asleep, but all that crying woke me up. Uncle Perry, I
hope you never go off like my dad did. He's made everybody not very
happy. And y'know what? He hasn't called me even one time since
we came down here. Do you think he will?" J.J.'s head is twisted
sideways against the seat back, his hand almost touching Perry's leg.
J.J.'s on the verge of tears himself.

"Sure he will, partner—yeah, of course. Listen," Perry says, "sometimes, well, it's like this—you know how when you go snorkeling
after a storm, like we did off Main Beach last summer, and the water's

all murky and you can hardly see your own hand in front of your mask? And how it always takes awhile before the visibility's any good again, mmm? Right? Well, people's lives get all murked up like that, too—same thing. And it's not easy. Just like you say, nobody's too happy, but you've got to wait it out; it's the only way. In the long run, it's usually okay."

"How long's the long run?" J.J. needs more than this kind of nebulous confirmation. He needs days to count down, a calendar date to anticipate—August 15 or September 22 or maybe December 25, a Christmas reunion where the family gathers to open presents, the "long run" finally up and everything back to normal. It's not the wait; it's the uncertainty.

Perry hangs a left at Mistuxet Avenue. There's a sign at Andy I's advertising EDIBLE ART. That same sign in downtown New London would be pornographic, but all this means is one-of-a-kind bakery goods at prime-season prices. As Perry's mom used to say about inflation, "The crazy, crazy cost of things!" Neil's got the big bucks, and Pauline's already talking about taking him to the cleaners, but it's J.J., even more than Virtine, who'll pay in the end, who'll be eaten up. Perry's doing his levelheaded best not to sound resentful of Neil, not to arouse even worse anxiety in J.J. "The long run's no set time," Perry explains. "It's just a phrase that means we're not going to stay glum forever." He leans toward J.J. and softly elbows his shoulder. "Right?"

"Timmy Reminschnieder—he's a friend at my school—he said sometimes when your dad leaves, the kids are sent away to the Oh Holiness Association, or off to Brightside."

"Whattaya mean, sent away? That's a bunch of malarkey. Cripes," Perry says, slowing down, turning right on Church Street. There must be two hundred cormorants on the rocks along the river. "What the dickens would he say something like that for?"

"He said the courts do it. They send real mean women to grab all the kids from broken homes, and it doesn't even count how good you've been or anything—they just snatch you away."

"And I'm telling you the courts *don't* do that. They don't interfere unless the children are unloved and in danger at home, and that could never, ever happen to you or Virtine. Both your parents love you very much—I can vouch for that, kiddo. So don't you let Timmy whatever his name is bamboozle you. You listen to your uncle Perry."

J.J.'s a worrier. He reminds Perry of himself around that age, right after Janine's death, when his mom turned riotous, his dad hush-hush. And Perry was left to decipher the world between them, Hank always off someplace else on his bicycle from morning until just before dark. Perry can still hear his mom's screaming falsetto, wasted on his dad, who'd turn and walk away, outside and out of sight into the barn or deep into the orchard. Though they've stayed together, that summer marked the end of their marriage, obliterated any sense of family from then on. If his dad speaks at all around Perry's mom, it's in short, clipped sentences, often single-word sentences—yes and no. It's as though, toting his silence for so long, even the simplest conversations seem doomed, Perry's mom chiding, "What's wrong? What's wrong with you now?" Perry seldom even calls home. "Face the facts," Hank told him one night as they both lay wide awake on their beds until very late. "You and me, we're as good as orphaned."

And now J.J.'s feeling that, too. He stops clicking the pinballs—Perry thinks of them as two large worry beads—and he intuitively knows the question that's coming, and when it does, he pulls off to the side of the road and shuts off the ignition. This is something Perry's dad used to do, just the two of them in the car, and then he'd fumble and fumble with whatever it was he meant to say to Perry, as if there weren't any words fit to decipher the complex puzzle of their lives. Pieces kept falling away, like voices, Perry thought back then, like rain. Then fewer and fewer attempts to say a thing, the car windows rolled down and Perry listening only to the onrush of wind across the open fields. He answers J.J., "You bet I will. You can count on it. Absolutely, but I guarantee it won't come to that—not ever."

"But if it does?"

"If it does, you'll come live with me and I'll always take care of you. I promise."

"And you'll be kinda like my father, right?"

"I'll be like a second father."

"And for Virtine, too?"

"Of course," Perry says, though he knows Virtine's as fearless a nine-year-old as he's ever met; the demons of divorce have not begun to converge on her as they have already on J.J. Not that they won't. But for now she'll continue to unearth, day by day, reasons to stay happy enough. She won't brood like J.J. and she definitely won't need Perry in this way. Uncle's fine, uncle's enough. But yes, he promises again that he'll be there for her, as well. "Deal?"

J.J. nods. His eyes are nearly cobalt behind the tinted blue of the windshield. He's staring up at Perry. "Deal," he says, and scratches his cheek with his thumbnail, and finally he half smiles before looking away.

Chapter 12

"The future's coming," Alden Grelling announces. Hardly an arguable proclamation, so Perry nods in agreement. He tells himself, That's right, and the past is behind us, the shaky present always slipping by.

But not quickly enough. Alden Grelling's a talker, and much less guarded than most who end up here talking to Perry. Alden has that disconcerting habit of mouthing whatever Perry says, as though he has to repeat it to himself to understand it. He's twenty-six years old and already balding, except for a wispy fringe above his ears, plus orange sideburns that taper toward his purplish and permanently disfigured lips. The result, last winter, of pressing them around the frozen keyhole of his car. He'll explain he had only two choices—remain on his knees praying all night, the temperature dropping and the snow knifing in, or tear free of the skin holding him there. Originally from Weeks, Louisiana, he presently rents a room in a boarding house over on Hempstead. He's between jobs and has eyes so deeply set that Perry has never been able to determine their color. Hazel—at least according to Alden's file.

Out of the blue, he'll issue forth with nonsense statements like, "No bottles for bait," then pontificate about how you can't have customers cashing in their empties for shrimp or pinfish. There's the can and bottle bin, and then there's the cash drawer. And there's a limit to everything. "Establish some rules," he'll say, "or like to be kicked around for your whole entire life."

"And those who break the rules?"

"One time, that's all, just the one stinkin' time," Alden'll argue. "A single miscue."

Report night is the second Thursday of each month. The reason Alden's sitting here in Perry's office? For stealing a boat he says he meant to fish the bayous out of back home. "Arrive empty-handed and the folks and friends'll wonder what you been up to out east for all that time."

The answer, not much, other than to exhaust his welfare benefits and then back his wreck of a Buick into Gauthier's Marina, locate a boat trailer to fit his bumper hitch, and tow a nineteen-foot Boston Whaler all the way to New Haven before being arrested on Route 91.

Perry sees as many as twenty probationers and parolees on this one night, a marathon check-in. No complimentary coffee in the waiting room. And no magazines, and almost nobody talking.

As usual, first in line was six-foot-six, 270-pound Marlon Beebow, who, at that size, should be able to hold his booze but can't, and, shut off, will sometimes nod and smile and stumble out into the bar parking lot, where he'll trash the windshields of cars with a lug wrench or baseball bat. Sober, he's one of the gentlest, least threatening men Perry's ever met. Someone, unlike Alden, you might really *go* fishing with. The essential line to check on Marlon's report sheet is the one that shows if he's missed any AA meetings. If not, he's out the door—it's that routine.

"Must be a thrill a minute," Alden offers up, "your job I mean, always blasting off on a joyride into the weirdo minds of criminals. D'you see *The Silence of the Lambs* yet? Man oh man, Hannibal 'the Cannibal' Lecter—now, there's one extremely disturbed but very intelligent dude."

Perry's struck half-dumb sometimes by the names these people invoke as heroes. But never surprised, and able on the comeback to say to Alden, "Strictly Hollywood, and morbid Hollywood at that." But who's forgotten that the Jeffrey Dahmers are alive in this world, too, the real psychos, whose misshapen minds consume and then act out the unimaginable.

Perry's listened to Steve Hazelton prosecute murder cases, arguing that homicide is homicide. Dead's as dead as dead gets, and the only just punishment—an eye for an eye. Shoot or gas or gangplank or hang or fry or lethally inject the bastards the way they do in the more enlightened penal states such as Kansas and Florida and Maryland. Perry opposes capital punishment on the grounds that it makes monsters of us all. Baloney, Steve Hazelton, who's witnessed an execution in Maryland, tells Perry. Steve says it's a lot like watching a movie, high-tension drama, and the acting is first-rate.

"It snagged how many Academy Awards?" Alden Grelling asks, then answers his own question. "A bunch, if I ain't mistaken. I don't mind confiding that I paid to see it two shows in a row, right down front, center-screen. Hannibal the Cannibal—my money says there's a sequel down the road and that they never catch 'em. He's too smart."

That's what Perry detested most about the film—ascribing genius to such a hideous character. Best Actor is exactly right. Crime has nothing to do with brains, but, rather, with bad decisions, and bad decisions everywhere—everywhere messing up. Like crawling under a car hoisted on a shaky jack, or not having a clue when to shut up and be mollified, inevitably escalating a situation way past where it

161 ✳

could and should have stopped. Or compounding an illness by refusing to seek medical attention. Barefoot and cutting firewood with a chain saw. As with Alden Grelling, the scars are visible wherever you see these people, their bit-part lives so *unremarkable* that when they die or almost die, nobody cares, nobody really gives a rat's ass.

Case in point: domestic violence— *The State of Connecticut* v. *Claude Albrecht*, who purchased a used twelve-gauge for the sole purpose of shooting and killing his wife, the late and unfaithful Colleen Davis Albrecht, mother of one from a former marriage, the child having been placed in the father's custody by court order back in 1968, when Perry had just turned fourteen and most likely was sound asleep in northern Michigan when Claude Albrecht murdered Colleen and then turned the barrel on himself and fired twice. Surviving, he stood trial and was sentenced to life, serving eighteen years, standard incarceration for second-degree murder. After Claude Albrecht's release from prison, Steve Hazelton, in a time of escalating brutal crimes, echoed the common sentiment when he said to Perry, "Whoever found that prick back then should have stood around just long enough to watch the motherfucker bleed to death on his couch, and saved the taxpayers all that money."

Claude Albrecht is one of only two murderers ever paroled into Perry's charge. He left the office, same as the B and Es and petty larcenists and small-time pushers, with his head down as he passed through the drab anteroom. Most of them, but not all, are punks with the brains of a sand flea—losers who in no way resemble the image Alden's concocted to portray them.

And only one no-show tonight—Roland Knudson. Unlikely an innocent miss, but maybe, maybe it is. Exhaustion from working all that overtime. Perry's feeling besieged himself, struggling like hell to catch up after being away, and then to keep pace. He stands and escorts Alden to the outer door, and Alden offers a chummy "Later," and

Perry's cautious nod says, Count on it, because these are the rules—
no bottles for bait. Then he hesitates a few seconds to watch the night
custodian deftly guide the heavy electric chrome floor buffer from
side to side at the far end of the hallway, the shiny black-and-white
checkerboard tiles seeming to waver ever so slightly back and forth
under a clear liquid light.

Perry answers his phone on the fourth ring. Marcia has not moved
back yet, but Perry says "Hi" out of habit. For years, Marcia has called
him every report night to see how late he's going to be. But it's not
Marcia anxious to hear that he's ready to bag it and head home. It's
Angela, who wants him not to. He hasn't seen or heard from her since
the Jet Ski debacle.

Fathers abducting their own children are not uncommon, and rarely
do they harm, and they almost always return them within hours, all
charges dropped. "Yes," she confirms, "he's got Corey with him, but
that's not the problem—that part's fine. It's Roland sinking into one
of his moods again that frightens me."

"But you're all right?" Perry asks.

"He hasn't hurt me, if that's what you mean. You know where
I'm sitting right now? On the stoop with the portable phone, because
he ripped out the one on the wall, then stormed outside into the front
yard and started swinging the receiver by the cord above his head,
around and around, and shouting like a madman for somebody to
answer him. For God, I guess. Has Roland ever told you how his
mom used to talk about calling God?"

"No, he hasn't," Perry says. "Not yet."

"He will. . . . He's been on that crazy kick again, but what I want
to know is, what on earth does God need to hear from down here
anymore?"

Everything, Perry thinks, every single living sound. If he were the
one dialing God, it would be from the edge of the ocean, the receiver

whipping and whipping through the cool salt air and picking up that lonely, accumulating wail of the foghorn. And the high torrent of waves breaking against jetties up and down the coast, the backwash pulling away from the rocks, away from the fluttering, rubbery ribbons of kelp, the mussels like slate blue clusters of ears listening underwater. The sound of wind across the barnacled underbellies of boats abandoned at the backs of shipyards, the stammering syllables of stars. There must even be a sound for the slow corrosion of pennies tossed from bridges at night. He should hear that, too, and the final oval-mouthed notes of a stingray washed up onto its back in the sea wrack. Marcia would call these "Mystic sounds." Roland, inland only ten miles, is demanding that God listen to other things.

"I was watching from the picture window when he let go of the cord," Angela says. "It flew so high and far, I didn't see it land. That's when Roland came back inside and took Corey. He pointed his finger at me like, Not one word. For a while, I could see the two of them out there, but I can't anymore, except when Roland lights a cigarette— then I know they're still inside the Firebird. I should've had it carted away to the junkyard while Roland was in jail."

Perry's suddenly conscious of his rising body heat, sweat beads breaking out along his hairline. He switches off the desk lamp and loosens his tie and unbuttons the top button of his shirt, then leans slowly back in his chair and asks Angela if she's walked out there to try talking to Roland.

"As far as the edge of the field I have," she says. "Twice already, but he won't answer me, and it made Corey cry both times he heard my voice, so I came back here to wait some more."

Trying to compose himself, Perry eases his way a little further into the conversation by continuing to ask the obvious factual questions. "Has Roland been drinking?"

"He's not inebriated, if that's what you're getting at—two beers, which I realize shouldn't even be in the house, but he's a construction worker now and comes home hot and tired out, and I can't say, 'No, you can't handle it, Roland, because you're a recuperating alcoholic.' I can't monitor him like you do. That part's your job, isn't it? I guess mine's to blow the whistle on him, which must be what I'm doing by calling you, blowing the whistle on my own husband. You told me once I should, and that you'd intervene to head off any trouble."

Or create another kind of trouble, Perry tells himself, though it would be a shame to deny what that spirit of recklessness can do for one's heart. Take this woman on the other end of the line for example, who excites in Perry the urge to dispute not the boundaries of love but the measured, debilitating boundaries of marriage. And take the way that he and Angela, having stopped just shy of trespass, still feel surging between them sparks enough to reignite that fire.

All reasons why Perry agrees to drive over so late instead of calling the cops to respond to a domestic dispute, though that's exactly how it should be handled—by the book.

But it isn't, and by the time he arrives, it's after eleven o'clock. He's been standing, first on the stairs, and then, for the past ten minutes, alone in the driveway. Angela has still not shown herself. He's about to go knock on the door again, but instead, seeing the flame of Roland's cigarette lighter illuminate the Firebird's interior, Perry walks across the dirt road and into the field.

It's mostly dark—old furrows underfoot—and the slow approach makes the distance seem much farther than it really is, the thin outline of the moon visible every now and then behind the clouds. He does not announce his approach, unless the grasshoppers springing wildly out of the way are loud enough, or the napweed and thistle scratching against his trouser cuffs. Perry understands that a man should never walk all the way up on another man who's been sitting for hours in a junk car with his infant son. So he circles wide, coming head on at

165 ✳

the Firebird, where he stops and lights a cigarette himself. He notices the hood has been closed.

"How 'bout a lift?" Perry says.

"Depends some on where you're headed, Mr. Lafond, don't you think?"

Perry shrugs, a wasted gesture in the dark, and before he can speak again, Roland flicks his cigarette butt through the busted-out windshield, the orange sparks carried to the left of Perry by the breeze. "Shhh," Roland says to Corey. "Shhh, little guy, your old man's right here to protect you."

What from? Those same screwups who demolished the Firebird, returning a little older and meaner with chains or blackjacks or sockfuls of quarters? It was the glass they came to shatter, not bones. No, *protection* is simply a word a father uses to shield his child from whatever oblique danger lurks out there. Tonight it's this strange man who angles around to the passenger side, then lowers his face even with the window and says, "No place special—wherever you're headed's fine."

"Hop in," Roland says, and Perry yanks on the door handle, surprised by how easily the door swings open, how little effort it takes to pull it closed. He wonders if Corey remembers him, if children this young even have a memory. This might be a real pleasant one—two men and a baby. Film this version—the baby relaxed and happy with a bottle, sitting in the front seat between his dad and his mom's almost boyfriend. A scene with bundles of possibility.

Roland lights his lighter again, this time to point out to Perry the relatively low mileage on the odometer, the pinstriped detailing above the dashboard, tight four-speed gearbox. Four hundred and twenty-seven cubic inches under the hood, three two-barrel carburetors. "Zero to sixty," Roland says, "in less time than it takes most people to wave good-bye." But it's not so much a car he's describing as a souped-up dream, a once-upon-a-time fantasy of speeding away toward a different and happier and better life. The tires have sunk to the hubcaps in the sand, the spare stolen out of the trunk, the trunk left open to the rain and the snow and the winds.

Nonetheless, the conversation begins to move, stalls, starts again. Backfires once when Perry interrupts Roland, saying, "That's not the answer." Roland warns him to stop butting in. "Let me finish what I'm saying for once, okay?"

Neither raises his voice across that arm's length of darkness occupied by baby Corey, his lips making a soft sucking sound on the nipple. His toes curl inside his booties, at least on the foot Perry's holding and lightly massaging with his thumb while listening to Roland, who says, "And my mom sat me down at the kitchen table—I thought, Here we go, my first lecture on the birds and the bees, but that wasn't it at all. She said, 'Roland, maybe it's sacrilegious for me to say this, but I think God's slipping—pretty badly where we're concerned.' She had a puffed-up left eye and bruises on her arms, and her lipstick wasn't on straight, like her hand had been shaking, and she said, 'Judas Priest.' And then she goes on to tell me, 'Roland, a mother shouldn't say this to her child, but I've come to believe some people have a free long-distance number to call God, and the others, like us, have to pay prime-time rates, and then some bored angel operator puts us on hold. No background harp music while you wait, like you half expect and maybe even deserve. You listen instead to this cavernous silence, which I guess is where castoffs like us are eventually headed, into a compassion-less, empty heaven.'

"Castoffs is right. No shit, everything we ever owned was second-hand. The car was and the lawn mower and all the furniture, the clothes on our backs, which she said didn't exactly go very far toward improving our station in life, now did they? Secondhand toaster and Sylvania TV with no remote control and a secondhand Electrolux to vacuum the secondhand carpets and rugs. 'Even a secondhand wedding

ring,' she said, calmly twisting it off, 'with somebody else's initials—
somebody L.W.' and the word *Love*—engraved on the inside. 'Look,'
she said again, so I did, I took it and looked and then she said, 'I don't
have the foggiest whose it was or where your father got it—somewhere,
maybe at the pawnshop downtown, and here we are, still makeshift
and living kitty-corner to despair itself. All our possessions,' she said,
'all of them added up wouldn't be collateral enough to guarantee even
one dignified day down here. Roland, look at me,' she said, and asked
that I forgive both her griping and her French, but damn it all, wasn't
life a bitch?

"I told her no, life was a bastard, not a bitch, which is what my
old man used to call her. Constantly—bitch this, bitch that, and always
raising his hand to her or to me. Abuse in our household was strictly
male, Mr. Lafond, strictly bastard. I wonder sometimes how many of
those bastard genes I inherited from him, and I pray to God that it's
not too many and that I haven't passed them along to my son. You
know that saying about the nut not falling too far from the tree? Well,
I'm trying to prove it wrong—I'm trying not to be another bastard
monstrosity like my old man, but I can see him in my eyes in the
mirror when I lean close some mornings. He's right there, hating
everybody so much that it makes me dizzy—it throws the whole
frigging world out of kilter, and it's all I can do to keep *me*, Roland
Kyle Knudson, Jr., from flying into a rage. Does that make even a
screwy sorta sense to you, Mr. Lafond? Can you understand any of
what I'm talking about? You ever once spend serious time reflecting
at this level of bitterness?"

He's raised his voice just enough to be heard above the descending
guttural drone of an airplane approaching the runway from behind
them. A Piper Cherokee, Perry guesses, or a Taylorcraft or Cessna, its
landing lights passing in less than a second across the length of the
Firebird and illuminating a swath of field the width of an interstate.

The sensation is that the aircraft stays stationary, and it's the two men and the baby speeding backward in the Firebird farther and farther into the dark. A real Rod Serling rush. Perry resists this eerie impulse to turn around, though he's almost certain of some apparitional presence in the backseat—the ghost of his own dad perhaps, who has endured his fair share of grief but harbors no bitterness. Or Hank, who does, but bears it so poorly that his life has become a series of forfeitures— a charge Marcia has lodged against Perry, who is both bitter and not bitter, a middle man of sorts, more befuddled by the commonplace than by anything otherworldly. He told Marcia once that if a spaceship were to land and open its doors to him, he'd board it and be transported far, far away from this dangerous and random and hopelessly unfair existence that nobody he knows has come close to figuring out.

Maybe the kids who are loved have, at least while they're very young, like baby Corey, who keeps squeezing Perry's finger, squeezing and staring up as if urging him, as Roland has urged God, to listen to what's *here*, right now: to the songs of the crickets, that scratchy timbre of their legs. Like strings, Perry thinks, a weedy orchestra of insects.

Of late, Perry's modus operandi with Roland has been temerity, a combativeness meant to subdue and to weaken and to force him to measure up. And now the doubling notes of the crickets like a hymn to this still moment when nobody is talking, though something incredible is being said.

It's Roland who disturbs the silence. He says, "So why bother to reshuffle the deck when your luck is always the same bad luck? You learn to play what you're dealt—is that a fair assumption, Mr. Lafond?— bluffing where you can for an edge. But I'm not bluffing now. The stakes are too high. I realize that, and maybe I can beat the odds. I've got a wife I love and a boy I love and a second child on the way, who I'll love, too—and a good job for a change that I can't afford to lose. And you're here to call me, the man always holding all the aces. The smart move is for me to fold, I guess, to say, 'You win,' and all because I missed an appointment."

"It's not a major miss," Perry says, "but you should have called. I'd understand," Perry insists.

"I'm sorry about that, I really am. But I had this other, more pressing appointment with my son. All day today, hauling cinder blocks, I'd catch myself thinking about him, wanting for the two of us to spend some quality time together, which maybe don't seem so quality to you out here in a junk car at midnight, but it is. Listen, I'm busting my ass and betting I can break the Knudson curse and make life right for my kids like I never had it, and like Angela never had it, either."

The sudden reappearance of the moon has brightened the field, as well as the Firebird's white interior, and Roland reaches across his body with his left hand to take the bottle from Corey, who has fallen asleep sitting up, his head tilted slightly back against the seat and away from Perry. There's a little drool that Roland wipes away with one knuckle from Corey's chin.

Perry remembers Angela referring to Roland as a good father, and when Roland says, "Start 'em loving you early," Perry nods. "Invest right from the get go and maybe there won't be so much hell for them to pay down the road."

Down the road, Perry repeats to himself, and baby Corey breathing so peacefully between these two men who have been there—different roads and different times, and with other people who mattered and then didn't, or mattered and simply disappeared without apology or explanation. So many words for that: *vanished*, or *parted company*, or *flew the coop*. Up and gone. Exited unexpectedly. Made tracks for some other place, hitchhiking, perhaps, on the outskirts of a town called Hopelessness or Cornered or Plenty Scared. Or how about Uncalled For? Or Free Advice, which, of course, is never free, whether you accept or reject it—there's a price simply for listening, isn't there?

Hightailed it, lit out, sometimes only as far as the next room, or the couch, or that motel sufficiently distanced between the argument and the making up and the leaving it all again. The miles accumulate until finally it's impossible to retrace all those steps that led you here—led Roland and Perry and even baby Corey to this spot on this night of a certain summer in Connecticut just far enough away from a runway not to see its lights.

"I'd bet," Roland says, "if I installed a new battery, the wipers would still work."

Perry imagines the blades slapping wildly back and forth without the resistance of the windshield, and he wonders why Roland would think of this now. There's no rain in the forecast. The clouds, in fact, have passed, the cursive scribble of the stars illegible to Perry except for the Big Dipper, its straight-handled, four-cornered ladle like a child's drawing, the only constellation Perry can ever find.

Roland's hand is on the shift, the clutch engaged, and Perry, along for the ride, slides lower on the seat, knees pressed to the dash, and he closes his eyes and believes he's closer to arriving where he wants to arrive than he's been in a long time. Not a place so much as a feeling—destination repose, he thinks, a peaceful sleepiness drifting over him, though he's not sure why.

"There's no trick to it," Roland says. "More like what I call 'heart magic,' and all that means is that you remember to love 'em, no matter what else you do. Don't much matter how you fail elsewhere, or how it is you disgrace yourself outside their presence. Oh, they'll sure as hell hear about you somewhere—on the playground, on the streets— your old man this, your old man that, but they'll forgive it all in the end if you loved 'em enough. Like here. Take *this* night—it'll survive in Corey's memory bank forever."

Such trust, Perry thinks, and such sadness, each surrounding the other, the crickets, for whatever reason, having stopped their serenade.

"It's weird," Roland says, "but I know it's true. You take a baby out here like this and part of him says, Man, I ain't ever leaving, though he can't even talk yet or form such thoughts. But something deep inside's already telling him he's located a tiny parcel of happiness and that it's his pop led him right to the spot. I ain't just spinning my tires, Mr. Lafond, when I say Corey's going to remember these trips we took together in a junked-out Firebird—him and me."

Then Roland goes suddenly silent again, and this time the silence fills the space around them like absence itself, like pure emptiness, and Perry opens his eyes to be sure he's not in some other place all alone. Marcia has warned him repeatedly that it's the direction in which he's been heading, further and further from everyone and everything he's ever loved and lost or is still afraid of losing. She's been gone for almost a week, so when Perry hears Angela's voice call out to her husband and son, Perry pretends it's Marcia he hears calling him. And he pretends Corey is *their* child, and he says, "Please, let me carry him," and Roland gets out of the car and comes around to open the passenger-side door.

"Thank you," Perry says, and even the door slamming shut does not wake the baby, safe in this man's arms.

Chapter 13

As usual after a nightmare, Perry has been up for hours, the bedroom door closed tightly so Marcia can sleep in. It's Sunday morning, the beginning of day two since Marcia's return. And like some bad omen, Perry's been waiting again for that huge flatbed and for those death containers full of tart cherries and water, and for the afterimages of all those faces to fade, as they always do, in full light. It's why Perry has pulled open the blinds so wide, and finally the first rays of the sun are expanding across the kitchen table, where he's been rubbing ointment onto the scar on his hand.

Ever since the stitches dissolved, the scar has turned an uglier and uglier hue of purple. The doctor has assured Perry it will become less noticeable after awhile, but he says it will never completely disappear. Big hurts never do, Perry thought. But as Marcia said, sometimes you have to accept the partial healing, and that's precisely Perry's new resolution, though it pains him deeply each time he admits to himself that he is indeed the guiltier party, the one who has damaged their marriage most. Yes, the one who sent Marcia packing, "which is another kind of recurring nightmare," Marcia said on the phone, "and one that ends here and now. No more, Perry. I'll come home and we'll talk, but I'm not so sure anymore that we're at all compatible. How could we be when we're after such different things?"

It was not really a question to be answered, but, rather, an answer itself, assertive and accurate and, Perry realized, equally painful to them both. He imagined her lips moving above the mouthpiece as she formed each word, and he wondered if her eyes were open or closed, if she was barefoot, if she felt weak in the knees like he did, if *her* hands were clammy and shaking, too.

"I hope this doesn't sound too simpleminded, Perry, but I used to believe that a life together for you and me was a matter of connecting the dots—from A to B to C. Fall in love, get married, have gorgeous, smart children to tuck into bed each night. Nice dark, straight lines to follow all the way to stability and happiness, to that feeling of permanence you said vanished in a flash after Janine's death, and that you wanted more than any single thing to recapture. You said you needed a center again, a grounding—me and a family. I never in a million years could have imagined that we'd get so sidetracked, and then so lost. It seems like we've been through the alphabet dozens of times, forward and backward, and when I try to retrace my steps, there's no way out of the snarl. Things are a real mess, Perry."

"Then let's start over," Perry offered, "right from scratch. It's still not too late—it can't be."

"It's seven-fifty-one P.M.," Marcia said, "on Friday, July seventeenth, 1992. There's not quite as much light in the sky as there was just a week ago, and the second wave of summer renters has already settled in on the Point. They'll be gone soon, too, and I'll head back to school and the bell for recess will ring at exactly ten-twenty-eight in the morning, always the same time but different days. I never told you this, but if the sun's at a certain angle, and if I stand in this one low place on the playground, I can watch the children's faces flash by me in a blur on the merry-go-round. The light makes it appear like they're glowing under halos, like angels. But I stopped watching because I started getting so dizzy. You know why? Not because they spun by so fast, but because every fall it's new kids, new angels, and it scares me how quickly they're here and gone."

The same way it scares Perry to think about all the awful things that can happen to them on any given day. But he did not say that, nor did he confess that he, as well, gets dizzy, and not only when he thinks about Janine, but also about kids like Marvin Ants and Cynthia Gunderson and, more recently, a six-year-old named Gloria Nofsinger, whose custodial uncle, while the girl's mother and father were both in jail, tattooed her legs—every inch of them: an intricate patterning of swastikas and samurai swords and black widow spiders, and, high up on the inside of each thigh, a serpent's forked tongue corkscrewing toward her vagina. The uncle owned Babe's Tattoo Parlor, a hangout for bikers and city cowboys, and when the child-protection people investigated, asking Babe why he defaced her like that, he said, "Advertising." And then he paused, cocked his head, squinted, and said, "*De*face—hell, I ain't got to that part yet. And I'll tell you what else— I say, 'Piss off' to those got no eye for art and no head for business."

Nor did Perry mention the flames on the Firebird, how, like the Phoenix, he'd felt reborn. In fact, he didn't mention the Firebird at all, nor the moon and the clouds and the brilliance of the stars. Nor the crickets, unremitting with song, followed by that eerie silence. He did not say any of the things he knew he ought not to say, nor any of the things he thought he might. Not one word about Roland and baby Corey, and certainly no attempt to clarify what Angela's calling out from the field's edge around midnight meant to him. What her sadness meant and means, and Roland's sadness, and how when Angela

175 ✳

stepped forward wearing a white scoop-necked nightgown and reached out to take the baby, Perry did not want to let him go.

He did not resort over the telephone to any abstract primping, no cheap-shot claims about having been transformed back into that man of passion and promise Marcia stood beside almost a decade and a half ago at the altar.

Mostly what Perry did was listen, but not to specific conditions and detailed ultimatums, because Marcia did not use the conversation to gain any leverage. She was beyond that, consumed, she said, by anxieties and doubts, "huge, converging doubts," she said, "that have all but suffocated me. This past week, for the first time in my life, I've imagined an end to our marriage. I don't want that—I never have—so I'm going to start again in a few days on the Pergonal, and maybe we can take a short trip to the Vineyard, and if this still sounds all wrong to you, just say so and I'll stay away. I don't mean to pressure you, Perry, really I don't. But if I come home, I have to come home as me."

"That's all I ask," Perry said.

"Is it? It hasn't felt like that."

"But it's true."

"All that's left then is to convince me."

"I will, if you'll give me a little time."

"It'll take time, Perry, a lot of time, but before too much more goes by, you're going to have to decide on some things."

"I already have."

"Good," Marcia said, "then you won't mind if I hold you to them."

Perry hopes she won't need to, but he equates his nightmares to a long-standing addiction he can't kick, can't resist alone in the darkness, though he's determined to embrace the spirit of Janine and let it live. She'd be thirty-three now, no longer afraid of the bogeyman. A grown woman, kids of her own, perhaps, and the fierce love Perry feels just imagining them exists in direct proportion to the grief of Janine's absence. So why this nightmare again? Why not some good dreams, some balance?

"Too much existential drift," *thus spoke* Marcia last night, her explanation for confiscating *The Portable Nietzsche*, imposing *her* will on deadbeat Fred's retirement to the bookshelf. "Let's give him a little time to think about what he said, and why it's wrong."

A second-grade scolding for Fred Nietzsche, who has bullied poor Perry Lafond into the worst funk of his life. But he'll bounce back once he stops looking over his shoulder all the time, once he learns to trust what's good in the world again. Marcia playing the wise, stern teacher made Perry laugh and feel young and innocent again.

And he feels momentarily even more like a kid when the phone rings and he hears his dad's distant voice.

"Perry," he says, "is that you?"

"Yes," he tells him, "it is, it's me."

It's only the second time he has ever called here, and Perry, not wanting to cut him short, tolerates the strain behind each faltering syllable. Then he closes his eyes and listens to his dad say, "Perry, I'm not calling from the hospital. I'm calling from the pay phone by the front booth at Twink's Petting Farm. You remember Twink's. It doesn't open until eight, but there's a llama staring out at me from behind the fence. And some Angora rabbits hopping around that Hank would like a lot, and one sheep that keeps on with an awful bleating. Otherwise, the animals seem happy." He pauses; then he continues with the news Perry knows is coming. "Your mother—she thought she had a cold and smeared on some Vicks VapoRub, and during the night she had another stroke. Which is what I meant to say, and that it's time now for you and your brother to come home—you come home, Perry. It's the right thing."

"Is she okay?" Perry asks, meaning, Is she alive for God's sake? What's her condition?

"She's not out of the woods yet," he says, "but she was sleeping pretty soundly when I left her. There's more deadness on her left side, so I didn't hold that hand. I held the other, and I could feel her try to squeeze. The doctor said that's a good sign, but I don't know your mother well enough anymore to be sure what she meant after all these years. What do you think she meant, Perry?"

He hears the robot operator interrupt to ask for another ninety cents, and then he hears the coins drop, and his dad is back on the line, saying he's out of change and has to sign off. "What a mess," he says.

"What's the number there?" Perry asks, but his dad tells him, "Hurry home, son." He says, "Don't call me here—it's just a place I remember you boys liked, and so I stopped. That's all."

"Hey," Perry says, and then he's shouting into the receiver, "this is a fucking emergency. Hey, you programmed bitch recording, you answer me—somebody answer me," but of course nobody does. Not until he hangs up and dials the travel agent, who says, "Can you hold, please?" and Perry answers, "No. No," he says again, "I can't," and he tells her about his mom and how the house was kept so quiet for her benefit after Janine died. He mentions the bleating sheep, and how it's simply not possible—"Believe me," he says, "I know"—to block out certain sounds so that they fade finally into nothingness. "They never disappear completely," he says.

"So this is a funeral you're flying to?" the woman says, and in a way it is, and Perry says, "Yes," and she explains—and he can tell she's very young—that he can fly half fare if he can verify the loss.

Which one, he thinks, and by whose consent? And if loss is the criteria by which we fly home cut-rate, isn't every arrival the occasion for mourning the past, every departure the guilt we carry with us for hurrying away?

"A copy of the death certificate will suffice," she says.

"Indeed," Perry agrees, indeed it should. He's confirmed on Northwest from Hartford to Detroit; then he'll have to go standby from there to Traverse City. The computer says he's number one on the standby list. It's the best she can do on such short notice, though sometimes that's how people die or have strokes, isn't it? He reads her his Visa card number, plus the expiration date. The flight, she explains, is open-ended. "Thank you," Perry says, and she tells him she's sorry and that she hopes she can help again under different circumstances—maybe for a getaway vacation.

"Getaway," Perry repeats, and he wonders with what restrictions, and at what price, and where to. Fucking Pluto might be far enough, but he does not ask if they have any planes going there, because this travel agent has meant no harm. His ticket will be ready in half an hour. His suitcase is stored in the basement, but first he has a few calls to make, easiest to hardest: Cal Hyde for more leave time, then his dad at home, and then Hank, who said too many times growing up that he hated their mother and that Janine's death was everybody's fault. Everybody's. And nobody's, Perry would rather believe. Or God's. And what an incredible waste that it ever had to be said, much less so damn often, and that the family did not then know how to go to Hank, nor he to any of them.

He lives in Bad Axe, down in Michigan's thumb, less than a five-hour drive back to the folks, a trip Perry's certain Hank will make alone. They'll both arrive solo. Their wives share this much in common: Lafond reunions depress them. Marcia talks about it not as a loveless family but as one without positive ties or reinforcement. And that's the bigger tragedy, she says, to have allowed such madness for so long.

And so then what's left? Small sections of orchards and pasturelands his dad no longer owns, having sold them off too soon and too cheaply. The house, the last time Perry saw it, had been painted with pink trim, and, from a distance and the daylight dimming, he saw his mom in her wheelchair on the front porch, and Perry believed it was the most beautiful color he'd ever seen. He waved, walking toward the house, and his dad, slump-shouldered, stepped out from behind the screen door, his glasses on, the evening newspaper still spread apart in his hands. One whole side of the stairs had been replaced by a plywood ramp and a railing. The visit was brief, less than two days, and briefer for Hank, who stayed only a few hours the following afternoon and who, on the phone some weeks later, told Perry he remembered it only as a blur. He said, "Is it true we were even there?"

"Yes," Perry whispers aloud, glancing at his watch. And yes, that it was much too little and way too late and that it was obvious to everyone that it would take a second stroke or a heart attack to bring the two boys back home again. Back to the mundane, as Hank said, which didn't *have* to be, but is now, the only existence left for their parents to live out. He said, "They should have sold the house, too. Aired out the ghost echoes and unloaded it along with the goddamn land." Perry almost said, "Why, so they could have moved closer to you?" But he's been almost as negligent as Hank, though certainly less inclined to determine what *should* have been, and hating his brother for referring to their mom as freakish, to their dad as an early riser out of need to run and hide, a weak and feckless man, an invalid himself. And Hank continues to refer to Janine's death as "that day." It's a phrase their dad used to use, but in a different context, to ask if his sons couldn't remember other things—that day of the God Bless America parking-lot sale, where he purchased the satellite dish and faced it south behind the house, right between the two outbuildings, and how the reception was so incredibly clear, and how they went from getting only two channels to over a hundred. Or that day the blue jay dive-bombed the cat in the barn, or that day, or that one, and isn't it a shame that they don't count?

Perry, standing by the open window, does not hear Marcia enter the living room, but he is not startled by the touch of her hand on his shoulder. If anything, he is weakened by it. Marcia can sense this, and she does not try to coax him into turning around, and he does not turn on his own. He cannot muster even that much exertion. There's a startling clarity as well as an awful vagueness about this moment, and in it Perry feels that he both exists and does not, his body so porous, it seems as if the cold breeze keeps passing right through him.

Of course the phone call is not unexpected; subconsciously, he has been waiting for it every day for years, every single day. Still, the timing could not be worse, and there's nothing that anybody alive might say to him right now that could possibly matter or change how he feels.

Marcia tries, but her words resemble static, her voice overloading the frazzled circuitry to Perry's ears and throat and brain. He can't hear or think or formulate a single response beyond the two small words that form on his lips. "My mom," he says, and Marcia embraces him from behind, feeling the chill, Perry suspects, because she, too, has started to shiver.

Perry's dad keeps talking about strokes as though they were earthquakes. He says, "We're just waiting now for the aftershock, except there's no telling for sure if there's going to be one or not—usually there is, but not always. There wasn't the last time. Her doctor, he's originally from Massachusetts, out east."

Yep, Perry thinks, that's where Massachusetts is all right, same as always. "Can she speak?" he asks.

"Oh, it's all garbled, Perry—a word here and there. *Yarn*, I think that was one, but she never knitted, did she?" Perry tries to remember seeing balls of yarn and darning needles on the couch, but he can't, so he doesn't answer. "She'll understand whatever *you* say, so ask her some questions. She'll shake her head yes or no, and she won't take her eyes off you, like she's half reading your lips and half hearing you."

"There's my bag," Perry says, glad to be stepping away from his dad for a few seconds. Where the conveyor belt comes out of its S-turn, Perry lifts off his suitcase. He'll carry it, he says. And no, he's not suffering jet lag—he hasn't even left the frigging time zone. Connecticut isn't exactly Borneo. His flights were okay, as is his hand, his job, Marcia, him—yes, he's okay, he's fine, he tells his dad on their way out to the car.

"Hank's en route already," his dad says, "and should arrive by early evening."

Perry gestures toward all the airport traffic, and his dad says, "Cherry Festival. You missed the Cherry Royale parade by one day. Wait'll you see the town, how it's grown and changed. I hardly ever drive in anymore, and never during the summer. Except for now, of course. Except to see your mother." He's brought the festival schedule with him, cut out from the newspaper. "Here," he says, after starting the car and rolling down his window, "see what interests you."

Perry almost tells him that nothing does lately, certainly not the Very Cherry Luncheon. Thanks, but he's not hungry, at least not for the cabbage and cherry slaw or the cherry pretzel tortes or the red onion cherry chutney—he'll admit to a weakness for sweets, but this sounds disgusting. Maybe they could stop for a burger at Don's on their way home from the hospital. And fries and a shake.

They pass the Goodwill store on South Airport. The sign advertises a Cherry Sale: EVERY RED ITEM, 99 CENTS.

"Hard to believe," his dad says, but he's not talking about red bargain prices. He's talking about the hoodlums who stole the Elias Brothers Big Boy balloon from the open space by the waterfront, across the street from the amusement rides. "A twenty-five footer," he says. "It was a marker for the lost children."

He means those separated from their parents, but the word *the* makes it sound as though he's talking about *all* the lost children, and about their miraculous reappearance under some inflatable monster balloon, and all this after so long an absence—little kids arriving by ones and twos, then in small groups, then packs of them out of nowhere. He imagines Janine waiting there, still a five-year-old, and their mom struggling in a wheelchair toward her through the crowd, Janine stand-offish at first, then withdrawing a few feet and finally running away in tears from the awful moans and grunts of this crazed woman she couldn't possibly recognize anymore.

But Perry will. His dad says, "Prepare yourself is all—it's a shock when you first see her."

It always has been, always, always, always, he thinks. And this, when he shuts his eyes—she's standing again in the early-morning light of the pantry, holding on to a box of Rice Krispies, Janine's favorite, with both hands, and staring out at Perry seated alone at the kitchen table. Hank has not come downstairs yet, and his dad is outside, and Perry says, "Mom, the funeral was weeks ago," but she's dressed in black and wearing a veil, and thumbing the edges of the cereal box in some kind of weird home worship. He wants to coax her out of there. He wants, more than anything in the whole world, for her to sit down to breakfast, just the two of them, and exchange smiles, something as simple as that, and as permanent.

"But nothing is," his dad says. "Nothing's ever for certain." He's predicting that she'll come out of ICU and then go home after two weeks, after beginning her physical therapy, and that, God willing, she'll make a partial recovery. "They don't allow patients to lie around too long anymore," he says. "It's the very worst thing for them." Then he cups his right hand to the base of Perry's skull to show where the stroke was. "Right there," he says, as though pinpointing the location of an ache or a kink. It's exactly where Perry likes to be massaged by Marcia—his "log jam of tension," as she calls it. She says it will kill him someday unless he learns how to relax.

There's an ambulance at the four-way stop—no siren, no panic in the lights—and the driver motions Perry's dad to go ahead and make the left. Perry acknowledges with a nod, then clears his throat and his dad starts into the turn, followed by a right into Munson's main parking lot.

There's no shortage of empty spaces, and Perry keeps staring up at hundreds of windows, the dazzle of sunlight turning them into mirrors reflecting the clouds and the sky. This is the same hospital where he was born, where Hank and Janine were born, too, both boys delivered on schedule, but Janine almost ten weeks premature. Early in the morning—Perry remembers that it was still dark outside and raining—the doctor came into the waiting room and said, "Mr. Lafond?" Perry's dad stood up slowly to listen to the doctor announce that it was a girl, three and a half pounds, which, under the circumstances, was a good birth weight, the chances of survival fifty-fifty. He said thank God it was a girl, because tiny girls fought harder, and that a boy this size—well, he said, he might never make it. "And my wife?" Perry's dad asked, and the doctor said, "Almost ready to get back into a swimsuit," a comment Perry, squinting up from his chair, didn't much like. The doctor predicted that if there were no serious complications, the baby could leave in about a month. It was the first time Perry ever counted off the days toward anything, a fat black X through each calendar square. In mid-July, a few hours before Janine arrived bundled in blankets, both boys went from room to room, closing and locking all the windows and turning off both ceiling fans, the thermostat set at eighty-five. Hank had been raising chicks that summer, Buff Bantams, which he intended to show at the state fair, and he said the house was as warm as his incubator. Their dad, turning the doorknob and pushing open the door, said, "That's good. That's exactly the temperature your baby sister needs for a while."

But he couldn't stand the heat, and he and Hank and Perry slept out on the porch every night for weeks, mother and daughter alone somewhere inside. Janine didn't cry or sweat hardly ever, but their mom sure did, her blouses always soaked, her damp hair pulled back into a heavy ponytail, making her face seem gaunt and angular and not very pretty anymore. Her only relief, a cold bath, a habit she kept for years and years to neutralize the hot and muggy and what she called "unlivable" days.

Like this one, Perry thinks, exactly like this one, and he's grateful for the coolness that washes by him as he steps into the hospital lobby, the automatic glass doors squeezing shut behind him.

They are told at the front desk that Perry's mom has already been moved to a semiprivate room on the third floor, last one on the left, room 392. "She won't mind that," Perry's dad says, and Perry thinks, Mind what? The location? The company? The first thing Perry notices is that there is none—the second bed, the one closest to them, is empty. Perry's right behind his dad, who's knocking lightly on the open door, knocking and leaning in and saying her name. "Arlene, look who I've brought to see you. Look who's here."

Perry steps by his dad into the room, as if from offstage. He's appropriately animated, because that's the object, isn't it, to act beyond the nervousness and the grief and the guilt? He's certain his first words will come out wavery and high-pitched and nonsensical, and he's surprised by how calm he sounds when he says, "Hi, Mom," and squeezes her foot lightly through the sheets, then continues around to the far side of the bed and leans over and kisses her on the forehead. His lips are dry and, for the instant his eyes stay closed, he believes he can disappear, that he can actually will himself away from this terrible paralysis.

But it's his dad who's vanished, the master at that—here and gone, like magic. And his mom is staring through the empty doorway. Perry knows that look. Passing her bedroom, he used to stop, and from the hall he'd say, "Mom? Mom, are you okay?" But she'd never answer or even blink, and after awhile he started hurrying by, scarcely glancing in. Hank said that it was a trance, and that a trance was a brain lapse. "When she's like that, she can't hear or see you, Perry. You're maybe like a ghost or a faraway echo is all. It's best," he said, "to let her go." Perry asked, "Where to?" Hank admitted that he didn't know for sure, except that it was where deranged people retreated inside their heads. Then he paused and said that it was impossible to lead a sane life around someone like her. "No kidding, Perry, it really is, and it's going to catch up with us, with you and me. It's unhealthy to live in a house like this, and as soon as I'm old enough, I'm leaving for good. That's what desire is," he said, "to want something deep down in your heart, and that's my desire, to get far, far away. It's your funeral if you think different." He said, "This here's a loony bin."

It's not *yarn* she's trying to say; it's *years*. And when Perry repeats it, she smiles and nods, though it appears more like a grin, since the muscles don't work on one entire side of her face. On the other half, her expression is apologetic and sad. It's alive, Perry thinks, with regret, and yes, it shows the years. Perry tells her she's got more than a few good ones left, and for all he knows, it's not entirely a lie.

There's an IV in her forearm, and she's thinner than Perry has ever seen her. He's been warned of this. "The doctors doubt that she can swallow yet," his dad said on the drive over. "They're afraid that she'll choke if she tries." His dad's also the one who used to have this joke about skin—he'd claim it's what kept the rain out, and he'd turn his face up to it, and sometimes he'd open his mouth. "Even cherries have it," he'd say. "Look how they glisten. Look how lush the orchard is, how we've been blessed again." But there's this dull gray tinge to his mom's skin; it feels papery and thin, like ash, like something already perishing.

"Where'd the flowers come from?" Perry asks, which sounds all wrong; it sounds as though they were scavenged from another room by the nurses, a discarded bouquet of wilting white irises. He recognizes the vase, and he answers his own question with another question: "Did Dad bring them? Your favorites," he says when she smiles. "You always loved irises." And day lilies and tulips and glads. Perry used to help his mom dig up and separate the bulbs and replant them around the yard. Perennials. Never anything that died and vanished for good after a single season. *Years* is right, and the renewal each spring of all that survives and multiplies and blossoms in a profusion of color his mom always referred to as the "curse of the blind." "What would it be like?" she'd say, staring out the window. "What in heaven's name would it be like to miss such splendor?"

Perry often has. He's promised Marcia they'll have a spectacular flower garden once they own their own house. One time, he randomly spread cosmos seeds alongside the garage, tiny seeds from a packet Marcia brought home after the school's Save the Earth drive. Perry explained to her that they'd never grow. But they did, waist-high, and then flowered. He's always loved that name—cosmos. But today, this is the world—his mom's vocabulary reduced to a single monosyllable. "Years" she says again, and Perry imagines a dictionary filled with only that one word, repeated over and over, and how there must be a trillion definitions.

"I understand," Perry says, and he begins to talk nonstop after his mom's eyelids begin to shut. As if he could ever catch her up, in a matter of seconds, on the past few years, on all the years. He lets go of her hand and fusses some with the fold of the sheet, smoothing it out, cupping her shoulder in his palm, kissing her again as she sleeps. And such an odd, distant visitor his dad has made, eavesdropping at the door. Perry's pretended not to notice him standing there. And Perry realizes again that whatever connection he's hoped for by coming here will always be lost to the larger, more permanent detachment that *is* this family's history.

187 ✳

Perry and his dad leave together, the hallway seeming narrower and narrower each time Perry glances back. He wants both to be leaving this place forever and to never leave—to sit in that hospital chair and wait for his mom to wake, to find him still beside her.

The hallway is saturated with greenish fluorescent light; it reminds Perry of the Mystic Seaport Aquarium, the dreaminess he always feels there. But the rooms here are not glass tanks of exotic fish, and Perry turns abruptly away from the woman who has struggled to take a single hunchbacked step outside her doorway, her hands gripping the chrome walker so tightly, they appear to be fingerless.

"Huh?" Perry says as they reach the elevator. "I'm sorry, what did you say?"

"I said that's Hurley Glen's wife—I'm sure it is," and as Perry presses the L button, his dad walks back to her to say hello. He points down the hall, then in the opposite direction toward Perry; these are the two imperatives of which he speaks, his wife and his son. That's because, in the end, you understand what should have mattered. Perry's dad is pointing that out right now, pointing it out, no doubt, as though it always has.

"In what way?" Hank asks. He and Perry have just crossed the driveway where the side yard dips gradually toward what's left of the orchard, a few acres of unpruned cherry trees, the soft fruit rotting on the ground. Fallen cherries, the kind that exploded against your chest or back or kneecaps whenever Hank and Perry fired them close range at each other, the juice red and sticky like blood. No arguments about who hit whom and where—they wore the stains on their T-shirts and skin. Back then it was fun playing harmless games of war to celebrate the end of each harvest.

What Perry would like to see now is a truce. It's nearly ten o'clock and still not completely dark, and Hank refuses to drop the subject of parents and kids. Perry does not need another run-through of his and Hank's tragic growing-up—it's wearying conversation, a duplicate of what followed their mom's first stroke. Perry's been hoping Hank might have softened some, but he hasn't—he's as bitter and unshakable as ever. He says, "Let me guess, you've been to a miracles seminar." He's taller and thinner than Perry, and the lines in his forehead have deepened into a permanent frown. "Absolutely nothing's changed," he says. "You've inventoried the house, same as I have—it's impossible not to—and it's like everything's frozen in time. Those same goddamn appliances—Jesus, Perry, that range and refrigerator must be over thirty years old, and the linoleum worn through in places right down to the underlayer. An old-fashioned farmhouse is one thing, but there's nothing quaint about this place. It's downright depressing is what it is."

"What's the point, Hank? What the fuck's the point of dredging all this up again? The revenge factor's too high, can't you see that? It's time to let it go—just let it go. Don't hate them like this. Haven't they paid enough? Haven't we all?"

"I've paid the most," he says, "and I'm reminded of that whenever I come back here." He pauses and then he says, "Do you remember how Dad used to joke to us, 'A couple three good harvests in a row and I'll be 'bout ready to make the mustard?' Remember him saying that? And promises about how the whole family'd drive off to Disneyland and Mammoth Cave and King's Island. We'd always be pestering him about the different places we wanted to see. And then the world stopped. Every night after that, I went to bed wishing it was me who'd died."

"Maybe we all felt like that," Perry says. "I know that Mom did, and she *is* dying now, and you can help by staying one night."

"No," Hank says, "I can't stand being inside that house. All those low-wattage lightbulbs—I take off my glasses and it's like I'm staring through crinkled plastic at old snapshots, or blurred slow-motion footage from that ancient Super-8 Dad bought so he'd capture our childhood. Janine's high chair's still in the pantry for Christ's sake. What, are they expecting grandkids?"

Perry knows about Hank's vasectomy, and Hank knows enough about Marcia's infertility to answer his own question. "No," he says, "there's no future here—they live in the debris of that awful past, which is why I'm leaving, and don't you try to talk me out of it, Perry. It's too late."

"Plus the animals," Perry says. "Don't forget to mention them—they always mattered more to you than people anyway." He's referring to the excuse Hank used earlier when their dad asked him how long he could stay. Wednesday's a surgery morning—he's sorry, but he has to hurry right back to the clinic—business has quadrupled since he and Connie opened their own small-animal practice. As Hank talked, Perry conjured up an image of him in a white coat, up at 5:00 A.M. and studying the medical chart of a poodle named Muffin or Shalimar, his veterinary degree from Michigan State framed and hanging on the wall behind the reception counter, the animals still asleep in their cages. Saint Hank of Bad Axe—perhaps he has the healing power to grow Basket more hair, to cure heartworm and cataracts and hip dysplasia. He's the one, at ten years old, who half filled a Pepsi can with pennies, then called the family together one evening and said, "Don't ever hit the puppy, not with your hand or with a folded-up newspaper or with anything else. Shake this can instead," he said. "Shake it at her like this whenever she makes a mistake, and she'll be housebroken in a couple weeks. She'll be afraid of the noise, not of us."

The noise, Perry reminds himself, was eerie and loud, but there's nothing frightening tonight about the peepers and crickets and the breeze in the long, bent-over grass. Nor the snap of the cards he and Hank heard as they walked past the kitchen window, their dad already playing a game of solitaire at the table. And what's left to learn from these late sounds? Perry wonders. He listens to the distant whine of a semi gearing down for the bend on Route 10. "Probably hauling Derald Thompson's cherries," Perry says, but it's a lame detour this late in the conversation, and Hank says back, "You want to know what part of the family shutdown *is* our fault? Should I tell you? Is it still too difficult for you to figure out?"

Perry can barely make out the movement of his brother's lips, the dim circuit of fireflies pulsing now behind him along the rim of the trees. The luminous dial of Hank's wristwatch glows green. It reminds Perry of a diver's watch. He means to be disarming when he says, "Not enough hither, and too much yon."

"You're wrong," Hank says, "dead wrong. None of it's our fault— zero, zilch. Can't you get that through your head?" Then he begins to sound like Perry when he says, "Little kids sign on to be little kids, and parents to be parents, who should never, under any circumstances, let happen what happened to us." But he doesn't stop there. He says, "We were abandoned, Perry, by both of them, and allowed to carry all this guilt into our adult lives. Enough, I say. Blame yourself for staying away if you need to, but I'm out of here. It was a huge mistake for me to listen to you. I tried to tell you that last time, and it's even truer now."

And whatever else Hank intends to say is not said because Perry cuts him off, asking, "How long did you spend visiting with Mom?"

"Why? What the hell difference does that make?"

"What room is she in, Hank? What floor is she on?" His voice has changed—it's slow-cadenced and challenging.

"Misery's room," Hank says, "on misery's floor, exactly where she's always been since that day, never once asking us to come in, refusing to let herself—to let me or you or Dad recover."

Perry can no longer judge the distance between him and Hank

191 ✳

now that it's completely dark—a few feet maybe. If Perry were to step forward, he's not sure if it would be to pummel or to hug his brother in this same hollow where they used to wrestle and then lie side by side, panting hard and saying nothing, their eyes wide open to the moon and the stars.

"Were there railings on her bed? Huh? Come on, answer me. Was there a pitcher and water glass on the nightstand?" Perry does not ease up even when Hank circles wide and walks away. "Did you hear Mom say *years* or *yarn*, which one, Hank? And is it her left or her right side this time that's paralyzed?"

Hank's van door opens and then slams shut and the engine starts, the high beams flooding the driveway. "Hey," Perry shouts, running after the van as it swings right onto the road. "Hey, tell me, how did she seem when you saw our mother, Hank? I want to know—how did our mother seem?"

Chapter 14

On hands and knees, Perry reaches under his bed. Of course the saxophone is there—of course it is. He pulls the dusty case out and snaps open both latches with his thumbs. It's a silver Buescher, a tenor, bought at the Calsibet's estate sale shortly after Norm Calsibet died. Perry can't recall what from—a stroke or heart disease or cancer. They all sounded alike back then, all killers. What he does remember is his dad saying, "If that's an estate, then Perry, my boy, we live in the Taj Mahal." Hank was off someplace banding or bird-watching, so Perry and his dad went over alone, his dad going on about how Norm Calsibet was no Coleman Hawkins or Ben Webster, but that for this vicinity of the world he was sure no slouch. His wife, Alma Calsibet, wearing dark, thick glasses because of cataracts, referred to the saxophone as a relic, and let it go, as Perry's dad joked later, for a song. Relic or not, it was all polished up and glittering, and there was a black neck strap in the case and two new reeds, and on the ride home when Perry twisted off the mouthpiece cap, his dad said, "Go ahead," and

Perry slid the mouthpiece onto the cork of the neck and puffed out his cheeks and filled the car with what he'd learn later was a low B-flat, not an easy note to play.

And impossible now that the pads are dry and warped, the keys all out of adjustment and a musty smell drifting up from inside the case. There's a music store in New London, just a couple of blocks from the courthouse, where saxophones hang in the window, and a sign that says INSTRUMENTS REPAIRED. But Perry won't carry this east; all he intended was to play a few riffs right here in his bedroom, at most to try and run a chord or two. That's all. Just tighten the ligature and lick the reed and improvise from the past. The only sounds possible tonight would resemble an amplified, high-pitched wheeze or shriek his dad would tune out by turning off his hearing aid. The house is silent, so Perry lays down the horn on the bed and goes downstairs and outside onto the front porch.

"The volcano," his dad says. "That's what I read in the paper, Mount Pinatubo—it's why the summer's been so cold—not so much tonight, but down into the low thirties last week, a record setter. Did you see the leaves, how they're already changing in July? The smell of fall's not in the air—fall's here. Next month, you'll see snowplows back on the pickups. It's a farmer's stock-in-trade—that's the honest truth—to be cheated one way or another. These are awful times to be growing cherries, even worse for field crops." He says, "Have you ever in your life seen such stunted corn? We had some good years, though, didn't we, Perry? Didn't we?" When Perry doesn't answer, his dad says, "But that's all over, now that those government scientists see how to slow the global warming. You mark my words, they'll invent ways to rupture volcanos all around the world. They'll put an end to summer as we used to know it up here, and that's a damn shame, forcing the seasons out of whack."

Until he spoke, Perry had not noticed his dad was there, but he strains to see him now, dim and sitting in the wheelchair in the darkness, a white afghan covering his lap and legs. He's peeling a hard-boiled egg, dropping the shells onto a plate. And Perry can smell coffee, freeze-dried Taster's Choice—he'd bet his life on it. And he'd bet that his dad has no idea what this image of himself as an invalid is doing to his son. Convincing him that what Hank has always maintained about their dad is true—that ever since Janine's death he's grown more feeble and weak-willed. "Can't you see that?" Hank insisted as recently as an hour ago, and Perry thinks, Yes, yes I can. Until this moment, he's refused to acknowledge it so completely, but as his dad flexes his fingers and complains about arthritis, Perry believes it's really a clot slowly forming somewhere in his dad's left wrist or forearm.

He wheels closer to Perry, into the filmy light cast from the door-way, and his face appears gray and lopsided when he cocks his head and points up beyond the eaves trough at the pulsing configurations of stars, and he says, "Some evenings, right after your mother come home from that first stroke, I'd push her up close to these stairs and lock the brake, and she'd stare out there for hours. I'd sit next to her, hoping some spur-of-the-moment conversation might distract her a bit, not only from the stroke but from everything that ever led to her sitting here and feeling the terrible sadness of it all. Don't ever believe she didn't love you boys, because she did."

The frayed cuffs of his dad's pajama bottoms ride up his shins, which are shiny and white, each slipper worn through above the big toe. "He's terminal," is how Hank described their dad, and Perry can't shake the image of him as a nursing-home patient, allowed out to the front porch to spend a few rushed minutes with his younger son, here all the way from Connecticut, but only passing through. Down the road, there will be no other way to care for him. Unload the house and the remaining five acres and exhaust that good-faith money before Medicaid reluctantly agrees to kick in for the rest—a year's worth or two or ten, a vision so fucking depressing that Perry reaches over and squeezes his dad's elbow and says to him, "I know, I know she loved us." The resignation in Perry's voice has nothing to do with disbelief, but, rather, with it being the extraordinary and, finally, undeniable truth. Had Hank visited her in the hospital, he'd have admitted to this, too. He would have. Which Perry assumes must be the reason Hank lied about going up there—love, unlived and unfelt for so long, becomes only another desperate gesture in the end, a final grimace at all the pain hoarded over a lifetime. Something close to that. An appeal, as far as Hank's concerned, that's wasted on him. A laugher.

But there's nothing funny about the way Perry's dad presses the back of his hand to his lips and breathes deeply in and out. And he shakes his head because he doubts, as always, that he can say what he needs to say, except to mention the absence of black flies with all this crazy late-autumn weather in July. But at least no welts to worry about, he says, no matter how long you sit outside.

Perry's still wearing a T-shirt and no shoes and, folding his arms, he stays seated beside his dad, who predicted early in the evening that the showers of the northern lights would be absolutely brilliant with these clear skies, "a festival," he called it. And then he said, "If only your mother could be here to see it with us."

Perry's heard a ton of "if onlys" in his work, but it's the "what is" that Hank has pointed out again, as it's the "what is" that Perry points to each time Lester Hoyos or Virgil Lewis or Carl Osbourne or whoever recalls yet again some blamable single event that seized and ruined their lives. And isn't that the real crime here, the Lafonds having brutalized themselves by refusing all these years to allow Janine's death to pass?

It's obviously too late to accomplish that now, but it's worth a try. Get rid of the high chair and call up Southgate Galleria to arrange for some new Congoleum vinyl flooring to be installed in the kitchen.

Plus wallpaper for his mom's bedroom—something floral and animated for her to return home to: a rose or lily or wildflower pattern.

It's not entirely out of spite that Hank condemned the house, though he wasn't talking as much about structural, as he was the need for major spiritual repair. Or both. And it's in that vein that Perry cuts off his dad, who's been wondering aloud, his voice washed-out and distant again, if there's really time for all that, as though it has to be accomplished tomorrow over lunch hour. Merciful Lord, Perry thinks. There's little chance his mom will be released before August, and he says, echoing Betty Benoit, "Doubt sees the obstacles; faith sees the way." The statement is so lavish and lofty and strange-sounding coming from Perry's mouth that his dad simply nods.

Perry, by contrast, pushes himself quickly up from his chair and backs all the way to the bottom of the wheelchair ramp, arms outspread in compliment of his dad's having taken such immaculate care of the house's exterior. From where he's standing, Perry can see, off to his left, what resembles the skeleton of a huge umbrella, what his dad, twisting the aluminum center pole back and forth into the poured concrete over thirty years ago, called a "clothesline tree," and under it right now a silver sheen on the grass. Perry has never seen the northern lights appear so bright and so suddenly. The barn seems freshly whitewashed, Perry imagining at this moment Hank walking out and staring up, a newborn goat cradled in his arms. If J.J. and Virtine were here, or if Perry had children of his own, he'd explain the aurora borealis to them by saying God sometimes turns up heaven's dimmer switch so high, the light spills over—it cascades down like shimmering, weightless water, meaning, of course, that it falls only partway, far enough to illuminate every leaf and needle of shrubbery, but never far enough actually to touch the earth. If it did, we'd all turn into angels.

Nothing exasperates Marcia more than when Perry refuses to visit her classroom during storytime. "They'd love you," she keeps telling him. "They'd love and remember you forever." And most likely swoon at the extravagant fact that 62,417 angels can sit down to dinner at once, elbow-to-elbow, on the head of a lightning rod. Times six, he'd say, because that's how many lightning rods Perry has just counted along the peak of the barn roof.

Strictly diversionary, Perry realizes, dismissively shaking his head as if to say, Nothing, when his dad calls him back from the fantasy. "You and Hank, you two shouldn't fight like that."

"Probably not," Perry says.

"No probably about it—there's no point anymore. It was foolish, Perry, foolish *and* so deliberate."

Guilty on both counts, Perry admits to himself—fool and aggressor. Is he sorry? Of course, in large part. But still resentful of Hank's' faith in the antidepressants he claimed he needed to help him survive this day, a defense that echoes the miserable whining Perry hears too often from the coke heads, from almost all the hard-core dopers. Blotto the world. Perry despises those punks, and maybe he said what he shouldn't have to Hank right then. He said, "Develop an addiction to oysters—they're a lot better for you than revenge."

That's when the conversation, chatty and friendly for a while after Hank first arrived, turned nasty, Hank pointing at Perry and warning him to cut the shit, to save the advice for the criminals. "And quit protecting Mom and Dad as though they're the innocent bystanders, because you don't believe that. Say it, Perry, say you don't believe that—please, just that much."

Perry couldn't, and Hank, puffing up, said, "Neglect is child abuse. You know all about child abuse in your work, don't you? Why can't you see it here?"

"This isn't a court case," Perry said, "so let's get off that."

"It should've been, and you can bet your life I would've testified about what went on in our past. I'd sure as hell have fingered the two of them. They weren't here for us, Perry, so why should we be here for them now?"

"Because that's what matters. Hang around long enough and maybe you'll figure that out," Perry said, the two brothers walking farther and farther away from the house each time they raised their voices.

"I heard every word," Perry's dad says, "from behind the screen door, where I listened and then watched you chase Hank away. He drove half a day to get here—the first time we've seen him in three years—and you chase him off the property like he's some trespasser."

"You act as if it's out of his way," Perry argues, which of course it is, the most remote place on the face of the earth—you'd need a whole other childhood to find it. There used to be a sign on Godfrey Street in Mystic that said DEAF CHILD, though some numbskull, using a can of black spray paint, altered it one night to DEAD CHILD. A sick joke, but Perry couldn't help imagining that sign on the roadside in front of this house. Would it mean accelerate and get by, or slow down and watch the dead child's mother walk out across the lawn to the compost heap and turn her colander upside down, tap the bottom, and then just stand there staring off into space? Or later, after her first stroke, sitting alone out on the porch, the dead child's father at the hedges with his shears. Perry glances up at the road, but there's no traffic, and no road sign, and in the brilliant plumes of light, the landscape keeps changing shape. There's a strobe effect, both Perry's hands appearing to tremble as he lifts them slowly to shield his eyes.

"More or less," his dad says, but Perry's drifted a few steps farther away from the porch, away from the fading conversation. Followed by the sudden cold cross breeze, and yes, the silver flecks swirling in the grass begin to resemble snow.

"Brrrr," Marcia says as Perry describes the night for her. He's trying to sound upbeat, forcing one of his dad's jokes. "Yup," he says, "in Michigan this year, summer fell on a Friday."

She's not exactly in stitches, but she does laugh, then updates him on how she and the kids spent the afternoon swimming at East Dock, the boards so hot that you could only walk across them after your feet were wet. Perry and Marcia have been on the phone about ten minutes, Marcia having called at precisely the arranged time, asking first about Perry's mom, then about his dad, about Hank. He's answered by explaining that he needs to stay a few days longer than he thought. "New wallpaper and flooring," he says, "to try and spiff the place up," and before she can interrupt for other details, he says, "Jesus, I really miss you."

"Good, because I miss you, too. We all do," Marcia adds.

"Everybody's okay there?"

"I guess, if you're inclined to see only the good in things. Mom bought some new Corning Ware at the mall and cooked a nice dinner, but you're gone and Pauline drove back to Boston around noontime to meet with her lawyer, so it felt pretty empty at the table. Virtine announced that she had certain rights as the firstborn—what it amounted to is that she wanted to stay out later than J.J. She insisted if Neil were here, he'd let her, but that only made J.J. cry. You should see him—he's sprawled out asleep on his back on the couch."

Perry's drinking a third bottle of his dad's beer—a Stroh's—and smoking a cigarette, a classic late-night combo guaranteed to embrace the loneliness already sinking in. After a short silence, she asks if he's still there, and he says, "Sort of," which verifies two things: he is in Michigan but doesn't want to be, or wants to be but has misjudged how absolutely miserable he'd feel by the time he finally heard Marcia's voice.

There's no pillow between his shoulder blades and the red oak headboard of his mom's bed. The thick, clear glass ashtray he's carried upstairs stays balanced on one thigh. How odd, Perry thought while waiting for Marcia's call, that the only extension should be in this room nobody dared enter after Janine died—a black rotary dial phone, the receiver heavy and clammy-feeling against his ear. He can't remember the year they switched from a party line to a private line, but he can remember the quick triple ring of the Lafond number. Perry's mom used to say that Blanche Vanpelt eavesdropped without the decency even to cover the mouthpiece, and that during any sudden pause in a conversation you could hear her breathing. Perry never could, though. Hank said kids weren't gossipy or hypocritical or private enough to interest adults. But wouldn't Blanche Vanpelt get an earful listening in now as Marcia, long distance, tries to cheer Perry up by exaggerating how she's going to fantasize about him tonight in bed. "And tomorrow morning, too," she promises, "and maybe again by late afternoon after my swim, while I'm rinsing the salt off my skin in the shower. Hello? Hey, out there, am I getting through?"

Perry notices some motion in the hallway, and he says to Marcia, "Hang on," and he sets his beer bottle on the floor and reaches over and switches off the lamp, which only makes the open doorway darker.

"Is somebody there?" Marcia asks.

"I don't know. I guess not. I thought so for a second."

"Block out the ghosts," Marcia says. "Good grief." But Perry leaves the lamp off and squints hard at the spot where he's certain someone stopped. He more than half believes, once his night vision focuses, that it won't be an apparition he's staring after. Whatever the presence, it's real in a way he hasn't felt before and, for a change, not the least bit threatening.

Marcia and Perry talk past midnight, agreeing there's no sense in him rushing back. "Though it felt so good to be together again," she says. "We're going to be all right, Perry."

"We'll work on it," he says.

"Fair enough, and in the meantime, you stay poised and level-headed out there. They need you."

Perry has told her nothing about the blowup with Hank. The percentage in that would trickle down to zero.

"I will," he says, "I promise," when she tells him to go right to bed.

"Don't stay up stalking around the house, or you'll turn into one of those ghosts you think you see."

"Scout's honor," he says, but after they hang up, Perry does walk downstairs. His dad's door is open a crack, and Perry can hear him snoring lightly. Whoever used the toilet last did not jiggle the lever, and there's that sound of water unable to level off. It's too late to fix it now, or to flush the toilet, so Perry eases open the front door, stepping out to the edge of the porch, where he pees over the side. The telephone books, dating back to 1960, are still stacked in three piles on the floor, to be recycled, Hank told Perry, into animal bedding. Not the reason he's returned, but son of a bitch if Hank's van isn't parked again in the driveway, the engine still ticking and cooling down.

Perry's careful and quiet placing the saxophone back into its case. Hank's in the other twin bed, under the sheet and blanket, a lightweight quilt folded back over his legs. Since entering the room, Perry's resisted the urge to shake Hank's shoulder, the way he'd do some nights, groggy with Sominex but unable to nod off for more than a couple of minutes at a time. He's battled insomnia since, but those early bouts were by far the worst. Hank never seemed to mind being awakened, no matter how late or how often, and he'd prop himself up on one elbow and yawn through a few shivery contortions before saying, "What's up?"

Always that same phrase—"What's up?"—and they'd resume their conversation about being brothers and having this special radar that maybe didn't go bleep, bleep, bleep across some screen but would nonetheless signal, and from anywhere, when the other guy was in trouble and needed help. Which means, Hank would say, that they'd never really be apart.

Perry has no trouble summoning that same pulse now—his heart beats so loudly inside his chest, he's certain Hank will all of a sudden sit up with him again, the light still falling like rain outside the window. But Hank doesn't move, and when Perry pulls the covers back on his own bed and slides in, he and Hank are facing each other—there's maybe three feet between them. Perry's mattress is softer than he remembers, the bed much lower to the floor. There's a bureau over which Hank has draped a pair of trousers, a white shirt on the doorknob of the closet. It's these details that calm Perry—it's as though their bedroom has slowly had to rearrange itself just enough to fit this moment and make it real. And complete, Perry thinks after shutting his eyes, at least for right now, their two bodies breathing in perfect sync.

Chapter 15

The first two flights out of Detroit to Hartford are booked solid—exasperating until Perry is given a standby seat in first class on the 5:15. Plus all the free peanuts and Beefeater he wants, and he's already on his third martini, waiting for whatever repair needs to be made on the landing gear. The seat next to him is still empty.

He told Marcia early this morning that it might be a long day and for her not to worry or wait around—he'd get there as soon as he could. If he ended up stranded in the airport overnight, he'd call. Otherwise, he'd said, "It's warp speed ahead."

Finally, the jet taxis out onto the runway, and within minutes, it is airborne and climbing. From behind the bulkhead, a baby begins to cry again, and the guy with the laptop sitting directly across the aisle from Perry leans out and cranes his neck and stares back prima donna—style to let the mother know he hasn't paid first-class fare to listen to this noise. The crying continues until after the plane reaches cruising altitude and the seat belt signs are turned off and the stewardess, smiling cheerfully as she passes, delivers the baby bottle. The captain apologizes over the speakers for the long delay, then assures everyone that he expects to make up a little time with a prevailing tailwind. "Now just lean back," he says, "and enjoy the flight."

Make up a little time, Perry thinks. How about making up for lost time, a much more difficult maneuver, but Perry's given it his best shot during the past five days. He'll call tomorrow to check on his mom's condition and to see if the new Congoleum has been installed in the kitchen. The pattern he finally chose is called Mythic Stone. Seamless installation backed by a ten-year Scuff-Tuff and Mildew-Protection Limited Warranty. He spent two tedious hours in that showroom, flipping through floor samples and talking with a salesman named Butch.

Hank, on the other hand, after sneaking into their bedroom that first night, snuck out again before dawn, Perry and their dad still asleep. When Perry awakened, no Hank and no note, and the phone directories gone from the porch and light rain falling. Nobody has heard a word from him, though yesterday a flower arrangement arrived anonymously to their mom's hospital room, and Perry told her it was from Hank and Connie. Then he placed it carefully on the nightstand next to Marcia's get-well card.

Perry reminds himself again that his mom has improved, her vital signs steady and the doctor optimistic that she'll be able to return home soon. As Perry is doing now, but not comfortably, because it has gotten suddenly too hot inside the cabin and he reaches up and twists clockwise on the air nozzle, aiming it directly onto his face. He's been traveling for almost twelve hours already, and when he tilts his head back, he drifts immediately into an early-evening gin nap.

He doesn't wake until the aircraft touches down with a jerk and tire screech, Perry's mouth very dry, the empty nip bottles gone and his tray in its upright position. The baby has stopped crying. If there's been a meal served, Perry's missed it, but he won't stop on the road for a bite to eat—not now, with only a thirty-minute drive to Mystic. Not this late, he promises himself, not after all this lost time.

Marcia and Angela are sitting shoulder-to-shoulder midway down the back stairs when Perry drives in. He can tell it's them even in the semidarkness, and he can tell they've been waiting for him to arrive. What he does not know is why, only that it must be bad.

Both women stand as he gets out of the car, and for a minute nobody moves. They stare down at him, and he up at the two of them. It's too dark and far to read anything in their eyes. Then Marcia touches Angela's elbow, as if guiding her first step, and Angela descends, but not rushing down to Perry—she's deliberate and slow, her left hand gripping the railing. Marcia turns the other way, up and into the apartment, closing the door behind her.

"Where are we?" Perry asks when Angela finally stops a few feet in front of him. He means where in the story, and why, and how much does Marcia know? Jesus Christ Almighty, it's been a long day, and is this ransom time or payback in some other unexpected way?

"It's not as if I followed you," Angela says. "You *showed* me how to get here—you wanted me to know. Your phone's unlisted. I tried that, and then I simply raced down the pathway you opened to me into your heart. Didn't you do that?"

"Angela . . ." Perry says.

"And doesn't that mean I should be able to come find you at home if I need to badly enough? Or have I completely crossed my wires? All I know for sure is that I've never needed anybody more in my life."

There are dark half-moons under her eyes, and either hickeys or bruises on one side of her neck. She's wearing perfume and lipstick, a short-sleeved blouse with the bra strap showing, and a pleated skirt. She looks like a schoolgirl.

"It's Roland, isn't it?" he says.

"It won't blow over this time. It wasn't ever going to blow over. Roland's specialty is screwing up. That's what he does—he screws up over and over again."

Perry steps forward and takes her hand, gently squeezing it. There's a light on in the bedroom window that faces the driveway, and Marcia is not there. When Perry glances up, Angela says, "Your wife is very beautiful. You never told me how beautiful she was. And smart and nice like you. We've been talking a long time about having babies."

"Where's Corey?"

"With Roland, but I don't know where this time. They drove away in the pickup."

"How long ago?"

"Midafternoon, three o'clock maybe—I'm not sure. Roland came home carrying the last of a six-pack of beer by the empty plastic loops, kind of swinging it by his leg, but right away I could smell whiskey, too. I heard a car toot and drive away. I don't know who it was or where Roland was coming home from. A bar, I guess. He said to pack what I needed because we were leaving right away for Texas, and then he started kissing me hard on the neck. He backed me right against the wall, and I kind of slid to the floor with him draped all over me. I couldn't get loose, so I shouted for him to stop, just stop it, which maybe was the wrong thing to say, because he went all limp and sat back on the floor, his legs spread wide apart and his head hanging down. 'Roland,' I said, 'Roland, listen to me,' but he started screaming no—long, wailing noes, like he was testing how loud and long he could do it without taking a breath. He sounded like somebody dying."

"And?"

"And what? I was crying and Corey was crying in his crib, and when Roland finally stopped that awful noise, it was like he'd frightened himself. You know that tan he's got? It turned white as a ghost, and he tried to talk then, but he couldn't, nothing I could make heads or tails of."

"Did *anything* he said make sense? Like where he'd been or what happened, the name of somebody or someplace? Anything about why he wasn't at work?"

"Something about not wearing his hard hat, and that the ocean inspector was going to write him up, but I said, 'Wait.' I said, 'Roland, what on earth is an ocean inspector?' From then on's when everything went berserk—nothing after that made even an ounce of sense."

"OSHA," Perry says, letting go of her hand, "not ocean. They're safety inspectors. That's their job—to check construction sites for safety violations."

"Perry, Roland's got a gun—it's not a new one, and I don't think he'd ever shoot anyone. I pleaded with him not to buy it, but he said it was a necessary evil, living so far out in the boonies. He's had it for a couple years, but he's never taken it out of the house before, not even to practice on bottles or cans. Never once."

"Until now, you mean." Perry pauses, and then he says, "Why didn't you tell me this before? They're going to throw the book at him this time, Angela, and there's nothing I'll be able to do."

She begins to answer, then presses both palms to her temples instead. "Can we go sit down?" she asks, and Perry says, "Hold on. Hold on a minute—I need to get a few things straight. You're sure Roland's not at home?"

"I'm positive. I've called every half hour, but there's no answer, even though I hang up after the first two rings and call right back— it's a code we have."

"A code?"

"Yes," she repeats, "a code, so he knows it's me. Is there something wrong with that?"

"No," Perry says, "no, there's not," but having insinuated otherwise, he apologizes. He says, "Let's stay calm—let's regroup and think this through. Maybe he's in the Firebird and can't hear the phone."

"No . . . he's not, he's not there, either."

"How can you be so sure?"

"Because Marcia drove me home."

"Oh Jesus, Angela . . . no."

"I didn't mean to get her involved, but my son's missing and I can't call the cops on Roland because he'll go straight to jail, and Marcia's the one who suggested we drive by. Not go inside or anything—just see if the pickup was there, but it wasn't."

Perry turns away, listening to the noisy approach of a car on Elm Street, then watches the sparks thrown up from the pavement by the bouncing tailpipe. Then, meeting her eyes again, he says, "Back up a minute. How did you get here?"

"My friend Brenda, she dropped me off and drove back to her place in case Roland called or showed up there. Perry, can we go inside? I have to sit down—I don't feel well."

"Nor do I," he says, and closes his eyes and bows his head and clasps his hands together. Angela, holding her abdomen, asks if he's praying for her, if that's all he's going to do, just stand there and pray. He doesn't think so, but he's not sure. He's only ever thought about praying from down on his knees like his dad taught him, and he hasn't done that for years, not in a church or by the side of his bed, not even at a funeral.

But Angela collapses hard to *her* knees, and then doubles over in the driveway by Perry's feet. There's no doubt that what she's whispering between moans is a prayer, and Perry hears the words clearly next to his ear as he lifts and carries her quickly toward the house. "Please, God," she says, "please don't let me lose this child."

*　*　*

There's a lot of blood on the sheet, thicker and darker than any blood Perry has ever seen. Like mucus or membrane, like shiny red gelatin.

He's alone in his bedroom because Marcia, after the ambulance sped away, has fled, but not before pointing at the blood and asking Perry, "Was it yours?" He shook his head no. On her way past him, she stopped and said, "A woman I've never met before arrives out of the blue at our house, crying and asking for you, and then miscarries on our bed. I'll never sleep in that bed again—do you hear me?" And to this he nodded yes.

He folds the sheet back carefully, and then over again from the foot of the bed, then up from each side, lifting it by the four corners with one hand, holding it away from his body. No, it's not his, but he acknowledges to himself that he's responsible in some major way for what has happened here, for this tragedy.

He thinks of the sheet as a shroud and he has no idea what to do with it. There's no hiding it as he did with Roland's cowboy shirt. He takes only one short step toward the bathroom and knows he cannot bring himself to wash the blood out by hand in the bathtub. And a vigil is all wrong—this apartment really would feel like a funeral home, Perry the strange, lone visitor to this wake.

Early in their marriage he made Marcia promise that if he dies first, she'll have him cremated, though he hasn't figured out yet where he wants his ashes to be spread. "You've got time to decide," she said, "or better yet, to change your mind."

Perry won't. There's no spot reserved for him in the Lafond family plot, and he refuses to be confined for eternity here among the Benoits, his arms crossed forever on his chest, six dark feet below a pink marble headstone. No, he intends to vanish completely after death, and it's with this in mind that he carries the sheet downstairs and places it on the front seat of the Subaru. He turns on the headlights and opens the garage door so he can find the can of gasoline. It's right next to the lawn mower, a red five-gallon can with a spout, and he listens to the sloshing inside when he lifts and shakes it. After checking his pockets to make sure he's got a book of matches, he leaves.

Once he's out in the country, the sky seems suddenly clustered with stars, millions of them pulsing and dimming and, over eons, dying out, their light traveling on and on. This vastness comforts Perry. He's not sure why, but he's leaning up close to the windshield, his forearms hugging the steering wheel as he drives, hardly watching the road. He believes that if he were to close his eyes, he would still arrive safely, because this is his fate and, although he's tried, there's nothing he can do to change it. He speeds up and then slows down. He swerves left and then right across the road from one spongy shoulder to the other, back and forth. All four windows are wide open and the flaps of the sheet rise and billow and settle back. A car passes going the other way, blasting its horn—somebody heading home, no doubt, to his wife and kids.

When Perry turns onto the dirt road, he sees that Roland and Angela's house is completely dark, abandoned-looking, a matchbox ranch the bank would just as soon see go up in flames, thus preventing the inevitable ordeal of foreclosure. Much simpler just to settle with the insurance company and be done with it.

Perry switches off the ignition but keeps the high beams shining on the front of the house like a crime scene. He wishes to God he had never set foot inside there. Because he did, he helped set all of this in motion. But he hasn't returned to torch the place. He's here only to cremate the remains of this unborn child who Roland does not even know has died. Or never lived, Perry tells himself, though Marcia's explained to him many times that a heartbeat begins at eight weeks. Already a person, she'll argue—eyes and ears, fingers and toes, a skeleton beginning to harden, all this with the embryo the size of a grain of rice. It's what she called "the biological continuum."

211 ✳

Perry pushes the cigarette lighter in with his thumb and kills the brights, then the headlights completely, the house disappearing in such total darkness that he flicks them right back on. The biological continuum, Perry thinks again, and he remembers suddenly how his dad snuck up on him one time inside the barn, where Perry had fallen asleep in the armchair his dad kept out there. It was the first warm evening that spring, and his dad, crouched right in front of him, whispered, "Perry," and when he opened his eyes, he was temporarily blinded by the flashbulb. Not really disoriented or scared, just not wanting to move until his sight returned to normal.

That is how Perry's feeling again, clicking slowly backward on the light switch until only the parking lights stay lit. He can make out his face in the rearview mirror, and more clearly once the lighter pops and he touches the round glow-orange coil to the tip of his Camel. He's beginning more and more to resemble both his mom and his dad, and seeing that, he turns away and gets quickly out of the car and walks across the dirt road to the field's edge and stays right there, staring. He's always had good night vision, and it takes only a few minutes under the starlight before the Firebird appears, then the outline of those yellow-and-red flames along the side.

He wonders if he'll be sorry for what he's about to do. He hadn't thought before about being sorry, or about this being wrong, maybe even being a terrible thing, some aberration of character taking charge, taking over without any forethought of guilt or grief or consequence.

It's as if there are two Perrys, the one who keeps walking into the field with the sheet and the can of gas and the one who watches. The one who lowers the gas can into the weeds and opens the driver's side door and places the sheet midway on the front seat, where Corey sat so peacefully between Roland and Perry. And the one who's nervous and afraid, listening to the gas splashing through the busted-out windshield and windows onto the white interior, then nodding finally when the one with the matches strikes a single match and glances back. And he nods, too, and lights the entire book, then retreats one step and tosses it into the Firebird, which explodes into real flames, the heat scorching Perry's throat and lungs so that he's unable to breathe. He's on his hands and knees, gasping openmouthed as he crawls away from the fire and the black spewing of fumes into the night air. It's the smell of gas and vinyl and plastic and steel, everything ablaze and roaring, shadows dancing across the weeds. He's sure the car's gas tank is going to blow—he's seen it in a hundred action movies, the hero always diving, by a split second, to safety. But the gas tank doesn't blow, though the fire burns and burns, Perry making his way slowly back to the road.

He can't even swallow yet, but he can see from his knees that there really is another person here, not his "other" at all—someone younger and taller and bigger through the arms and pointing a pistol at Perry and saying, "Things are heating right up, Mr. Lafond. Seems like hell is spilling over and all the sinners are out, and what are the chances anymore of the likes of us growing into happy old men? I don't think all that good. Whatta you think?"

It's the "us" that Perry responds to when he says, his voice raspy, "Speak for yourself." The pistol does not frighten him at all.

"You haven't committed a crime, then?" Roland says. "This is okay what you've done? Justice is a crazy game, but I still trust you, at least with my son, and that's all that matters for now. This," Roland says, and he points toward the Firebird with the pistol barrel, "this I don't understand. Kinda pretty, though, a Firebird."

Perry turns at the waist, and he can see that the flames flapping from the windows resemble wings, and when he closes his eyes again, it's to pray.

"Our Father . . ." he whispers, and he does not look up again until he hears the front door of the house open and close. And it opens again a few minutes later, and by the time Roland carries baby Corey down the stairs and across the parched lawn, Perry is standing. Roland has put on his yellow hard hat, the white pistol grip sticking out above the waist of his jeans. He's still wearing his work boots.

"Take him," Roland says, and he hands Corey, whose eyes are wide open, into Perry's arms. "This is becoming a habit," Roland says. He says, "Look at 'em—he knows it's time for his old man to run again, and he's not gonna make a fuss, 'cause me and him, we're gonna rendezvous in a bit, soon as I get settled. He's very beautiful, isn't he?"

"Too beautiful to leave," Perry says. "And where's there to go, anyway?"

"You call it chasing fool's gold, but I like to think of it as the land of beginning again."

"That place is right here," Perry says. "It always has been."

"You talking to me or to you?"

"To both of us," Perry admits.

"Then you're at least half-wrong. I stay, I face assault charges, and I don't guess you can fix that fellow's jaw for me. Not without a magic wand you can't, and I can't do more time. This here's a dead end for me—bad cards again, Mr. Lafond. It's time to turn away."

"How bad was it—today I mean, with the OSHA inspector?"

"He wasn't like you. I explained how my job was on the line. I said, 'Here, look,' and I reached over to where my hard hat was on a stack of pallets, and I put the hat back on and I said, 'There, we're okay now. Everybody's safe,' but he just kept writing me up. He refused even to look at me. And then, snap city, where my permanent residence seems to be, and I reached back, and pow, down he goes like a sacka potatoes. Except that the cops ain't been here yet, I thought sure as hell I'd killed 'em."

"They'll be looking for your truck," and saying that, Perry scans the peripheral darkness, and, not seeing the pickup, he understands

Roland's getaway plan, and he says to him, "Don't do it, Roland. Car theft'll only add fuel to the fire."

"Interesting way to put it," Roland says, and they both stare out at the halo of light glowing above the Firebird in the field under all those stars. And they stare at Corey and then at each other, and at the Subaru parked askew on the dirt road, the parking lights still on.

"Keys in it?" Roland asks, but of course he already knows they are, so when he reaches out, it's to shake Perry's hand. Both men squeeze firmly before letting go.

"At least give me the gun," Perry says, and it's not a surprise when Roland does, handle first.

"A Colt," Roland says, "and it'll cost you whatever cash you can spare."

Perry turns around, holding the baby and the pistol while Roland takes the wallet from Perry's back pocket. There's maybe seventy bucks, and a Shell credit card, which Perry tells him to take, too. "The registration's in the glove compartment," he says, and still facing away, he finally tells him, "Roland, Angela lost the baby."

It feels like a long time before Roland says, "Turn around," and when Perry does, Roland leans forward and kisses Corey on the forehead. "I love you," he whispers, and Corey smiles, his thumb sliding partway out of his mouth.

"Let me get my suitcase," Perry says, as though he's arrived as a friend or family, here to baby-sit a few days and watch the house while Roland's away, while Angela recovers in the hospital.

"I'll get it," Roland offers, and he walks over to the car and pushes the back of the seat forward, then lifts the suitcase out of the back and carries it up to the porch, Perry following. "Corey's ready for bed, and there's a bottle made up for when he wakes—two in the morning, like clockwork. Just heat it up and test the formula on the inside of your wrist. It's a piece of cake, Mr. Lafond."

"Why didn't you answer the phone when Angela called? She needed you."

"Sleeping it off," he says. "And when I woke up, I decided to write it all out, everything I could think to say, which ain't enough, but it's all there in a letter for her on the kitchen table. It won't make any of what's happened all right, but it tries to say some things."

"At least call her before you go. Call her at the hospital."

"I can't do that," Roland says. "Last I saw it, one phone was boomeranging toward God. And that portable job—well, nothing personal, Mr. Lafond, but I couldn't leave something like that around once you arrived on the scene. Just couldn't take that chance."

Perry nods—on that count, good, now he won't have to worry about whether or not to blow the whistle. And Perry does not respond when Roland says, "For what it's worth, thanks. Thanks for a lot." Then to Corey, he says, "Little man," and he kisses him again and simply leaves and gets into the car, the parking lights dimming before the engine catches. Perry crouches and lays the pistol at his feet, and he takes the baby's hand and waves it as Roland backs up and brakes and shifts into first and then turns on the headlights and drives away. Only then does Perry let go of Corey's hand, the tiny fingers spreading open and dancing back and forth all by themselves.

Of course Perry could walk out to the main road and eventually flag a ride, or even angle across the field in the direction of the runway and find the lights and follow them back to the hangars, where there must be a pay phone.

But Corey's asleep in his crib, and Perry's standing in the dark living room at the picture window, watching the last of the flames die out in the Firebird. He wonders where Marcia is, and Roland, and if Angela is awake or asleep. And he thinks about how, reaching out to him from the stretcher, she said, "Find Corey and stay with him," and Perry has, and he wishes he could call to tell her that. And tell her that the pistol was unloaded, and that there's a letter in an envelope that's unsealed on the kitchen table from Roland, and Angela's name is on the outside in block letters, each one separately underlined, and would she like Perry to read the letter to her? He wants to very badly. He's curious to know what it is a man says to his wife under these conditions, and if it constitutes a conversation, or the realization that that time has permanently passed. It must happen often, not one word in a million able to find its niche, not here in Connecticut or in northern Michigan or in Texas, not anywhere in all the dialects of failure and loneliness.

And then what to do with the aftermath of silence, with everything you might have said over the years and instead said nothing, which Perry guesses is why Roland tried to write it out—tried to collect his thoughts and probably couldn't, digressing all over the place. Perry would. He always does, every single time he talks to himself, yapping it up and driving himself half nuts with the effort to make even the simplest, most obvious connections, trying to be heard clearly for once, and to hear what is truly being said.

He tells himself it's exhaustion talking, and that he should go to bed. But it's almost 2:00 A.M. and Corey will be waking up. Perry's already checked on him a dozen times, tiptoeing into his bedroom, the Barney night-light glowing lavender on the wall opposite the crib, below the bassinet. He already has water in the saucepan, the pan on the left-front burner of the stove, the baby bottle in the fridge. A jar of Beech-Nut custard on the counter, a spoon and napkin. He's fussed around with a Huggies disposable diaper, trying to figure out how it works, if there's a front and a back. He likes the idea of adhesive instead of safety pins.

"Like clockwork," Roland said, and now the *beep-beep-beep* of

Perry's watch alarm, set just in case he dozed off, though, by standing and walking around the house, he's straight-armed sleep each time it circled and closed in. And by smoking his last few cigarettes, by popping open and pouring beer after beer down the kitchen sink, and by hiding the pistol between the mattress and box spring on Roland and Angela's bed. Then retrieving and hiding it again: on the back of the closet shelf, then outside under the stairs, and finally in Perry's suitcase, wrapped in a souvenir T-shirt Perry bought for Marcia in Traverse City.

It's all part of some convoluted cover-up plan that Perry hasn't the energy even to try and figure out—except to visualize a man holding a baby and a suitcase and walking slowly down a dirt road, away from a smoking car in a field at first light. Like refugees, Perry thinks, like survivors. But he turns away from that image, and away from the picture window when he hears Corey stir in his crib and then cry for Angela or Roland, whoever's turn it is to wake and go to him.

Chapter 16

Perry's not under arrest, not even under the kind of suspicion, he's been told, that could land him in jail, but there are questions still to be answered. How did he become so personally involved with the Knudsons? And why? And did this relationship constitute aiding and abetting in any way? Why was Roland, as a condition of his initial parole violation, not enrolled in AA? And why is so much of the recent paperwork on him—home visits, report nights, et cetera, et cetera—blank?

How was it that Angela was at the Lafonds' apartment on the night before her husband was killed—he having fallen asleep at the wheel of Perry's Subaru and hit a tree head-on? The only tree, by the way, on that entire stretch of road large enough to crush a car so completely. Which leads us to consider suicide, doesn't it? And to ask ourselves this: could his death have been averted had Perry followed normal procedures? After all, how did Roland get so far without the car being reported stolen? And who honestly believes that two miles was too far to walk in the dark, and what kind of person, given the circumstances of July 23 and July 24, could fall so soundly asleep on the couch and not be awakened until Officer Janulis and Officer McKelvey entered the premises and nudged Perry with their batons?

And let it be further noted that, according to those two officers, Perry Lafond showed no emotion when confronted with this news, only asked if Angela had been told, and remained silent when Officer Janulis said that no, she hadn't yet been located. Why, right then, didn't Perry offer up information about the miscarriage and about her being taken by ambulance to Pequonock Bridge Hospital, instead of waiting several minutes, until Officer McKelvey lifted baby Corey screaming from his crib? Screaming and reaching out for Perry, who said, "Let me take him to his mother." They couldn't do that, they said, but they allowed him to change and feed the baby, but never out of sight of one of them.

They didn't know, and so they couldn't tell Perry it wasn't Marcia, but, rather, Wayne daSilva who walked into the morgue in New Hope, Pennsylvania, to identify what there was of the body, much more of it, Wayne reportedly said, than lots of bodies he'd seen and that it definitely was *not* Perry Lafond. Marcia was waiting in the hallway, hysterical at first but eventually calming down enough to ask if there was a child in the car. Whose child? Hers? Was there kidnapping involved, or was this simply trauma talk? And does that excuse her, after mentioning Roland's name, from saying nothing, as Perry said nothing, about the whereabouts of the deceased's wife? Was this a conscious withholding of information or not? All very odd. Until the pieces of the puzzle fit, Perry will remain on suspension, without pay.

He's sitting alone on the deck of the houseboat in the sun, his eyes closed. He's given Roland's handgun to Wayne to dispose of miles out in the ocean. Let somebody locate that piece of the puzzle! Wayne, taking the gun, asked no questions. He's on his lobster boat now, hauling pots. The catch has been light lately, and most of the tourists have sailed or motored away. Even the dock stragglers have that look of leaving in their eyes.

Angela has asked Perry to say a few words at the funeral tomorrow morning, a simple graveside service. He has Marcia's Bible on his lap, and he's remembering Janine's funeral, he and Hank standing between their mom and dad, listening to the priest read from the Twenty-third Psalm: "Yea, though I walk through the valley of the shadow of death, I will fear no evil." There was a canopy they stood under because of the rain, the smell of incense hanging in the heavy air, the priest swinging the censer back and forth above the coffin. His vestments, at their dad's request, were green, the color of hope, he later explained to his sons, but all Perry could think about was how it was the same color as those spaded squares of sod piled behind the grave.

Perry does not know the Bible well. He's looked up the word *children* in the *Concordance*. Proverbs 17, verse 6: "The children's children are the crown of old men; and the glory of children are their fathers." He might read this passage; he's got it marked with the black ribbon.

Roland was not a good husband, and not a good father, though Perry believes he wanted to be and that he loved his wife and loved and worshiped his son, whom Perry did not hand that morning to Angela. A cop named Marie Garcia did, just moments after Angela was released from the hospital. It was also Marie Garcia who delivered the news about Roland, despite Perry's plea to be the one to do it. "Please," he said. He said, "That is not something a stranger should do."

She drove Angela and Corey home in the cruiser, and she reported later that Angela had pointed at the Firebird and said, "Look what Roland's done," and until that moment she hadn't even cried, and then she couldn't stop. There was enough food in the house, and the department would arrange for a telephone repairman to stop out the

221 ✳

next day. The pickup, located by midafternoon behind one of the hangars at the airport, was towed into New London—Angela owes Dino Londrico & Sons ninety dollars. She's got thirty days.

Perry was not detained long, but he was told in no uncertain terms to keep "it at arm's length until the dust settled." "It," Perry thought, and "arm's length," and "dust." What a language. He was certain Roland's letter did not speak like that, and he delivered it to Angela, driving out that night on his Harley. Marcia did not object, not to that, nor to his decision to move out. "It's been coming," she said. "Closer and closer." The timing was bad, but any time would be bad, wouldn't it? School starts for her in a month—she's got meetings to attend and bulletin boards to get ready. She said, "When I thought you were dead . . ." but she couldn't finish, and she hugged Perry and said, "I can't stop thinking about that, how it felt like nothing else mattered, nothing," and neither of them pushed to clarify anything more. The bed had been remade, the tennis ball can with the syringes pushed to the back corner of the bureau. On his way out, he could see where she'd slept—on the comforter on the living room floor.

He withdrew $2,600 from the savings account, what would amount to half the insurance settlement from the Subaru, all hundred-dollar bills. As he enclosed the money in Roland's envelope, he saw the salutation: "Dear Angela, Dear Angel . . ."

What are you doing, Perry chastised himself. Read it or don't, but don't use this cheap excuse of stuffing in a wad of death cash to get a peek—don't add this to the guilt list. He lifted the bills back out and then licked the glue on the inside of the flap and sealed the envelope, then got a second one and placed the money in it. He didn't know then and does not know now what it cost Angela to have Roland's body driven back to Connecticut in a hearse, nor what the funeral expenses will total. He's never tried to tally in dollars and cents before what a life lost can set another person back. Emotionally, he knows exactly the price one pays.

Perry drove his Harley into the driveway. The outside light by the side door was on and, after taking off his helmet, that's the door where he knocked. He helped to shoulder it open when he heard Angela pulling on the doorknob.

"I was hoping you'd come," she said. "I sent my friend Brenda home just in case you did, and here you are."

Perry followed Angela inside, through the darkened kitchen out into the living room, where he handed her Roland's letter. "He asked me to give you this." When he offered the money, Angela refused.

"Life insurance is not expensive at Roland's age. For all his recklessness and debt, he never let his policy lapse. He joked that it fit his character—that it put a price on his head. 'Look what I'm worth,' he'd say, and point to a figure that doesn't make me rich, just not destitute. Unless they can prove it was suicide. . . ."

"They can't," Perry said.

"Do you think it was? Did he talk like he'd do something crazy like that?"

"No," Perry said. "Just the opposite," but he's wondering now if suicide was what Roland meant by "the land of beginning again."

Angela set Roland's letter on the floor by the playpen. Perry sat down on the couch, Angela on the recliner, exactly where they sat and talked less than a month ago. This conversation, of course, was not about saving Roland from jail, but much of it was about Roland, who wanted desperately to get a grip on his life and to watch his son grow up and away from that terrible male Knudson curse. Corey will be told someday, not so far in the future, that his father was killed in an auto accident, and maybe that he'd had a scrape or two with the law, a topic Perry hopes Corey won't want to hear much about. Maybe Angela will remarry and Corey will think of that man as his dad.

Which isn't to say that these things were even mentioned that night, because they weren't. The conversation was slow and quiet and calm. An airplane flew low over the house, and Angela got up once to make coffee and to check on Corey. Before Perry left, they stood facing each other, and he reached out again and brushed her hair back from her forehead, but without that funny feeling in his stomach.

He asked if she needed a ride to the cemetery and she said no, that Brenda would drive her and that she could stay with Brenda for a while after the house got sold. They'd built up a little equity, plus the remodeling. It could be attractive to the right buyer—maybe advertise it as a starter home out in the country. And she said that she was going to miss Roland something terrible but that she wasn't going to mind being alone with only her son, and did that sound wrong to say about a man you'd known and loved almost half your life? A man you grew up with? It didn't at all; it sounded honest, Perry said.

Then he told her Wayne's phone number, which she wrote down on the pink highlight of a calendar picture called "Night Island." Perry could see that a dark X was penciled in the square on the day Roland died. She thanked Perry for coming and pushed up onto her toes and kissed him on the cheek.

He did not swing left out of the driveway. He drove straight into the field and stopped when the angle widened enough for him to see Angela standing in the living room, reading Roland's letter. She wiped her eyes several times and turned the letter over and read that side, then slid it behind the next page and continued. When she finished, she stood hugging herself as though she were cold, her head down. It wasn't until several minutes later that she leaned into the lamplight and turned the lamp off. Perry waited until the bedroom light went on, and then he looked away. In first gear, he concentrated on his headlight beam as the Harley bounced across the ruts and weeds. He hit his brights and stared up, and he could see that the Firebird's painted flames had blistered and peeled. It resembled something abandoned in *Mad Max*, skeletal and bleak. He continued beyond the car before turning in a slow arc and coming back onto the dirt road, where he shifted into second and then into third, opening the throttle wide into fourth before finally slowing down to try and get his bearings.

It's going to take awhile—one careful step at a time, Wayne advised. Rush it, he said, and you'll never climb back onto safe and familiar terrain. Wayne's told Perry he's welcome to hide out on the houseboat until hell freezes over.

There's a cool breeze blowing, and no clouds, and Perry can see all the way downriver to the train trestle where the Amtrak rattled past just before daybreak, its lighted windows barely visible through the mist. "The ghost commute to Boston," Wayne calls it.

Now, from the shadow of the dock, a family of mallards swims again into the current, the five babies in a straight line behind the mother, the surface water fanning into a V. Perry wishes he could simply praise these images in his eulogy as he could for Wayne—the river flowing and the blue sky and the coming closing of another summer—"To every thing there is a season, and a time to every purpose under the heaven."

Perry's always understood the *time* part—it's the *purpose* that causes all the trouble. Which is what Angela said once was Roland's middle name, Trouble, and that it all stemmed from him never knowing from one minute to the next why he was put on this earth in the first place.

"Not to zip boys into body bags," Wayne said of himself, but that's what he did his final two weeks in Vietnam after being called away from the front. And dug latrines, and tried not to think about why and what that war had done to his life. He said one morning the chaplain stood without his Bible among the bodies, with nothing to say, bombs exploding in the distance.

There's cold lobster in the refrigerator, and mayonnaise, and Wayne has told Perry not to be shy, because he's going to earn his keep once the funeral's over. Perry's looking forward to getting out on the ocean.

"It'll help clear your head," Wayne said, and Perry believes him.

His doubts are about saying the right things tomorrow to the mourners, however many or few there are. So far today, he hasn't spoken to a soul, though that's exactly what he's been attempting to do. It'll come, he knows, and as he gets up to go inside for lunch, the only cloud of the morning covers the sun. And the drawbridge begins to rise, the pigeons scattering upward in a wide spiral from underneath. Not too far away, Perry can hear the shrieks of gulls following the first of the fishing fleet home.

Before Wayne left this morning, Perry asked him for a piece of paper, not a paper towel. But that's all there was, that and a blue felt-tip pen. So far, Perry's written down tomorrow's date and Roland's name. Because he does not want even that much to blow away, he folds and places it under the Bible on the chair seat. And the sun reappears. Wayne, who listens every morning to the weather forecast on his marine radio, told Perry it's going to stay cool along the coast, and cool inland, and that there won't be any rain for the next two days. He meant, of course, for the funeral.

It's always dark stepping inside out of the sun, and Perry will give himself a few more minutes for his eyes to adjust. Then he'll call Angela for cemetery directions and to ask what time she wants people to gather—the *purpose* clearly clear for once, to put her husband to rest.

Chapter 17

The cemetery is surrounded by a wrought-iron fence—like an endless row of heavy black javelins, thousands and thousands of them—with only two entrances, and Perry has driven past the main gate in favor of arriving undetected from the lower, shady backside where the oldest graves are located: almost all flush markers, dull-edged white marble, the names and dates and inscriptions cut too shallow into the stone to withstand the wearing away by wind and snow and rain. Most are unreadable. More ferns grow here than flowers.

Perry has already parked his Harley under a large-domed locust, one of many. Someone has carved his initials, J.W., and the year, '83, into the bark. Perry thinks the tree must be a century old, its roots clinging and spreading out under the earth of this graveyard.

Perry has not worn gloves, the morning so cool that his fingers actually ache, and he flexes them before taking off his helmet and combing his hair. Then he reaches into the saddlebag for the chamois cloth that he uses to wipe the dust from his shoes. And he unbuttons his suitcoat and straightens his tie. Lastly, he checks his watch—not quite 9:30. He's half an hour early.

Except for the crows cawing somewhere out of sight, it's quiet, the only movement a man who guides the silver disk of his metal detector back and forth above the graves—loose change from the dead? The not so recently departed sending up their jewelry?

The road curves off to the left, but Perry does not follow it; he heads straight up the gradual slope through an avenue of headstones, his eyes focused on the hedgerow of blue spruce at the crest. It takes him only a few unhurried minutes to get there. Almost squatting, he makes his way crablike under the branches and needles, then emerges on the other side, where the ground descends.

There's full sunshine here, the headstones upright and much larger—mottled browns and reds and grays, the granite polished and shiny. Perry counts half a dozen mausoleums, and he has to cup the match in his hands against the breeze when he lights his cigarette. The yellow lopped-off heads of dandelions lie scattered where the mower's been through. Perry can smell the cut grass.

But he cannot see inside the caretaker's shed, though its double doors are wide open. It's too far away, the opening dark like a cave. And there's something prehistoric about the arm of the backhoe that protrudes from behind and above the roofline.

Until this moment, Perry has always thought of Janine's grave being dug by hand, maybe one man or two digging carefully down all day, then returning to shovel the dirt back in. But Perry never saw them. After the committal service, only he and Hank and their mom and dad remained graveside for the lowering of the casket, Perry fighting off the panic to yell that it was too deep—the hole they dug was way, way too deep.

He hadn't even realized he'd been squeezing and squeezing the rose stem, and when he tossed it, that bowl of white petals seemed to hang motionless in the air before falling in slow motion. He closed his eyes right before the rose hit the lid, and when he opened them, his hand was bleeding. His mom had already taken her first step away, so when Perry reached out, it was to his dad, who refused to hold it— both *his* hands were covering his face.

Perry's not positive that the grave he sees is Roland's grave. There's a mound of dirt, and the silver lowering device in place, and stacked squares of sod. He's going to wait up here for the procession of cars to stop and for the mourners to get out before he starts down.

The fender flags on the hearse are orange, and the headlight that's out resembles a bad eye. Perry recognizes the car directly behind; he's seen it parked in front of Brenda's house, a dark blue station wagon that's inched up so close to the rear bumper, it looks like the shadow of the hearse. There's a large gap after that, then a pack of three cars, and all by itself a beat-up red van with a lot of rust and a noisy muffler and a spare tire strapped on top.

Three doors of the station wagon open simultaneously and three women get out, Angela from the backseat. She's carrying Corey. Perry nervously waves to her, but she hasn't seen him yet. Only the undertaker has, and he watches Perry's slow and odd approach—except for the minister, they're the only two wearing suits. The pallbearers have gathered in a solemn group behind the hearse. Perry doesn't recognize any of them. They're all younger, Roland's age, and they all look as though they've borrowed sport coats that are either too large or too tight, one a rumpled blue-and-white seersucker that Perry's certain will split up the back as soon as the guy lifts on his side of the coffin.

But it doesn't split, and Perry stands to the side as they pass, followed by the minister, who holds his Bible in front of him with two hands. Angela, who does see Perry now, moves away from the woman beside her, and Perry steps forward to take Angela's elbow in his hand as though they've rehearsed this, like it's where he's supposed to join them as part of the ceremony, as Roland's special friend. The undertaker brings up the rear, his arms full of flowers. Perry has had lilies sent.

There's no canopy and no chairs, so everybody stands facing the casket, which is black and glitters in the sun—not even enough people to form a semicircle. Perry's in the middle of the line next to Angela. To his right, a woman with a cane who stares up at him and then away. Perry's almost certain from her eyes that it's Roland's mom, though she seems much too old.

"I am the resurrection and the life, saith the Lord: he that believeth in me, though he were dead, yet shall he live: and whosoever liveth and believeth in me, shall never die."

The minister clears his throat. "O, Heavenly Father . . ." he says, but Perry listens instead to Corey, who has started to squirm and fuss, but he relaxes again in Angela's arms when she pulls back her sleeve so he can play with the stretch band of her watch.

". . . and we are all innocents once again in God's Kingdom. . . ."

Perry can hear those crows, and he can hear the woman next to him sniffle into a white handkerchief at the mention of "Our beloved brother Roland," who, as he understands from talking briefly with the family, endured his share of torment, "But Thine is the power," he says, "and the grace of forgiveness shall be in the asking. . . ." He opens his Bible again and reads: "So when this corruptible shall have put on incorruption, and this mortal shall have put on immortality, then shall be brought to pass the saying that is written, Death is swallowed up in victory."

Perry bows his head, and out of the corner of his eye he watches the hem of Angela's black dress move in the breeze.

"Can you take him a minute?" Angela whispers. She means Corey, but he refuses to go to Perry; he's crying now and kicking and becoming even heavier to hold.

The minister raises his voice above the pained screams of this child whose mother can do nothing to make him stop.

"And God shall wipe away all tears from their eyes; and there shall be no more death, neither sorrow, nor crying: neither shall there be any more pain; for the former things are passed away."

He bends at the knees and reaches for a handful of dirt, then turns and casts it onto the coffin, which is perched on canvas straps above the vault.

"Forasmuch as it hath pleased Almighty God, in his wise providence, to take out of this world the soul of our deceased brother, we therefore commit his body to the ground; earth to earth, ashes to ashes, dust to dust."

"Amen," the woman next to Perry says, the word rippling in a short chorus left and right—*amenamenamenamen.*

Perry thinks the minister is going to trip the rollers to lower the coffin, but he's simply moved aside so Perry can step forward to speak. What he's written down is not at all what he means to say, it's too flowery and long-winded, so he does not even take the folded sheet of paper from the inside pocket of his suit coat.

He smiles sadly at Corey, who has stopped crying because Angela has lowered his feet onto the grass. He's wearing nothing black—white shoes and a brightly embroidered sweatshirt and red corduroy pants with straps that cross in the back. He holds tightly to Angela's thumbs. And he's craning his neck and staring up at her and thrusting forward; he wants to walk out from between his mother's legs.

So Perry stoops to one knee, but Corey does not make a stiff-legged rush to him. He watches Perry like a stranger—all eyes are on this man. Except for Angela, they're all wondering who he is. And Perry's eyeing them now. Even dressed up, the pallbearers look as though they've just stepped into a police lineup. All they need are identification numbers on cards hanging from around their necks.

The minister clears his throat and Perry stands, Angela nodding to him like everything's fine, which of course it's not or they wouldn't have gathered here in the dead silence this moment's become.

The undertaker, whose hands are folded, keeps twitching his thumbs, his cuff links glinting gold. Brenda squints, her head cocked to the side—her way of asking what's up. And that older woman—there's something so lifeless about the way her shoulders sag. Her shadow is almost touching Perry's feet. He's almost certain he's going to turn away and bolt back up through the headstones, ducking again under the hedgerow of spruce into the tomblike shade and be gone.

He actually feels short of breath, as he always does in the dream after running all that way from the orchard to the flooded backyard where Janine keeps screaming his name.

"Perry . . . ?" Angela says, and the minister, as though she's really addressing him, begins: "Here the soul occupies an earthly house, a frail tent—" But Perry says, "No, wait." He says, "Sooner or later . . ." but he stops again.

"Dissolving and perishable," the minister continues, and Perry interrupts a second time. He says, "I once saw Roland rub the tip of his little finger on Corey's gums because the baby was cutting teeth and that soothed the pain. Which Roland couldn't figure how to do with other things in his life, but he could with his son, and a man who loved children like that was a gentle man."

"There it will be a building of God . . ." the minister says, raising his voice because this time the backhoe's diesel engine has just started up with a plume of blue smoke. Perry glances over there, and then at Angela, and at the old woman, whose free hand has a tremor but is making the sign of the cross.

"Let us pray," the minister announces, and he begins: "Our Father, who art in heaven . . ." Perry steps back into the line, accidentally nudging Angela's hip with his hand.

The minister finishes reciting the Lord's Prayer and then implores his listeners to have faith and to journey forth into the mysterious but beneficent future of God's divine plan. He says, "God bless us all," and he offers his final condolences by stepping forward and shaking Angela's hand.

The pallbearers, breaking rank, light up on their way back to their cars, their ties already loosened, their conversation a hum.

Someone tugs on Perry's sleeve; it's the woman with the cane. She says, "You were Roland's friend." It's both a question and a statement.

"Yes," he says, his voice overtly penitent, "I was."

She examines him up and down. "I'm Roland's mother," and Perry tells her he knows—the resemblance is unmistakable. She nods, and her eyes turn vacant and misty, her lips squeezed so tightly together, they disappear.

"Roland's father," she says, "we don't even know where he is to tell him what's happened, to say, 'Roland senior, you have a grandson who's almost a year old, but your own son is no longer with us.' I doubt the news would change him one way or another, but he should be told just the same." She says, "Always so much bad news, you'd think God was taking pains to create it and send it our way. Bad news our whole lives, but never to compare with this. This . . ." she says, but she can't finish. She can only shake her head and turn and walk carefully away in the direction of the others.

Which leaves only Angela and Perry—Corey has been carried back to the car by Brenda. The caretaker, though he's half running, half walking, has not yet reached the burial site. When he does, Angela lets go of Perry's hand, and she tells him to go. "Please," she says, "and thank you." He does not stop or glance back or cover his ears or scream out himself or do anything else but walk, left foot, right foot, the enormous grief rising from Angela's mouth as the casket descends.

Chapter 18

Perry's back and arms and shoulders ached worse from three days of hauling pots than if he'd been lifting weights. But multiplied by weeks, he's worked himself into decent shape, his face and neck browner than they've ever been. Au naturel, as Wayne said—sun and wind and spray and rain. An all-seafood diet: steamers and striped bass and blue crabs fresh each day from the docks. Perry's down to 165 pounds—he hasn't felt this good physically in years.

Wayne's taken to calling him "Old Salty," especially since Perry's beard has grown beyond the Clint Eastwood stage. *Old* is indeed correct, Perry said, referring to all the gray—old and grizzled but getting his second wind.

"It's all a matter of pacing yourself," Wayne said, in what he calls "the rat race to the end of the millennium."

Or bow out altogether, Perry amended, and although he's felt revived by the elements, he's known all along this escape on the high seas could only ever be temporary. Reinstatement of his job means he begins that other life again tomorrow. Or doesn't, and he's been contemplating the consequences of that decision. He wonders if Marcia will support whichever way he goes with this.

Though neither of them has used the term *trial separation*, that's what it's been, and five weeks has felt like an eternity. Whatever each of them needs to be cannot be determined by the other's absence. They need to reopen the lines of communication, the reason for their date tonight, their first since splitting up—dinner at Bravo Bravo.

On this last voyage out on *The Greta Garbo*, Perry is taking it easy. He's learned to navigate the lobster route, so he's at the helm this morning, throttling down and sliding deftly inside of the buoys before kicking the engine into neutral. The surface water churns slate gray in the dull September light, the buoys half red and half white, each numbered for identification. Wayne reaches out for the marker with his gaff, yanks forward, and fastens the trawl line to the hydraulic winch, then presses the foot pedal. This has been the recent hot spot, though only in comparison to the overall sparseness of the past couple of weeks. These are Wayne's deepest pots, almost eighty feet down.

Ever since the catch has dwindled, the two men, pouring from their separate thermoses of coffee while motoring downriver, have placed daily bets on which pot will hold the largest lobster, and Perry's twenty bucks rides on this one that he can see now is empty except for two huge spider crabs, their long, silty legs pinching what's left of the stringy white skin of halibut.

"Shit," Perry says, both for losing another bet and because the average has dropped to one keeper for every four or five pots. At $2.75 per pound, Wayne's barely covering his operating costs.

"Hey, you sitting on any hot lottery hunches?" Wayne asks over his shoulder, then swings the pot onto the platform attached to the side of the boat. Like Perry, he's wearing a yellow slicker and yellow rubber bibs and black rubber boots, a glove on the hand that reaches in and tosses the spider crabs back.

"Captain Fucking Ahab," Perry says, a reference Wayne acknowledges by pretending to stomp an ivory leg two steps to the bait barrel. Lashed to the gunwale, a sawed-off harpoon with a sharpened barb. A hardbound *Moby-Dick* is one of only two books Perry has ever seen in Wayne's possession—the other is *Trout Fishing in America*, from which Wayne reads long passages aloud some evenings on the houseboat when he's high and mellow.

Perry's not looking for the white whale—he's simply turning away from the defeat of four consecutive losses: double or nothing on double or nothing. Different lobster pot, some goddamn result, Wayne cackling behind him like a hyena.

Wayne does not have a license to fish New York waters, but Perry can clearly see the mansions of Long Island, the fussiness of manicured shrubbery, the green nap of the lawns like putting surfaces that slope all the way down to the white sand of those long private beaches. Boathouses or gazebos at the ends of the docks—no weekly summer rentals over there in *Great Gatsby* land. On the opposite shore, the toned-down version that's become Groton Long Point. Less pretentious, but still a thousand light-years from the farmhouses and fields of northern Michigan.

Wayne claims the "*land* of the free" is a vagary. He'll pause in his work some mornings and bum a smoke from Perry, then light up and exhale slowly and say, "They've sold their souls to greed and decadence." Then he'll gesture to Perry and to himself and to the deep drafting of the V-shaped hull through the chop and the swells; to the bell clanging of the channel markers; to the heartbeat of the bilge pump after Wayne or Perry scoops and then empties a bucket of seawater across the deck. In a certain slant of early-morning light through the mist, Perry has noticed Wayne staring at the phosphorescent glow of plankton on the floating eelgrass torn up by a storm, or at the two palm fronds staple-tacked above the cabin door. His anthem is to "the *sea* of the free." He'll say, "A sweet, sweet deal, this life."

Also undervalued, although almost nobody's clamoring to buy in at any price—the hours are too long, the work too hard and dangerous and unpredictable. And charmed, Perry believes, for the few who've survived running two- and three-pot trawls. And survived the sudden gales and the fog and the floating debris that can shear a prop clean off, or, worse, can sink a twenty-three-foot craft like Wayne's as though it were a toy. Wayne claims to have watched a house float by, everything but the peak of the roof submerged, the TV antenna sticking up like the remains of a periscope.

Perry politely referred to it as a "misestimation"—a *piece* of roof maybe, blown off in high winds, or floating timber from a salvage barge.

"No way, skipper," Wayne insisted, "it was a house."

"And the closets still full of shoes and clothes, I suppose," Perry said, "and a cheesecake in the oven."

"It's a zany-strange world out here," Wayne said.

"Not that strange; you've been smoking some bad shit, my friend."

"Not a chance," Wayne said. "I saw it straight—a whole house floating by. You stay out here long enough, you'll see things you can hardly believe."

Perry sort of has, last night, in fact, but only in a dream: Main Street underwater, empty dinghies and dories floating loose and bumping up against the plate glass of the storefronts. And Perry motoring slowly by in a runabout—he doesn't know whose. He's late to meet Marcia at the restaurant, but she's not there yet at the window table. Or she's been there and gone. Only the waiter is visible, dressed entirely in white and staring out at Perry like he's a ghost or some shipwrecked sailor who has finally washed ashore. The boat's floor is slippery with sludge and seaweed and snails, and even if he can find a place to tie up, he can't go in looking like this. Where's his sport jacket and slacks? Where's his razor and comb? His Sperry Top-Siders?

Perry wishes Wayne hadn't rousted him from dream sleep—not this dream—he wanted to see where it ended, whether Marcia showed or not and, if she did, what got decided over dinner. He guesses he'll find all that out tonight, and tomorrow he'll give the sea back to the real loners like Wayne who belong out here with their visions.

"Cough up," Wayne says, and Perry takes the twenty from his billfold and slaps it on the console, moving the brass measuring gauge on top so the money doesn't blow out and away. From the eye socket to the back of the carapace, Wayne instructed Perry the first morning out, and if the lobster was a keeper, Perry would press open the banding device and slip a wide red rubber band over each claw, the crusher and the ripper. Otherwise, Wayne said, they'll mangle one another in the holding tank, which, so far, holds fewer than two dozen—hardly worth the trouble of stopping at Ford's, the fish dealer on the Noank docks.

But Wayne's not giving up—he reaches into the barrel for a fish head and twists it onto the bait spike, then latches the pot and heaves it overboard and reaches out with his gaff for the next one. Empty again. Then a short and a cull. But they finish the day by hauling up a granddaddy, a three-plus-pounder, which Wayne holds out like a dark green trophy.

The thick tail snaps and snaps, the lobster attempting to swim backward out of this man's grasp, and away from the hostile oxygen and the brightness of the noontime sun breaking through. But already there's a filmy bubble forming over its mouth, its BB eyes so solidly black, it's impossible to tell where they're looking, both claws wide open, the long antennae wavering in every direction that panic knows.

* * *

Panic's not what Perry feels as he steps off the houseboat and onto the dock, but he is plenty nervous. Until three nights ago, he'd talked with Marcia only twice on the phone, conversations that were cordial and brief and for the purpose of warning her that he needed to stop by the apartment to pick up this item or that. Both times he did, she was gone.

He's seen her once, the day after the funeral. He'd gone for a ride to Westerly, Rhode Island, on his Harley, just to get away for an hour. On his return, he did not speed up to try to beat the descending black-and-white-striped arm of the safety gate—no crazy visions of Evel Knievel airborne across the Mystic River. Perry approached slowly and switched off the ignition, lit a cigarette, and watched the drawbridge open to its full pitch—all this to allow a single yawl to motor through, its jib sheet flapping.

When the ramp of the drawbridge flattened back into West Main, Perry saw Marcia's car facing him, the two of them staring at each other as though from opposite sides of a border crossing. It was a foreign feeling, like no other Perry had ever experienced. They passed like strangers, Marcia slightly lifting her chin and lowering the visor so that Perry couldn't see her eyes through the windshield.

And now they're going to face each other across a table. It was Marcia who suggested they meet on neutral ground, and Perry's already made the short walk from the houseboat, where Wayne's got spareribs cooking on the grill, to the frosted, beveled glass front door of Bravo Bravo. He pulls it open and steps inside.

Marcia's already seated, and Perry smiles and points to her when the maître d' asks if it's a party of one. Jesus, no, Perry thinks, it's certainly not, not this evening, and he makes his way over to the table he requested by the window. Marcia sips from her glass of ice water, never taking her eyes off him as he sits down and leans back and pulls open the pleats and folds of his linen napkin.

"It's called the bird of paradise," Marcia says.

"What is?" Perry asks.

"The fancy way the napkin's folded. It's very elegant," she says.

Perry agrees—it's a welcome change from the squares of paper towels Wayne tears off from the roll and slaps down for every meal.

"It's funny, isn't it," Marcia says, "how seldom we dined out over all these years—candles and flowers? We should've made a point of treating ourselves better. And of treating each other better, don't you think?"

Perry shows that he does when he asks the waitress, who introduces herself as Willow, for a wine list. She's pale-skinned and very tall and looks like she might have played some basketball. She has that seductive Geena Davis overbite, a pleasant, accommodating smile.

"Yes, before dinner," Perry tells her, and she returns cradling a pricey bottle of Bordeaux. An excellent choice, she'd said. Full-bodied. Perry indulges the formality of smelling the cork and testing the first dry sip, which, of course, he approves. "Very nice," he says, and Willow pours, two half glasses, finishing with a practiced no-drip reverse twist of the bottle, which she then sets down.

"Enjoy," she says, "and I'll check back in a few minutes to take your orders."

Perry and Marcia both nod, and each surrenders to the silence as they wait for the other to propose a toast. Neither does, and they simultaneously look away, first out the window and then at their menus. Perry's eyes stray from the appetizers to Marcia, then back again and down the list of entrées. But he's not really reading them. Or he is, but his mind registers only isolated words: *Florentine*, *en croûte*, *julienne*, *almond glaze*, so when Marcia asks what he's decided on, Perry says, "What do you recommend?"

"For starters? That we move carefully—that we not attempt to say too much too soon. Let's concentrate on *this* evening. That'll be enough."

"Doesn't sound like you," Perry says. "Usually you're the one—"

"No," she says. "I was hoping you wouldn't do this."

"I'm not—I mean, I have just a couple things—"

"And you think I don't?"

Perry shrugs, and although he does not intend it to be, it's much too dismissive a gesture.

"Right," Marcia says, Perry focusing on the magnified wedge of lime Marcia's pushed below the ice with her spoon, and he follows the lime all the way to Marcia's lips as she lifts the water glass and takes another sip. Her eyelashes are long and dark, and for the few seconds her eyes stay closed, Perry wishes he could disappear, reenter the restaurant, begin the evening all over again.

"You drive?" Perry asks, attempting to reroute the conversation, and Marcia points out the window to where her car is parked diagonally across the street.

"And you know what was on the radio? That Paul Simon song—the one about slip sliding away—and I thought, There's our anthem. You slipping in one direction, me sliding in another. It's strange, Perry, being close enough to reach over and touch you, yet feeling so far apart, so remote."

Perry offers his hand, palm up, halfway across the table, but Marcia only stares at it, then, meeting Perry's eyes, she says, "I haven't had a bite to eat all day, so I'd have an appetite, but I'm not the least bit hungry. Why would I be with my stomach churning inside the way it is? Don't make me feel any worse, Perry, by rushing ahead to things I'm not ready to talk about."

"So where do we begin?"

"With a compliment?"

"You look spectacular wearing pearls," he says.

"You bought them for me for a ten-year-anniversary present."

Perry remembers buying them, perfectly matched Mikimotos, the

241 ✳

rose luster so fine, he could see his reflection clearly in each pearl—it was as if he'd picked up a strand of tiny round mirrors. The jeweler said they'd keep their shine from the natural oils on a woman's chest and breastbone, and so they should always be worn with a low neckline. He complimented Perry on having exquisite taste, then asked if Perry wanted the pearls gift-wrapped. Perry said yes, and the jeweler, disappearing into the back room, called out, "Your wife's a very lucky woman." Marcia might not agree, not anymore, but she is wearing the necklace, and she's absolutely stunning, flawless, Perry believes, and as she leans slightly forward, he watches the candle flame dance from pearl to perfect pearl.

This past June, he forgot their anniversary for the first time, and the late rain check he offered for a fancy dinner out never materialized. Until now, of course, delinquent for over three months, and it's true: "The nearer your destination, the more you're slip slidin' away."

Just hang tight, he tells himself. Whatever you do don't—I repeat, because you're a dumb fuck sometimes, Perry Lafond—don't lose this foothold. No, toehold is more like it. If Marcia would only take his hand. He needs her help more than ever if he stands any chance of climbing back into the world. But he refuses to beg—she's made it perfectly clear that she's not ready to hear about any big dirt, or about how he's changed now and that this time it's for keeps, or about how he *does* want a kid, a house at the end of a certain cul-de-sac, a different job, and to hell at last with all the would'ves and could'ves and should'ves that have consumed his life. But Marcia's not going to buy it, not in a repentant gush, so Perry folds both hands in his lap and asks simply if a compliment can still be a compliment if it's solicited.

"Your beard, you mean?"

"You catch on fast," he says. "You like?"

"Umm—ask our waitress what she thinks. I'm too used to you the other way, without."

"I'm not interested in waitress Willow," Perry says. "I want to know what *you* think."

"I think kissing you would feel like kissing another man."

And there it is—small miracle—she's opened the door, be it just a crack, but enough for Perry to get a glimpse of what she sees in this "other" man. He's no Mel Gibson, but acceptably handsome, early middle age, all tanned and in pretty decent shape, obviously a man who's been working outdoors. He's well dressed and smiling and sitting up straight, but there's a mix of something else there, too, something he can't hide and doesn't even seem to want to. Sadness, perhaps, which can be awfully attractive on someone who has faced and come through it. Some gray in the hair and beard, but that's distinguished, mature. He doesn't seem at all like the pushy or the swooning or the cocksure type, does he? All he asks, in fact, is that this elegant woman in pearls and a black dress get to know him. Hey, after those awkward first words, the good-talk subject of kissing might even go somewhere if only Perry could signal Willow away.

"Have you decided?" she asks, pen and pad in hand, and Perry says, "No, not yet," because the decisions are all Marcia's. If it were up to Perry, she'd fall immediately back in love with him and take him home, which may or may not be out of the question—it all depends on the ebb and flow, their degree of intimacy, the wine, the right or the wrong thing said. Luck and timing. Trust.

"Could we have a few minutes more?" Marcia says.

"Of course," Willow says, "take your time," and she leaves, heading back toward the kitchen.

"You've lost weight," Perry says.

"So have you."

"A few pounds, but I needed to. It's all that fresh, clean air."

"You look good, Perry, you really do."

"Even with the beard?"

"Even with the beard," she says, and Perry strokes it in a mock show of self-congratulation. It's a weak smile she gives him, and when her eyes focus again on the menu, Perry asks, "You think you can eat—maybe something light?"

"I'm going to try," she says. "Wouldn't want it said that I was the one who ruined the date."

"Do you remember our first one—not when we met, but our actual first date?"

"The real question is whether *you* remember it."

"As if it were yesterday," Perry says. "I picked you up at your dorm. It was snowing hard—big, slow, wet December flakes that you'd catch on your tongue as they floated down through the security vapor lights. You were wearing a red sweater and matching earmuffs, and we walked together all the way across campus to the library because I had a biology exam the next day."

"Which you barely passed. *D-* wasn't it?"

"The life cycles of moss," Perry says. "It never dawned on me that moss *had* sexual parts—I'd always assumed it was something soft to lie down on in the summertime by a lake or a stream, and correct me if I'm wrong, but didn't we—"

"It was great," Marcia says, but in a way that makes clear how these recent years have paled by comparison. Ann Arbor was the beginning of their future together; each had imagined meeting the other there, and almost as soon as they did, they felt an urgency to finish up and get their degrees and get married. They felt giddy, like young kids, after Marcia's graduation, and even more so the following May when Perry walked from the stage, clutching his diploma. It was the excitement of dreamers on the brink of something colossal, that magic love time before growing up and entering life's school of hard knocks. Hands-on courses such as Compromise and Concession 101, and Personality Flaws and Its Resentments 102, prerequisites to those more advanced classes in pettiness and provocation and treachery and deceit and disappointment. The offerings seemed endless: classes in tedium and insinuation and reasonlessness. A seminar Perry must have aced in all the fucked-up permutations of conscience and guilt. A thorough education, Perry's concluded, complete with fire drills for when your best-laid plans finally curled up in flames.

After that? You submit, as Perry's dad has, to defeat, or you don't. If you don't, maybe you invite your wife to dine out fancy at Bravo Bravo for the purpose of asking her to take you back. To take *me* back, Perry enunciates to himself, and he says, "So anyway."

"I'm going to try the swordfish," Marcia says.

"Sounds good," Perry says, but when Willow returns, he orders prime rib, the sixteen-ounce cut. "Rare," he says. "Horseradish on the side."

Marcia does not protest when Willow adds more wine to her untouched glass. No need to worry anymore about alcohol impeding fertility, though Marcia makes no move to cynically toast that, either.

"Cheers," Perry says, but they do not clink glasses. Marcia does not even lift hers. She ticks the rim with her fingernail, the hum vibrating between them.

"How's your mom, Perry? I've sent a few cards, but I haven't called, not since you left there."

Perry calls at the same time every other day from the houseboat, Wayne napping, and Perry on the deck, staring up or down river as he tries to decipher the partial words his mom chokes out. "It's painful to listen to," Perry says. "My dad takes the phone every minute or so and says, 'What your mother means,' but I don't believe he really knows. Or, worse yet, has ever known."

"I wouldn't be so sure," Marcia says. "People who've been together as long as they have find ways to communicate."

Not in this case, Perry thinks, imagining his mom enthroned all day in her wheelchair, the pink hue of her bathrobe even pinker where she sits too close amid the splashing colors of TV light, the living room shades drawn tightly to the sills.

"Makes sense," Perry says, sounding unconvinced. He's fiddling with the salt and pepper shakers, and now Marcia does reach over, and she strokes the back of his hand, right where the scar curves down toward his palm. Perry's afraid if he shifts his gaze back to her, he'll burst into tears. He's already close, but able to squeeze away the moistness under the pressure of his lids.

"Perry, listen to what your dad once said to me. It was the evening I first met him, and he and I were alone outside, and he said, 'Marcia, we have eighty-five species of trees in Michigan. That's more than any other state, more than all of Europe.' A complete non sequitur in a conversation about you boys, about you and Hank. Not what you'd call subliminal, but lying awake that night I thought, Of course—he wanted you and me to consider putting down roots closer by. He was afraid of you going away for good. Your mom, too—I could tell by the way she kept staring at you all weekend. They love you, Perry. That's all they're trying to say."

"Tough to interpret sometimes," he says.

"Like tonight."

Perry nods, then repeats what she's just said: "Yes, like tonight."

"Maybe it'll get easier after awhile."

"You don't sound all that certain," Perry says, and he doesn't need any help interpreting her long pause, and then her response: "I'm not," she says.

Willow arrives with their spinich salads, brings each separately from the tray to the table, then grinds clockwise on the pepper mill until Marcia says, "That's fine." Perry declines. "No thanks," he says, and reaches for his glass of wine.

He'd sure like a cigarette about now, but Bravo Bravo is smoke-free. He could excuse himself and step outside for a few minutes into the semidarkness, but he's afraid he might just walk away, walk the half mile through town, then uphill to Elm Street, take a right to the apartment and wait for Marcia there. He's got his house key with him this time. He could simply unlock the door, turn on the lights. He could load *Mystic Pizza* into the VCR, pop some popcorn in the microwave, take his place on the love seat so that when Marcia got home and changed out of her dress and into her nightshirt, she could curl up next to him and he could push the play button and put his arm around her and everything would seem like old times. Nothing to it—just turn back the goddamned clock, a concept so ridiculously stupid that it's not a concept at all, but, rather, a delusion.

To move at all is to go forward into the unknown of the coming days and weeks and months until it can be determined whether or not Perry and Marcia Lafond can ever truly feel married again. They're both still wearing their wedding bands, and certainly neither of them has mentioned divorce. That it should even occur as a possibility to Perry is so threatening that he can only respond by wetting his lips and swallowing hard. He hasn't touched his salad and he probably won't, and he'll end up asking for a doggie bag for that large portion of prime rib he'll be unable to finish, and he'll forget the doggie bag on the table when he and Marcia get up to leave, because the last thing on his mind will be leftovers for tomorrow's lunch. He'll be concentrating his full attention on Marcia, trying to brace himself for the moment she says good night and turns away. He's got less than an hour until that moment, and he's cautioning himself again against any testimonial dirges, against any quick-fix spiel, because that sequence of words doesn't exist.

Instead, some chitchat, a few guarded laughs, some looks, naturally, the wine bottle almost empty by the time their dinners arrive, so Perry orders half a carafe more. The food smells delicious, and it is—what they manage to eat of it.

"Perish the thought," Marcia says, talking about Neil, "that he should ever begin to act human. They converse only through their lawyers, and do you have any idea how expensive divorce talk can get when the clients have money? And how messy?"

Perry hadn't even realized that Pauline and the kids had pulled up stakes at the beach and headed back to Boston. Makes sense that they would, but he feels lousy about not having called, and even worse that nobody from *that* side of the family made an effort to contact him, as though whatever comfort he might have offered could possibly matter anymore.

"And the kids—how they holding up?"

"J.J.'s already missing days at school, and that's after perfect attendance all of last year. Virtine? She's been a handful, saying some really terrible things to Pauline. Which isn't abnormal for an intelligent, rebellious nine-year-old who blames her mother for the marriage breaking up. But it's not nine-year-oldish when you slam your bedroom door after being sent to your room, then immediately open that door and yell back down the stairs, 'La-di-fucking-da.' Where do they even hear that?"

Marcia's not soliciting an answer, and although Perry's the right person to ask, he doesn't provide one. The plates have been cleared and it's completely dark outside, the days getting shorter, the sporadic drift of traffic vanishing both ways. Perry and Marcia have passed on dessert, but they've said yes to a hummer and two straws, and as they drink at this window table where the candle has burned all the way down, their foreheads touch.

It's not only the wine and the Kahlúa and the rum—it's also hoping against hope that Marcia will have a last-minute change of heart and invite him home. The evening has gone well, considering, and Perry cannot keep his eyes off the back of her neck and her shoulder blades, the slight bounce of her hair as she walks in front of him toward the door. She's carrying her sweater, which he takes and holds open to her before they step outside into the cool air. Then it's arm in arm down the stairs to the sidewalk, where she thanks him and asks him to think hard and honestly about how he feels. "About you and me, Perry. About everything that has led to us standing here."

Perry shoves his hands deep into his pockets, afraid he's going to reach out and cradle Marcia's face and guide her closer to him than she wants to be.

"I don't know why I'm quoting our dads so much tonight, but my dad told me once never to run too far from a marriage I meant to save. Slam a few doors, he said, even the car door if you have to get out of the house. If it's raining or snowing, go ahead and start the engine to keep warm, but never drive away. But that's what I'm going to do, because I have to. Call me," she says. "Or better yet, surprise me and stop by the school—I'll be working late the next few nights."

"I might just do that," he says, and Marcia opens her purse and takes her keys out, dangling them. Perry does not hold out his palm, not even as a joke. "Good-night," she says, and steps up and kisses him on the lips. "I miss you," she says, "a lot, but don't ask for too much right now, okay? Okay, Perry?"

He nods and then watches her cross Main to the other side, where she opens the car door and slides in. When the engine starts, Perry takes his first backward step from under the lighted restaurant window, then turns and walks in the direction of the houseboat. He thinks, A man slightly tipsy who's returning to his friend's floating bachelor pad should feel less married, more happily *unattached*. But it's the other way around, and it's dark where Perry stops midway out on the upriver side of the drawbridge. For a change, he does not light up. And it would not be an act if he turned his face into the breeze and cried. It even feels like the sensible way to spend a little time alone, given the countless times he's resisted this same urge late at night. So he presses his forehead against the flat steel of the railing, and before he closes his eyes, he sees the stars reflected and rippling on the water. Is it an oar or a keel he hears, as in somebody being ferried away in the night? If so, where to? And is arriving there always so full of tears? Then let them flow, Perry thinks. Let the starlight shimmer and spill, and the silver hull of the gibbous moon continue its slow course above the rivers and towns and bays, above the cemeteries of grief, and the orchards and the sheets somebody's forgotten on the clothesline. And yes, above a burned-out Firebird in a field of weeds where not long ago a baby fell sound asleep between two men who talked about the future.

Perry's crying so hard now, his whole body rocks and rocks in the wake true sadness always leaves as it passes.

Chapter 19

Off-season's a tourist-town word, but since his resignation, Perry's been thinking of it as the more permanent condition. Like Nietzsche, Perry challenges the concept that "the value of an act must be measured by its consequences." Fuck the consequences, Perry's decided, and let the *act* be. And then move on in your own sweet time to whatever the will decrees.

Marcia, told after the fact, was elated by Perry's decision to quit. She called it his liberation, and he *is* feeling more than a little bit liberated on this last day as a parole and probation officer, but mostly he's feeling it for Walt Bolobas, whose early discharge has been approved. Perry has already called from the houseboat to give him the good news, and now Perry's driving out there on his Harley, the paperwork in one saddlebag, a bagful of apples for Rocky in the other.

The morning is sunny but brisk, and Perry's driving slowly out of town and by the shipyard, where the boats are shrink-wrapped in dry dock, past the gift shops that have closed until spring, and the bed-and-breakfasts that have already taken their awnings down.

On the Walkman, Perry's singing along to Lyle Lovett:

> "And if I had a boat
> I'd go out on the ocean,
> And if I had a pony
> I'd ride him on my boat."

He likes the crazy connectedness of the lyrics, "'And me,'" he continues on the chorus, "'upon my pony on my boat.'"

But it's a different tune that Walt's playing out on the front porch when Perry drives up and dismounts and applauds the accordion music.

"For my money," Walt says, "Myron Florin's still the greatest artist ever lived."

Either the news of his early discharge has not sunk in or Walt does not know how else to respond.

Perry rattles the papers as he walks to the top stair.

"Finally free," Walt says.

"Indeed," Perry confirms, "as free as a bird," and he smiles and gestures toward the bird hotels, which, like the hotels in Mystic, suddenly have plenty of vacancies.

"The theme shows," Walt says, "'Way Out West' or 'At the Circus' or 'Aloha Hawaii,' and it's a-one and a-two," and Perry confirms that he's just old enough to remember how that bubble machine spewed bubbles into the air behind the orchestra. Champagne music, and this conversation insists on celebrating *that* past, decades before Walt's arrest and conviction, when Lawrence Welk was still snapping thumb to forefinger.

"Half of America tuned in," Walt says, "not only to hear those polkas but to see Myron Florin's beautiful on-screen smile. All of us repeat attenders. Live TV—entire families gathering each week to watch that show."

It's true, Perry's mom and dad side by side in their identical Barca-Loungers, Janine always sound asleep next to Perry or Hank on the sofa. Perry guesses the Lennon Sisters must be pushing sixty, and what *were* the names of that dance-team couple? "Sure, Bobby and Elaine," Walt says.

Perry has no idea if they're even alive, but Myron Florin's alive, Walt says. "I saw him just the other night on PBS, still smiling and playing up a storm."

Walt slides his arms out of the straps and lays the accordion on its back on the porch swing, takes the papers from Perry and lowers them like sheet music, then gives the swing a push with his foot, and it's that image Perry can't shake from his mind—an accordion on a swing, the keys so white and black each time they move from the shade into the sun and back. Perry would only be flattering himself to mention that he used to play the saxophone. He and Walt have never had to fish around for conversation—since early on, they've enjoyed each other's company, and Perry knows they will both miss these talks and the short jaunts out back to the paddock.

But that's not where they're headed, because Walt has already put the apples on the stairs and said to Perry, "Follow me," and he leads him into the woodworking shop and closes the door behind Perry. There's plenty of light coming through the windows.

Walt stoops and reaches under the plywood bench and says, "Here," and he uncovers and then lifts a rocking horse from the floor. "A rocking pony," Walt says, and it's a spitting image of Rocky, a miniature: the same long grayish tail and spotted rump, the eyelashes jet black when Perry brushes aside the mane, donated, Walt explains, by Rocky himself.

Like the saddle, the rockers have been painted red, the bridle and the reins and the cinch underneath the belly all made of real leather.

Walt has even fashioned aluminum edging around each small hoof to resemble horseshoes. He must have been working on this ever since Perry mentioned that he and Marcia were trying to have kids. That seems like ages ago.

"For your firstborn," Walt says, "and you bring that baby over here someday to meet and ride the real pony. You'll do that for me, I hope. Will you do that?"

It's the first favor Walt has ever asked of Perry, who says, "For sure," and he means it, though making good on this particular promise is a long shot at best. What did the doctors say—12 or 13 percent success rate with the Pergonal for women Marcia's age? Whatever, the odds weren't good enough. Not yet, and the fertility talk has been put on hold, and they've not slept together for over two months.

"You take care," Walt says, and extends his hand. Perry shakes it. What he usually says to discharged parolees is, "Stay clean." To this man he says, "Thank you," and turns away and opens the door and steps back outside into the bright sunlight with his farewell gift. He resists the urge to go see Rocky, and instead heads straight for his Harley.

He sees Mrs. Bolobas peeking again from between the blinds, and this time Perry pauses and waves to her, but she does not wave back. The accordion is still on its back on the swing, the bellows spread open between the keyboard and buttons, the discharge papers blown onto the floor.

And Walt stands staring from the doorway of his woodworking shop, but he does not smile like Myron Florin—not even when Perry raises the rocking pony into the air to thank him again. Then he straps on his goggles and helmet, starts the Harley with the electric start, and places the rocking pony between his knees, the red rockers straddling the gas tank. This'll work, and when Perry glances up at Walt, he's nowhere to be seen, and the blinds are closed again in the living room, the swing perfectly still.

✳ 254

Perry does not toot or flash his headlight. He simply shifts into first and U-turns into the slow weave he makes down the driveway, avoiding the horse chestnuts that have fallen since he arrived.

The morning feels full of farewells, especially when Perry sees the FOR SALE sign in Angela's front yard. BY APPOINTMENT, the sign says, but Perry's not here for a showing—he's viewed the house inside and out. He's spent the night here, and he's fed and changed the baby, made himself coffee, found the laundry chute in the closet while searching for a place to hide the gun. He's felt his stomach knot up in the close presence of the woman who owns this property, and to whom he later made an offer to become intimately involved, to forfeit everything, which she rejected, and he's not here to counter with another. He's not entirely certain why he's stopped by. If it were to touch her again, he wouldn't be this relaxed when she answers the door. She's wearing flip-flops and shorts and one rubber glove and she's holding a bottle of Windex, her nipples erect against the stretch fabric of her tank top. Perry can see Corey in the playpen behind her—he's watching a single red balloon bounce across the ceiling, propelled by the sudden draft, a white string trailing. It reminds Perry of a kite.

"Hi, Angela," he says, and she says hi back, but she seems surprised to see him standing there, then immediately embarrassed by what she calls her "Cinderella getup." Perry wishes he could think of something witty to say about the prince and the glass slipper, but he can't.

"I don't know why I'm spiffing the place up so much," she says, "mopping and dusting everywhere and doing the windows until my arms ache. I guess maybe I just want the new owners to like the house better than I did."

"You mean . . . it's already sold?"

"If the people get approved, it is, which I don't think can be all that difficult, considering Roland and I got approved."

"Wow," Perry says, "was that fast."

"It was like magic, Perry. The realtor walked them through—by 'them,' I mean this young guy and his wife—and later that afternoon I get a call saying the couple are motivated to buy but they feel the asking price is a tad high and blah blah blah, until an agreeable figure is reached, and now I'm cleaning like a woman possessed. They want to set the closing for as soon as possible, so I'm going to start packing right away."

"And move in with Brenda for a while—isn't that what you told me?"

"It is, but I've changed my mind. I'm going to live with my mom in Massachusetts. She said I should be with family now, and I think she's right—I do. At least I hope she is." Angela reaches out and touches Perry's sleeve and says, "Come in," and she closes the door behind him.

"A year old," Perry says when he sees the cake, the vanilla frosting covered with colored sprinkles, a single half-burned-down candle in the center.

"He loves when you light it and sing to him and then blow the candle out."

Corey's standing, his fingers poking through the fishnet of the playpen. He keeps staring at Perry, who picks up Roland's lighter, his initials—R.K.K.—engraved in fancy script. Perry clicks it open, his thumb flicking against the striker wheel, and when it lights on the first try, Perry begins: "Happy birthday to you . . ." the candle spitting like a tiny pink sparkler. He takes a step toward Corey and bends to one knee. "Make a wish," he says, and maybe that's what Corey's smile is—a wish smile. Perry says, "That's good," and he blows out the candle. Corey looks over at his mother when she claps, the rubber glove making a kind of spongy applause.

She asks Perry if she can cut him a slice, but he declines. He says,

"I've got a present for Corey—let me go get it," which he does, and carries it back inside.

"My God," Angela says, "it's so beautiful, Perry. Where in the world did you get it?" She strokes the mane and the tail, pats the spotted rump.

"Okay, cowboy," he says, and Angela lifts Corey out of the playpen and lowers him into the saddle as Perry rocks the pony. "Giddyap," he says, and when he looks at Angela, she's staring right at him, and Corey's laughing and kicking his legs.

"I wish I had a camera," Angela says, and Perry's impossible wish is that it could be Roland kneeling in a birthday snapshot with his wife and son. "I know," Angela says, as if reading Perry's mind, "I know."

And the rest is good-bye, which, Angela says, needn't be drawn out. Perry's tied the balloon string to the pony, and Corey is on his back in the playpen with a bottle. Perry's hand is on the doorknob. He's wearing boots and he feels much taller than Angela, who says, "Not all that long ago—three years or so ago when I had ear surgery—they had to give me two shots in recovery to bring me out of the anesthesia. I must've not wanted to come back. But here I am," and Perry's eyes travel from her feet up the entire length of her body, right to the part in her hair, then back to her face, the high cheekbones, the lips he bends to kiss.

It's not a particularly long kiss. And even though neither of them actually presses against the other, Perry can feel all of her, and everything that has gone unsaid and will go unsaid now that she steps away, and he turns the doorknob and opens the door and closes it slowly behind him. He does not pause or turn around.

There's a flatbed truck backing across the field toward the Firebird, its removal part of the sale agreement, Angela said earlier.

"You the one paying?" the driver yells out to Perry. "Who then?" he shouts when Perry shakes his head no, and Perry points toward the house. The guy waves in acknowledgment, but he's going to get out and walk over there nonetheless and settle up before he'll cart the junker away.

Perry's almost sure it's a borzoi he sees in the passenger seat. The guy, climbing down from the truck, tells the dog to stay. He calls him Buster, and Perry thinks Buster's a good name for a borzoi who doesn't bolt or bark or show any alarm from the noise of the twin-engine plane as it banks around from the west and descends above the Firebird and the flatbed and the red gas can somebody simply left, for whatever reason, to rust in the weeds.

Chapter 20

Perry does not speculate excessively on the number of minor changes. Nor does he approve or disapprove. Nor detect any meaning beyond the inevitable shiftings brought on by his absence. A new mattress on the bed. A bar of glycerine soap in the shower, filmy-feeling on his skin, and perfumy, like a magazine scent strip. All the freshly folded laundry hers—panty hose and bras and nightgown, the balled-up socks on top, and her side of the bedroom closet encroaching halfway into his. The bulk of it, he's noticed, is a new fall wardrobe—wool skirts and sweaters and a waist-length camel's hair coat he likes. The sunlight is all different through the windows.

His first night back was last night. As Marcia said, after most of the summer and early fall away, and without having taken their annual excursion to either Block Island or Martha's Vineyard. She's admitted to enjoying their dates more and more, but before making love, she said, "So, here we are, back where we started."

Perry rephrased it to sound more optimistic. He said, "The honeymoon begins again," and although Marcia stayed silent as Perry led her into the bedroom, he believes he can retrieve what's been lost and make it spark and then catch fire again.

There have been no heavy-duty discussions about what he'll do next for a job, though he's been kicking a few ideas around. He's already received a letter from a defense attorney in New London named Simon Covert, nicknamed "Simon Convert" by those who'd like to see the guilty go down hard. He's asked Perry about any interest in working for the firm as a counter PSI—a presentence investigator, meaning he'd draw up favorable profiles of the accused. An "exaggerate all the positives" kind of job. Which is basically his reputation anyway, the letter said, so he wouldn't even be jumping sides. But jumping into the same trap, Perry thinks, though he's not ruling any offers out. Marcia's encouraged him just to be a husband for a while, and who knows, maybe a father, but she hasn't pushed on that at all, saying she's discovered that a baby cannot be their victory or their defeat. Perry's the one who keeps bringing up the subject—the combination of house husband and dad doesn't sound half bad.

"You're a sore loser," Marcia says after swishing her third consecutive free throw—all underhanded. She's barefoot and wearing shorts and a University of Michigan sweatshirt, blue and gold. Perry insists the color scheme of their alma mater is blue and maize. It has nothing whatsoever to do, he argues, with the eye of the beholder.

He can't distract her with this or any other argument. She's fully concentrated, and deadly with this old-fashioned technique: legs bowed and bent at the knees, and both heels lifting just slightly, then touching down on the hardwood at the instant of release.

Perry has never seen a basketball float so slowly—it's as though the slight reverse spin intends to neutralize all forward motion. Almost nongravitational, he thinks, and stares beyond Marcia, stares at the moon and stars through the wire-mesh window, and conjures up a planetary image: lunar ball, but only until the net snaps straight up after another made shot. When he attempts to duplicate it, the ball rims out. He's already an H-O-R-S—one more miss and Marcia wins her second round of H-O-R-S-E.

He challenges her to show some spunk, some versatility—a slashing cut into the paint for a pull-up bank shot, or how about a long-range jumper, a three-pointer, or a Kareem Abdul-Jabbar skyhook. That's invention. "C'mon," Perry pleads, "anything to rescue the game from the horizontal 1950s." He'll settle for anything that's even fractionally crowd-pleasing. "Consider the fans," he chides, "who've paid good money to be entertained—winning's not everything. They want style—entertainment and style."

"Accuracy *is* entertaining," Marcia says, "and stylish. And don't flatter yourself, Mr. Michael Jordan, because there's nobody here except you and me." She points emphatically to each of them. "You," she says, "and me."

"Every shooter plays to the crowd," Perry says. "You have to crank up the volume in your head—you have to imagine them in the bleachers, Marcia. Otherwise, what's the point?"

"Well, whoever's there," Marcia points out, "isn't saying boo—they're simply watching you get trounced. Now throw it here."

Perry's standing underneath the basket again, and he skips her a two-handed bounce pass, like his junior high coach taught on your basic give and go.

"Learn to lose gracefully," she says, the slap of the ball echoing in the empty gymnasium as she dribbles back to the foul line.

"Hey," he says, "you've got great legs," and signals time-out by tapping the fingers of his right hand against the other palm.

"Won't work," she says. "You're done for—admit it."

"Not until the fat lady sings, I'm not," he says, and Marcia forces the basketball up under the front of her sweatshirt and breaks into a gushy rendition of "Just a Closer Walk with Thee," the opening track from *White Men Can't Jump*, Perry's afternoon video rental, a film he and Marcia saw together at the theater last spring and will watch again later tonight.

From a standing position, Perry jumps straight up and grabs the rim, and before letting go, he says, "White *women* can't jump."

"But they can dance," Marcia says, hands on her hips and appearing as though she'll simply squat and give birth any minute, but not before Perry walks over and switches off the overheads. From the dark stage, he watches Marcia waltz into the spotlight of the moon at midcourt. She has slid both hands inside the sweatshirt pouch, palms pressing the ball.

Perry claps and whistles, and Marcia says, "I can hear the cheering now," and she pivots up onto her tiptoes, twirling and bobbing as if following the weight of her enormous belly.

Perry wishes at this moment that she *really* were dancing with the unborn, and he the expectant father cheering her on. He knows they are both lost in the fantasy of what her body would feel. But of course there's been no morning sickness and no fatigue, and her breasts, still upcurved, have not started to enlarge.

Before coming down to shoot hoops, they stopped in Marcia's classroom, where Perry agreed he'd visit the kids next week during story time—he's got in mind a story about a talking jellyfish, but nobody knows he's talking, because they can never find his mouth. Something in it about being heard but never listened to, which is no fun, is it? And have any of them ever felt like that?

"No," Marcia said when Perry asked. "Hero Lachapello is a boy, an adopted Korean child." Perry saw Hero's name on one of the twenty-two paper apples on the limbs of the paper tree on the bulletin board. Each apple had two leaves and a stem and, above the tree in multicolored letters, YOU'RE THE APPLE OF MY EYE. Perry walked up and down the aisles, the miniature desks only as high as his knees. Even if Marcia were to conceive tonight, which she won't, it would be seven years before their child was assigned a seat in a second-grade classroom, Perry and Marcia closer to fifty than to forty by then. Which is the way with time, with all good things, Marcia says, that eventually come of age.

She pirouettes into a perfect plié, heels together, toes pointing away 180 degrees, stomach still bulging like an overdue ballerina. It crosses Perry's mind to lift her up from behind by the waist and carry her in and out of the moonlight. Her head is tilted back, arms outstretched but cocked at the elbows and wrists like the spread wings of a stork. And Marcia holding a different position each time through the light, a kind of strobe-effect pantomime, an exotic midnight concert.

Perry keeps expecting Marcia to invite him to join her, some silent cheek-to-cheek like smitten teenagers, which is what he'd like. But this is going to be a solo performance, the choreography strictly female. So Perry sits down on the edge of the stage, dangling his legs, hands folded in his lap.

Though he cannot remember more than the gist of it, the Nietzsche passage he keeps flashing on is this one: ". . . and if this is my alpha and omega, that all that is heavy and grave should become light; all that is body, dancer . . ."

She's balanced on one leg, the other extended straight back, the arabesque held motionless until her fingertips reach for the floor, and she rotates slowly onto her back, arching it, knees bent and pointing toward the rafters. Perry cannot see her face—it's blocked by her belly, the low-luster glitter of light spreading beneath her like water.

He's read about women in labor submerging themselves neck-deep in birth tanks, their babies born underwater, a warmer, the article said, and less shocking arrival into this world. Perry doesn't buy it. If Marcia ever does give birth, he intends to be there in the delivery room, but not to watch the freaky occurrence of his child rising to the surface, tiny fists opening like fins. He understands all about our biological past—webbed fingers and toes, gills instead of lungs, scales, not skin. It's all too cold-blooded. Perry will take a rain check on the primordial.

Marcia hugs her belly. She's squatting now, her running shorts very white on her thighs; then she scuttles crablike into the perimeter dark, then back again, in and out, as though pulled by the waves. If Perry'd brought Marcia's Walkman, he'd play Van Morrison's *Moondance*. Not to slam-dunk to, but just to hear Van sing it's "a fantabulous night to make romance." Perry wonders what tune Marcia's imagining—she's mouthing lyrics and thrusting her hips from side to side until the basketball is shaken loose. After executing a simple layup, she carries the ball over and hands it to Perry.

"Okay," she challenges, "duplicate it." She's panting and laughing. "Any questions? Any part of it you'd like me to repeat?" She squeezes Perry's bare knees, wedging them apart so she can lean forward, her head turned sideways and resting on Perry's bare chest.

Those are the rules—you observe carefully, then appropriate not only your opponent's made shot but every move preceding it; you make all of it your own. There's no way Perry can redo what he's just seen. He remembers clearly every detail, and will continue to remember, replaying each one over and over in his mind's eye. And concede each time that he cannot compete at this level—it's a mismatch, and he presses his hand to Marcia's back. Her sweatshirt is soaked. Perry has hardly even broken a sweat.

She leans far enough away to give him a high five, then one with the other hand, and they interlock fingers and draw back together and make out for a long time in the semidark. They're acting like they're sixteen again and cutting class. But older, too, and Perry lowers himself off the stage and down onto his knees and lifts Marcia's shorts even higher up her legs and starts kissing them on the insides of the thighs. They taste like salt, like the sea.

"Not here," Marcia says, "not at school," and this time she *does* take his hand and leads him into the faint, soft spotlight of the moon, to the very heart of this dance floor where they stop and embrace but do not move. Not one inch. Not yet. And then together, they do.

✳ 264

LUCKY MAN, LUCKY WOMAN

Jack Driscoll

DISCUSSION QUESTIONS

1. In the opening sentence of *Lucky Man, Lucky Woman*, Perry is reading this passage from Nietzsche: "When marrying, one should ask oneself this question: Do you believe that you will be able to converse well with this woman into your old age? Everything else in marriage is transitory." How is this philosopher important in understanding Perry's great despair? And how does Perry's job as a parole officer contribute to this free fall?

2. Fertility is an issue throughout, but more as a device to exacerbate Perry's deep-seated fear of bringing a child into the world. How have his childhood and his job convinced him that his fears are real and justified?

3. How do Perry's and Marcia's jobs define, at least in part, their attitudes toward family, children, and the future? How do they represent the two different worlds Perry is attempting to negotiate? And how do their very different backgrounds contribute to the distance Perry feels growing between himself and his wife?

4. Why is Perry so drawn to Angela? What, ultimately, does she teach him about love and loss? The novel suggests that it is possible to rise above one's past. How is this particularly true of Angela?

5. What is so attractive to Perry about his friend Wayne's life? And why, after a period of lobster fishing and hiding out on the houseboat, does Perry decide to reenter the domestic world he has so willingly abandoned?

6. How does the lyrical prose of certain sections resonate in ways that magnify a character's sadness or remorse? And how do the accumulating details of landscape help the reader to feel the weight of such powerful emotions?

7. What drives Perry's recklessness? Is Wayne's explanation satisfactory?

8. After Roland, Walt Balobas is the most important of Perry's parolees. Why does Perry feel so close to him? Why does he intercede to get Walt's sentence reduced?

9. Marcia—responsible to marriage, family, job, and a hopeful future—stands as one of the novel's few "centered" characters. Is this her great strength, or her weakness?

10. Perry suffers from recurring nightmares in which Janine drowns again and again. No matter how deep he dives, he can never rescue her. Why does Perry feel so responsible for his sister's tragic death? How does the jet-ski accident relate back to this incident? Does Perry's traveling to Michigan help in any way to put closure on this family tragedy? Is there any reconciliation between him and his long-estranged family?

11. In the Firebird scene, what does Roland teach Perry about fatherhood?

12. Does the "dance" in the elementary school gym that concludes the novel suggest that all is well? Or is it less certain, less triumphant? What do you think will happen to Perry and Marcia after the end of the novel?

13. *Lucky Man, Lucky Woman* has been called a novel of forgiveness. Who has been forgiven, and why?

14. What is the meaning of "luck" in *Lucky Man, Lucky Woman*? Is luck the same as fate or destiny? Or can one change one's luck?